Deal With The Demon Lord

DEMON PACT BOOK 1

KACEY LEE

For those still finding their place in the world.

CHAPTER
One

I PULLED MY HOOD CLOSER TO MY FACE, COVERING my fiery red hair. It drew too much attention, and even though it had been centuries since the fall of the world, my stomach still flipped when I entered the Demon District.

The air had a sulfuric scent with an undertone of smoke and alcohol. I walked in a zigzag pattern to avoid broken bottles and unknown splotches on the concrete. My pace was brisk. The sooner I got out of here, the better. The atmosphere was thick with energy, from nerves, excitement, and the undercurrent of power from the collective demons in the area. Most cities had nice areas and seedy areas, but in today's world, it was all rundown.

I never saw it in its glory days when humans were still around. When I was a kid, I came across a map once in a library of old Earth. Apparently, this city used to be called San Diego, but now all the different areas of *Tenebris* were broken up into districts for the supernatural races. What once was the Gaslamp District was now run by the demons.

Speak of the devils, no pun intended, a drunken group of them tumbled from a club's door in front of me.

I halted in my tracks, tracing their movements with my peripherals without looking up.

"Bro! You should totally hit up that sexy succubus!" a green demon with yellow eyes hollered to a larger male with curving horns as long as my arm. You know what they say about large horns... he was... always compensating for something.

"Nah, man. She's so overrated," Horny-man replied with a smug look.

Yup, definitely overcompensating for his personality. My eyes dropped to his too-tight jeans. And for something else too, it seemed. Double whammy.

Greeny smirked, a long, forked tongue splicing between his lips. "Can I have a taste, man?"

"What about the bro code?" a smaller demon, who looked closer to human minus his fingers which turned into blackened claws, whined.

"Nah, it's fine. I'm hoping to weasel my way in with a siren. I met one on the Supes app," Horny claimed.

I rolled my eyes. I had never tried it, or rather, I didn't dare due to the ill effects when a Supe touched me. I'd heard it was filled with supernaturals looking for a "good time", not a mate. A waste of time, in my humble opinion. Plus, one of the few benefits of being a Supe was having a matebond, and it was incredibly rare to find your mate on such a thing.

"Sweet!" Greeny fist-pumped the air.

"Dude, I totally wanted the succubus!" Claw-boy groaned.

"The more the merrier." Greeny winked. He turned to his horned friend. "How the hell are you going to get into the Siren District?"

"She said she'd sing a song just for me that would allow me passage across the water." Horny towered even higher over his friends when he straightened his back to puff out his chest.

I stifled a groan. Yeah, and she'd probably kill you as soon as you made it ten feet from shore even if she sang a song so others wouldn't. Classic siren, stupid demon.

"Nice, man. Make sure you decide on a safe word." Greeny high-fived his buddy, the sound drawing my head up.

"What're you looking at?"

I jolted when I realized Claw-boy's brown eyes were trained on me.

The three stepped closer until they made a semicircle around me.

My hand reached for the dagger concealed at my hip. Thank the fates for witches. "I don't want any trouble," I warned.

A warning they stupidly didn't pick up on.

"Let's get a closer look at you." As quick as a frog's tongue, Greeny reached out, scales glistening across the back of his hand, and peeled off my hood.

I didn't flinch. No, I raised my head to look them square in the face. "Can I help you?"

"Bro, look at her hair!" Claw-boy ogled.

Horny's eyes flashed with interest.

A breeze blew through the strands, sending my scent over to them, and Greeny moaned while his eyes rolled back in his head.

"Fuck the succubus." He leaned over to take another whiff. "You smell like dessert."

"Looking for a good time?" Horny's eyes roved over my leather-clad body. Definitely not my preferred look; I'm a jeans and t-shirt kind of girl, but I needed to blend in. What I wouldn't give to wipe the smug look off their disgusting faces by plucking out his intrusive eyeballs. Too bad I'm trying to lay low. Demons weren't my favorite species to begin with, but this lot were literal scum that clearly had no respect for women.

"Hey, what about the siren?" Claw-boy's black fingers twitched at his side.

Ew, like any of them had a chance in hell in the first place.

"Yeah, so," I interrupted, "I'm going to need you fuckers to move out of my way."

Their eyes widened for a brief second.

"You should be happy we like a little fire, otherwise you'd be dead, witch." Greeny's slithered voice matched the movement of him running a finger across a strand of my ember hair.

I warned them. Well, kind of.

My right hand pulled the knife from my hip, turning it visible, but it still wasn't enough time for Greeny to pull away his hand before I sliced off the finger touching me.

"You bitch!" He grasped his hand, black blooding dripping from the wound.

Horny swung his meaty feast at my head, which I easily avoided.

Swooping under his arm, I pulled a bag of charmed salt from my pocket. Whispering a few words to ignite the spell, I threw it at his back, freezing him in place.

The third lunged at me, black claws swiping at my face.

I backpedaled, moving my head side to side to avoid his strikes.

I murmured another phrase in Latin, igniting a different spell, and blew a handful of salt into his face.

Smoke wafted from his sizzling skin as he screamed.

I turned back to Greeny. "If you three ever try to lay a hand on me again, I will murder you."

He had the audacity to laugh. "You would never kill a demon. Everyone knows that's a death sentence."

"You say that with the assumption I'd get caught." I

couldn't help but smile when his face paled. "Hope to *not* see you around." I wiggled my fingers in farewell as I walked past them.

Honestly, he was right. I would be absolutely nuts to murder a demon. Or any supernatural, for that matter. I mean, if I really had to, I would, but I didn't need to draw any more attention to myself or my reason for being here.

The supernaturals of this city needed to believe I was one of them, or I would definitely be dead. Thankfully, I had found a way to make a living and paid a witch to provide me with charms so others believed I was one too. As long as no one caught us in the same room together and realized we had the same scent, it would work perfectly.

The problem was, she was expensive. Really freaking expensive. But there was always a price to live in today's world. I should be happy that mine was easily handled with money or information, which was exactly why I was in the Demon District now.

The very last place I wanted to be.

Don't get me wrong, I've slipped into the Demon District more times than I could count to get information, but the Supes here coiled my stomach more than anyone else. They had less rules and were ruthless when they wanted something. Not to mention, their Demon Lord was probably the worst ruler of all the different Supe species. I'd heard he could kill someone with a snap of his finger, turning them to dust within a second; that he didn't even care if his own kind lived or died. At least the leaders of the other supernaturals cared about the wellbeing of those they oversaw.

It was harder for me to blend in here than most other districts, probably because I was constantly fighting my flight response. Let's just say I didn't do this for fun, and I only came here when I desperately needed the money. Like right now.

I shoved my hood back over my head and continued on my way. Thankfully, there were no more setbacks.

Stopping in front of the entrance to a bar, hung a sign with a giant pink flower. *Peonis.*

Yup, this was the place. Despite the fact they couldn't spell, I still snorted at the flickering "o".

Shaking my head, I opened the blackened door, and smoke smacked me in the face. I waved my hand to clear the air and pushed further into the busy bar. The bottom of my boots pulled at the sticky ground, and I tried not to think about the reason for it. Alcohol, blood, seed, piss. In a place like this, it could literally be anything and everything.

I swallowed down the bile rising in my throat, trying to breathe as little as I needed through my nose. Demons were disgusting.

My eyes naturally scanned the crowd. The joint wasn't big and a bit run down, definitely a hole in the wall. There were three exits, and the one to my left was the closest. The crowd was filled with various aged demons, plus a few shifters and some vampires out looking for a good time. The bartender looked human except for his tail, making him a low-level demon. A woman with a shaved head grinded on the leg of a shifter, noted by the flash of his yellow eyes, as he stroked the little wings on her back. The one thing everyone had in common, aside from being all Supes, was they were smashed.

Perfect.

To help blend in, I sauntered over to the bar.

"What'll it be?" the bartender asked.

I didn't even look his way when I answered, too focused on finding my target. "Whiskey. Neat."

When I heard the clank of the glass on the table, I threw down some money and walked away. I sipped at the whiskey and grimaced. Bottom-shelf shit was what he gave me. I should've been more specific.

The writhing bodies on the dance floor made me want to toss back the whole glass, but it was easier to blend in with a drink in hand.

Slipping through the cracks of people, I found a dark corner against the wall to bide my time.

Five minutes later, my mark walked through the door—Darius, a warlock and suspected philanderer. The witch who hired me had tastes that ran powerful, but no matter how strong, she had to be off her rocker to have dated the right-hand man of the Demon Lord.

Shit. I really wished I had enough money to pay her right about now so I didn't have to do this. Getting involved with anyone close to the Demon Lord was not conducive to survival. But a girl's gotta do what a girl's gotta do to keep breathing. I had to give Kyla credit, though, she definitely knew where to get information on her ex-boyfriend. Dive bar would not have been my expectation.

I knocked back the whiskey, relishing the burn. With my sights set on Darius, I threw my jacket off, putting it on a stool to retrieve later. Glancing down, I checked the ladies were displayed front and center, and quite well I might add. Maybe I should add some leather halters to my wardrobe. I preferred to be unobtrusive unless I needed to be seen. Today, I was the bait and the trap.

Faces turned my way, and I straightened with confidence. Hopefully the stench in this place would cover up my scent because there was no going back now.

Darius's gaze locked onto me, and a coy smile toyed the corner of my lips.

I sashayed over to him, hips swinging and head held high, and people automatically moved out of my way, giving me a straight shot.

"Hey, there," I purred. I held up my empty glass. "Wanna buy me a drink?"

His eyes sparked with excitement and satisfaction. He wasn't great looking, pretty average actually, and the same height as me when I wasn't wearing heels. He wore an old navy suit, not fitted to his body, and his brown eyes and hair were forgettable. "Follow me, sweetheart," he said.

His hand landed on my lower back, and revulsion spiked in me from the skin contact, just like it did for every Supe who touched me. I swallowed down the rising bile. What I was and what they were didn't mix, and my body rebelled every time I got close to one. Problem was that the revulsion was one-sided. If anything, they only got touchier as time went on. At least he was a warlock, which made it easier to handle because they were more closely related to humans.

The bartender smiled at me, giving me more attention now that my hoodie was gone. "What can I get you, doll?"

"She'll have a rum and Diet Coke," Darius interjected.

The bartender frowned when Darius spoke for me, but his lips parted in surprise when he recognized the man I stood beside. Everyone knew Darius had the Demon Lord's ear. He composed himself and nodded. "Yes, of course, sir."

My fists clenched at my side. I fucking hated rum, and a *Diet* Coke? Who the hell did he think he was?

Initially, I felt bad doing Kyla's bidding—finding her ex, giving him a truth serum, and asking some probing questions to see if he cheated on her. He wasn't her matebond, something unique across all supernaturals, so I didn't understand why she cared so much, but she wanted to know. It was petty, but it got me what I needed to hide my true nature. He did a wonderful job at giving me no regrets; screw this guy.

The bartender returned with two glasses, placing the rum and Diet Coke in front of me. I stared longingly at the top-shelf whiskey he handed to Darius.

"Oh my." I batted my eyes at a couple in the corner getting really close to taking their dry humping to the next level.

Darius turned to see what I was fake-surprised by.

Quickly, I pulled the capsule from my cleavage and broke it open above Darius's drink. The liquid inside mixed with the amber in under a second, and my hand was firmly back at my side, empty capsule shoved in my pocket, by the time he turned back around.

"Don't come to Demon District very often?" he asked.

"No." I hid my face behind my hair in a shy act.

"Yeah, I think I would've noticed you." He brushed a strand of hair behind my ear.

My stomach turned, and it took everything in me not to snap his finger. "Cheers!" I brought my cup up, pushing his arm away from me.

"To a glorious night," he agreed, bringing his glass to his lips to take a giant swig.

I mimicked the movement but didn't actually take a sip. Again, I really didn't like rum. It left a bad taste in my mouth, just like being touched by a Supe.

In order to ensure the potion was working, I asked a random question that could seem harmless. "So, what are you doing in these parts?" It was something common to ask when it was clear someone wasn't from the district they were in. I expected him to answer in a roundabout way.

"I work beside Lazarus, the Demon Lord. You could say I help run this district and know all the ins and outs. Those fools were shortsighted to kick me out of the Magic District, but I'm more here than I would've ever been there."

I blinked in surprise at the brutal honesty of his answer. Damn, this stuff was strong.

His eyebrows furrowed in confusion. I swept right in to keep him talking before he had chance to deduce what was happening.

"Have you had any serious relationships?"

There was a pause before he answered, "Yes."

Crap, he was starting to fight the effects whether he realized or not.

"Tell me about her... or him. How long were you together? Why did you break up?" I pressed.

"Her name is Kyla, and she's a witch. One of the strongest in the Magic District. I thought I could get ahead with her, wanted to learn her tricks. It took me a couple of years, but I finally did, and once I had upped my power and learned everything I did, it was time to move on."

"Move on?"

"Yeah, Gia is even more powerful, and she has a great ass." He froze with a gaping mouth.

My hand curled tighter around my glass. He totally just figured out what was happening. My eyes drifted towards the exit sign, and an assortment of excuses to escape crossed my mind. I found out what Kyla wanted. I needed to leave—stat.

But before I could grab my coat and high tail it out of there, his face turned blue.

My head cocked, and I took a step back when his hands raised to grab his throat. His brown eyes turned milky white, and he collapsed. Dead.

Well, this didn't go as planned.

I placed my cup on the counter, readying myself to leave, but when I looked up, all eyes were on me.

CHAPTER
Two

THREE SECONDS. THREE SECONDS WAS ALL I HAD before the place erupted into complete chaos. Demons used their magic to shimmer out of the joint, vampires used their lightning speed towards the exits, and the werewolves howled.

The bartender shimmered from behind the bar, disappearing from where he had stood to materialize right in front of me.

I reached for my magicked salt. My brain rapidly ran through what spell to use, but I didn't have anything for a job going this wrong. My heart hammered against my ribcage. This was bad. I was good at what I did because I stayed unknown. Never had someone died with me beside them. I needed to get out of here ASAP. I barely had pulled at the string of the little bag before the bartender wrenched my hand behind my back, slamming the side of my head onto the tabletop.

"Oh, no you don't," he growled, pressing all his weight into me.

My muscles tightened, and fear weaseled into my gut. If I was a real witch like my charm bracelet made everyone believe, then I could've used my powers to knock him away. But without the special salt Kyla gave me, I had nothing.

"Get off of me," I grunted.

The bartender laughed. "You just killed the Demon Lord's main crony and you think I'm going to let you go? Think again, buttercup."

Wait, what? Dread coiled through me. They thought I killed the guy. Oh shit.

Sadly, time wasn't on my side. I didn't even get an extra second to convince the demon otherwise before more shimmered into the joint.

They were high-level demons. I could tell by the sulfuric stench they brought with them. With their matching suits, it was easy to deduce them as Lazarus's top guards.

"That her?" one of them asked.

I watched the Matrix once when I was a kid, I found an underground movie house which aired human movie specials. The night I went was the night the Matrix debuted. I never got to go back because a week later it was discovered and burned down with everyone still inside.

That was the Supes' way of solving everything that reminded them of the time before they owned the world. Make it disappear.

All these men needed were some black shades and they would look exactly like the agents from the movie. Too bad I didn't have some slow-motion moves to get me out of this one.

"This is her." The bartender shoved me into the arms of an awaiting guard.

I wiggled in his grasp, but it barely fazed him. Cuffs

clinked over my wrists. The cool, magic-dampening metal hummed against my skin. Little did they know that the magic-dampening did nothing. They were still hefty devices and effective enough with their own spell that I couldn't get out of them, and based on the initials on the side, only one demon could take them off me.

I swallowed down my rising panic.

The bartender pointed to Darius's lifeless form still on the ground. "No blood. You don't need to worry about any of the cleanup; I've got it." He was practically fawning over the Demon Lord's peons, too scared to disrespect them, even though Darius definitely shit himself based on the smell.

The guard holding me nodded to another, who stepped up to Darius's body. With his hand on Darius's shoulder, the two shimmered away.

The guard's hard eyes swept across the joint. "Is there anything else?"

The bartender pointed to the glass. "Just that. I saw her slip something into it."

I blanched. He saw? And... now Darius was dead! If Kyla gave me something more than a truth serum, I was going to kill her.

"It wasn't me!" I cried out, but they ignored me.

"Bag it," my guard told one of the other men.

Once everything was accounted for and the bartender's statement had been taken, I felt the guardsman's hand tighten on my arm.

"No! You can't do this! I have rights!" I screamed, lashing out. I tried to knee him in the nuts, but he easily avoided it. When I shoulder-checked him, I only received an annoyed frown.

This didn't dissuade me. There was no way in hell I was letting them take me.

Raising my hands above my head, I twisted my body to

bend his wrist and snapped forward to break his hold. I raced for the closest exit. Freedom was two feet from my grasp when a hand locked at the base of my neck.

"*Soxnus*," the guard said in ancient daemon.

His power hit me, and everything went dark.

The pounding in my head increased the more aware I became. My cheek pressed against the cool ground, and the magic of the cuffs sizzled around my wrists. Pins and needles pricked my left leg.

How long had I been knocked out for? Stupid demon. Using ancient daemon wasn't fair. But no one played fair, not in today's world. If ever.

Blinking away the last of the drowsiness, I saw I was in an expansive room. Everything was made of black stone with the moldings in a golden paint. Guards lined the doors on the far wall.

The Demon Lord's tower.

This was the absolute last place I would want to be in all of *Tenebris,* all of Earth. I'd managed to avoid it for two and a half decades, yet here I was.

I flipped onto my back with a grunt. My chest rose with a deep inhale, and my lungs locked. The air was thick, choking me and making it hard to breathe. What was this power?

I turned my head towards where it emanated from and looked up a dais. Sitting on a black and gold throne to match the room was him: Lazarus, the Demon Lord, in all his glory.

His broad frame sat rigid in the chair. He turned his head away from the demon he spoke to, and pulled at the cuff of his grey suit. Black hair fell across his forehead, and his jaw was as sharp as the rest of him. He squared his wide shoulders, focusing on me. Silver eyes locked me in place. His power radiated around me, keeping tight control of my breath.

He nearly looked human. Literally the most sinfully sexy human to ever exist, except for one thing. Behind him rose giant, bat-like wings with a single white claw at each tip.

"You killed one of my best men." His voice strummed through the air and along my spine like ice water had been poured down my back.

Finally able to release my breath, I answered, "I did not."

A dark eyebrow arced up at me, proving to me he hadn't expected me to answer like that. No one spoke to the Demon Lord without revere or fear. Unlucky for him, I wasn't just anyone.

I pushed myself onto my knees. A glint in his steely gaze made me shudder until I realized my submissive position. With a flip of my hair over my shoulder, I stood and tried to make myself seem taller than I was.

A guard stepped forward on my right, clearly displeased at my disrespect.

Lazarus held up a hand in his direction, and the guard stepped back against the wall. "Do you have a name?" the Demon Lord inquired.

I narrowed my eyes at him and pressed my lips into a hard line.

"I *could* force you to tell me," he added, steepling his hands in front of his chest.

He could sure as hell try. I would never go down without a fight, even when faced with one of the worst beings on Earth, but I knew when to choose my battles. This wasn't it. Getting something sometimes meant giving first, and if I wanted to make it out of this alive, I needed to make him believe he was winning.

"Name," he demanded. His eyes flashed red, matching the rhythm of his lashing power as it wrapped around my throat. His face stayed passive, but his invisible magic tightened in warning.

"Serena," I choked out. I was innocent in all of this and didn't need to piss him off or give him further reason to unleash his wrath on me. I balled my fists to hide how they shook.

His power loosened, and I took in a staggering breath. "I am Lazarus, the Demon Lord." His magic laced his words, so his quiet introduction transformed into a sonorous tone buzzing through my limbs.

"No duh," I mumbled under my breath in hopes of easing the tension building in my body.

In the corner of my eyes, the guards went rigid. Stupid Supe hearing.

"What shall your punishment be?" Lazarus mused to himself with narrowed eyes. A white fang glinted when he spoke. "A life for a life, perhaps?"

My jaw unhinged before I snapped it shut with a glare. "I told you. I didn't kill him."

"And yet you drugged him," he retorted without hesitation.

"Yeah, a truth serum! Not to kill the guy!" I folded my arms over my chest like they could protect me from his enveloping powers that humidified the air around me until it was difficult to breathe.

There was a barely perceptible twitch in his jaw. "A truth serum?"

Shit. I literally just told the Demon Lord I tried to gain

unsolicited information from one of his top guys. This wasn't good.

"What was so important you needed to know from him?" Lazarus leaned forward, and with this slight movement, I felt a pull towards him.

This wasn't magical. It couldn't be. The only feeling I ever got around Supes was pain followed by the need to vomit. This had to be something else, a trick of some kind. Yet the slightly smaller distance between us had my feet shifting towards him. What the...

I shoved my heels into the ground and clamped my mouth shut. I didn't give information unless I was paid, Demon Lord or not.

My defiance was not received well. He rose from his chair and moved down the dais towards me. With each step, I was more and more drawn to him. He pinned me in place with his silver eyes, and his magic snapped in place, freezing my limbs. I couldn't move, couldn't blink; even my lungs were frozen so I couldn't breathe.

"You have two choices: cooperate or suffocate," he leered.

Shit. He meant business, and I was the dumbass pestering the most powerful Supe in the city, potentially the world. I tried to nod but couldn't. My eyes burned as they dried out, one tear leaked from my right one, and my lungs screamed at me for oxygen. Finally, his powers released me.

Through gasping breaths while wiping at my cheek, I answered, "His ex wanted to know if he cheated on her. That's all. Cross my heart." Sorry, Kyla, but desperate times called for desperate measures.

"Interesting." He prowled closer. By the time he stood three feet from me, I couldn't look away. I could barely breathe. "There's just one problem."

I bit my lower lip as warmth filled my center.

His silver eyes tracked the movement, landing on my lips and stealing what little air I had.

"W-what?" I breathed.

"I still have a dead warlock I entrusted with many secrets, and only one suspect." His assessing gaze turned from interested to accusatory in a split second.

"It wasn't me!" I stammered. "I swear. I'll prove it!"

His head tilted in a predatory way. "Willing to make a pact?"

I sipped in a surprised gasp, taking half a step away.

A smirk pulled at the corner of his lips. "Well?"

A pact with any demon was bad. But with the Demon Lord himself? A direct descendent of Lucifer?

"And if I don't take it?" My tongue rolled in my mouth like I was having an allergic reaction to something. Maybe I was. Demons and I definitely didn't get along.

He frowned. "Then I will assume you are guilty and kill you." He said it so matter-of-fact that I had no doubt he would.

"Can I think about it?" I asked.

He nodded. "You have ten seconds."

And the bastard started counting down.

"Ten..."

I could try to fight my way out, but if the rumors were true then I'd be dead within seconds.

"Seven..."

I could strike a deal to throw Kyla under the bus. Shit, but then there goes my primary stream of income and I'd be screwed.

"Four..."

There was no way I could pay him off. He owned half this town, and the only reason he didn't have all of it is because he chose not to.

"Two..."

Fuckity-fuck-fuck. If there was only a way…

"O—"

"Okay! I'll do it!" I blurted, mentally slapping my forehead, causing a small wince at the realization of what I'd just done. For fate's sake, at the first sign of pressure, I caved! I didn't plan on playing poker against him anytime soon.

His eyes flashed red with excitement. "Oh, little witch, you should always know the demands of a pact before agreeing," he *tsk*ed.

The fear in my expression must have been clearly written because a cruel smile slipped onto his face, showing the points of his canines.

"You will help me find the real killer and will remain here until proven innocent," he explained.

"Here in Demon District?" I clarified, my heart sinking in my chest. I couldn't be around Supes that consistently, or… or…

"Here, in my tower."

Oh, crap. I chewed on my bottom lip. I needed to find a way out of this. I had agreed to the deal too quickly, and I was going to get screwed over if I didn't do something, and fast.

His gaze fell to my raw lips, a flash of hunger taking over. My heart hammered in my chest. I needed to do something *now.*

"I will help you find the killer, and I will earn my innocence *and* my freedom," I clarified. "And I get my own room! Plush! High-end! Top notch service!" I screamed out the last few commands, worried he'd agree before I got a chance to finish.

"Look at you, little witch, learning already." This time when he smiled, it was deadly. "Deal."

His steps were light as he closed the distance until he held out his hand for me to shake.

I held my cuffed wrists in front of his face.

"After the deal," he stated.

With a sigh, I twisted my left hand out of the way and placed my right hand in his. I braced myself for pain, which is exactly why I couldn't stifle my gasp at the intense pleasure when our skin touched.

And that's how you make a deal with the devil.

CHAPTER
Three

"THE CUFFS?" SERENA RAISED HER LINKED WRISTS IN front of my face, an angry pout adding a crease between her eyebrows.

It took me a moment to register what she wanted. I was still reeling from our handshake. What the bloody hell was that? It had taken all of my self-control not to scoop her into my arms and shimmer to my bedroom. My palm was still hot from the touch of her.

I reached out, careful to make contact with the cool metal and not her skin. With ancient daemon on my lips, the cuffs disappeared.

She heaved out a sigh of relief. "Well? My room?" Her hand landed on her cocked hip.

I stifled the smile threatening to escape. When people spoke to me like this, I killed them, but for some reason the audacity of this little witch amused me. I nodded to a guard at the door. "They'll show you to your room."

"Top. Notch. Service," she reminded with vigor instead of fear.

No one made demands of me. I should throw her over my knee and spank her tight little ass for speaking to me like that.

"I will have a meal sent up," I said because, even so, a protective need thrummed in my veins. I was losing my touch. The dungeons were the only place she should be sent to, and yet here I was giving her a suite in my tower.

She looked over her shoulder one last time before following the guard out of the room, her sunset hair swishing over her back.

I sat back down on my throne. My wings twitched, vying to go for a fly.

"Leave me," I ordered my guards.

They all shimmered out.

I allowed myself to relax, running my hand over my face in exasperation. What the hell just happened?

I knew she didn't kill Darius. We searched her while she was asleep, confiscated a bag of salt, and found a broken capsule. We tested it, and it did indeed have a truth serum but traces of nothing else. I wasn't the Demon Lord without my own ways of discovering the truth, and no lies passed on her full lips when she said she didn't kill him.

Nothing pointed to her or gave her reason to kill him. In any other circumstance I would have let the person go. Well, not without scaring them a little first. I did have a reputation to uphold, after all.

Nonetheless, she was hiding something. I knew it the moment she stiffened when I called her 'little witch.' I heard her heart skip a beat and breath stutter. Unnoticeable to anyone else. Reactions she couldn't control herself; she may not have even realized she reacted. But I noticed and was officially intrigued. I had ruled Demon District for centuries, and it'd been a long time since something had caught my attention, since something of interest had piqued my curiosity. Poor girl. I hoped it wouldn't be the death of her... or me.

And don't get me started on her smell. When she woke up and her underlying scent hit me, she had no chance in hell of escaping.

My fangs pricked the inside of my bottom lip from simply remembering it. It was nothing like I'd ever come across. I wasn't talking about the perfumes and charms to override her scent but her true essence. There was something different, and I couldn't put my finger on it. But damn, did it smell divine. It took all my self-control not to taste her myself. I wanted to run my tongue over her supple skin, feel the beating artery in her neck, and draw her essence into me like sipping on fresh mountain air. My cock throbbed at the thought.

A knock sounded on the door.

"Come in," I announced.

The guard who escorted her to the room walked in. My men were well trained; they knew to never shimmer into my presence without being called.

"And?" I asked.

"I put her on the tenth floor. I made sure to lock all exits."

I nodded in approval. The upper section of my tower was the safest, and he made sure to keep her on the lowest level of that. My own personal penthouse resided on the thirteenth floor.

"Anything else?" my guard inquired, standing in the open doorway.

"Put a tail on this 'Kyla' the witch mentioned," I said.

"Do you want us to bring her in?"

I shook my head. "No. Gather whatever information you can on her. I want to see what we can learn about her habits and who she meets with before we take any further action. This is purely intel based for now." Plus, I bet she'd be the first person Serena would go to when she started her own investigation. That's if Kyla was truly who put her up to this. I was curious to see how the scenario played out, and I couldn't do that if I had Kyla locked away.

The guard bowed and exited, sure to close the door behind him.

Darius was a bastard, a real tool. He thought too highly of himself and was incredibly egotistical. Granted, he was a powerful warlock, but he wasn't the best in the city. Although, he sure acted like it. However, he had been good at his job, and it would be hard to replace him.

I may know Serena didn't kill him, but someone did, and I needed to figure out who and why. It took priority, and I couldn't let myself get distracted any more than I already had.

Raising from my seat, I rolled my shoulders and flexed my wings. I wouldn't get anywhere with a muddled mind. I resolved to do something about it and go feed to get her out of my head.

I passed through a door behind the dais and followed the narrow hallway until I reached an elevator shaft. I placed my hand on the electric pad. It scanned my hand, and with a green light, the door opened. I pressed the '13' button, and another device scanned my eyes.

The elevator was quick, and a sense of calm washed over me when I stepped into my home. I crossed the open floor plan, ignoring the grey tones of the bare space minus the crackling fire with my favorite painting of a swirling night sky above it, and headed straight to the double doors on the opposite side. I threw them open, and fresh air pushed into the enclosed space.

Stepping out on the balcony, I took a deep breath before flaring my wings out to the side. There was no railing. There was no need for one when you had wings. Anyone stupid enough to come to my private chambers deserved whatever fall awaited them.

I jumped off the side, spiraling for five seconds and wishing it could be longer. My wings caught the breeze, and I soared between the buildings with an ease that came from hundreds of years of practice.

The more distance I put between myself and Serena, the more I relaxed. Yes, a clear mind and space was definitely what I needed. There was no better way to let off some steam than with a succubus, so I banked right and headed straight for one of my VIP clubs on the edge of my district.

CHAPTER

Four

I DANGLED MY CHARM BRACELET IN FRONT OF MY face. Last night, the adrenaline of everything that happened wore off quickly, and I totally crashed after being escorted to my suite.

Floor-to-ceiling windows took up the outer walls, which was why I was woken up by the sun this morning. By the time I found a button that darkened the windows—talk about money—I was too wide awake.

I had drifted around the apartment, which took up the entire tenth floor. Considering I had never had more than a studio at best and a corner in an alley at worst, I was a bit shocked. Although, it was a little too pristine for my taste.

I was fairly certain these were Monet paintings hanging in this house. Yes, the originals stolen from museums after the humans and angels fled to another realm four hundred years ago following The Great Genocide. The battle of Lucifer and Michael left the world in ruins, but no one ran. Then The

Great Genocide wiped out eighty-thousand lives within seconds, no one understanding how or why, and the angels fled to safety with the humans at their sides, leaving the rest of us to rot. A whole other way of life was completely gone, and all we had left was art and ashes.

The paintings screamed wealth and made the space feel even more like a museum. The white walls and marbled floors didn't help either. There was nothing to snoop, and eventually I got bored in this minimalist-styled suite.

My stomach gurgled.

I must've been asleep when they swung by to deliver food this morning. At least they didn't let themselves in and drop it off. It would've been nice to wake up to food, but I was glad demons had some sense of decency.

I rose from my place on the soft cream couch and headed to the elevators. I pressed the button, and nothing happened. I pushed again. Still nothing.

I folded my arms, and it dawned on me. I was losing my edge. I wasn't a guest here; I was a prisoner. I stood there gaping at the closed doors. Those a-holes locked me in! Or the very rich equivalent of locking me in. I was ten stories up with no way out; there was no way I could escape out a window or anything.

With a stomp, my fists flew to my sides.

I reached for my pouch of salt and found it missing. Double crap. This wasn't good. I was stuck in the Demon Lord's tower, after being idiotic enough to make a pact, and was now completely defenseless.

Well, not completely. But I hated using my single-use tools when it wasn't an emergency.

I pushed the down arrow one more time in good faith.

Nope.

Okay, this wasn't necessarily life or death, but it could be if I didn't get more salt from Kyla soon. Plus, these demons needed to learn I was no one's kept pet. No matter who they thought they were.

Goosebumps covered my arms. Lazarus was everything I had heard and more. Deadly, cold, and cunning. What I hadn't expected was how the world disappeared when you looked at him, or the playful edge that could cut like a knife if you weren't careful. Power seeped from him like sweat, yet the rigidness in his stature showed he was actually holding back. And those eyes, the way they sparked with interest, captivated me with a single glance. Never had I wanted to peel back the layers of someone before, and for whatever reason I wanted to do that with him. He had secrets, and my skill set made me want to reveal them all.

I held my silver charm bracelet in front of me.

The hourglass suppressed my scent, the flower provided the witch smell, the eye helped detract attention to blend into a crowd, the feather was one time flight, the door was a single use shimmer, the fish would give me gills for an hour, and the pentagram was the deadliest of the bunch.

Half of these were to help hide me in plain sight, and out of the others...

I looked between the feather and the door. These would both help me get out of here. I didn't want to use the shimmer; it cost me a fortune and was my most versatile charm. Not that I'd admit it to anyone but myself, using a flight charm for my first time so high above was terrifying, and there was a good chance I would be seen.

Shimmer it was.

I grasped the door between my right forefinger and thumb, just the way Kyla taught me. I closed my eyes and envisioned my flat. A tiny space in the Magic District with my mattress on the ground, my kitchenette five feet away, and a door to the bathroom at the foot of my bed. Small, but mine.

"*Lacus*," I whispered.

The charm warmed between my fingers, but I didn't break concentration. There was a whoosh, and when the charm cooled, dead of all magic, I opened my eyes to find myself back at my apartment.

First things first, I needed to change out of this leather outfit. Sleeping in it had been a terrible idea; I needed to remember extra lotion from all the chafing, and there was no way I was going to sleep in my underwear in that place. It was too vulnerable, making it hard to escape if I needed to take the time to throw pants on. Even in my own place, half the time I slept in my jeans. That was usually only after a big job when I was a little more cautious, or rather jumpy, and the situation I was in now definitely meant I would be sleeping fully clothed.

I shuffled over to the trunk against the wall and flipped open the lid. Rummaging around through my pile of clothes, I found clean underwear, a pair of jeans, and a vintage style t-shirt that said "Practice Safe Hex" with a circle of candles and gems in the center. I ditched my wedges for my black pair of biker boots—or my ass-kickers, as I referred to them.

I opened my mini fridge and frowned at its emptiness. Oh right, that's why I took the job for Kyla in the first place. In the cupboard, I found one last granola bar and shoved it into my mouth.

When all was said and done with getting ready, I scoured my bedroom. I shuffled to my small twin-sized bed and pulled the bedframe away from the wall. The paint was untouched, at least to anyone who didn't know what they were looking for. Drawing my finger along the wall, exactly sixteen inches above the ground, I traced a pentagram. Above, below, and to each side, I spoke the Latin words for the four main elements: earth, wind, fire, and water. The paint glowed a faint biolumi-nescent purple with the pentagram I had created. Spreading my fingers to line up inside of the five points, I pressed while speaking a spell in a foreign tongue, a mixture of angelic, demonic, and fate only knew what. I never asked Kyla for a translation; all I cared about was that it worked. The wall glimmered away, leaving a black hole in its place. Magic symbols still covered the interior of the opening, keeping anyone from feeling the power emanating from the object inside.

Careful of the sharp edges, my fingers wrapped around the cool metal handle, and a calmness settled in my chest. It was still there. Not that I expected for it to disappear, but it still brought me peace of mind every time. I didn't dare take it out of the magicked space for fear of its power emitting and alerting a Supe. If any Supe found this, it would be disastrous. There were charms on the blade itself to keep it from detection, but I couldn't risk anyone finding out about it. A part of me still questioned whether I should bring it with me. I had never been without it; it was the one link to my past, and I hated the idea of leaving it here.

It was safer this way, both for the blade and for me. With hesitation, I placed it back down and said the necessary spells to conceal it once more. Sighing, I pushed my bed back into place and pressed my hand against the wall. Head hanging, I squeezed my eyes shut. I would be okay. I didn't need it to protect me, I could protect myself. I had done it for twelve years already.

Spinning around, I walked away from my second biggest secret. There was one last thing I needed before going to Kyla's.

I pulled open the middle dresser drawer with a frown. Reaching underneath, I found the envelope I was searching for and ripped it free from the duct tape securing it to the underside of the drawer.

My fingers clenched the cash. It was everything I had to my name. A pit formed in my stomach. Again, this was for emergencies only.

I knew Lazarus would come for me eventually with the

pact in place, and if they kept confiscating my salt, I would need something bigger. Money I could earn back, but my life I couldn't.

I shoved the envelope into my jeans at the base of my back and covered it with my shirt.

Hopefully, Kyla was around to see me.

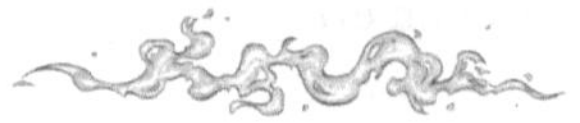

"Look what the cat shifter dragged in." Kyla looked up from a potion she was brewing. She wore one of her many multi-colored dresses, and her 4C curls were plaited. It was her preferred hairstyle when she had a lot of work to do.

The door of her shop snicked shut behind me. *Deja Brew* was tucked away on a side street of the main strip, which used to be known as Liberty Station in San Diego. It was a decent sized shop. Well, anything was decent when I compared it to my apartment. She was lucky enough to own the space above it too; she only needed to pay a single rent to the High Priestess for the space. The High Priestess was the leader of the witches and warlocks, so they were one big coven. Being the closest thing to humans on Earth, witches needed all the strength they could get, and this definitely had a 'more the merrier' mindset for magic users. What the High Priestess did with the money, I had no clue, but it brought safety to the Magic District, so no one complained.

Herbs, incense, and candles gave her shop a spicy-earthy smell. Much better than the acidic aroma of Demon District. I preferred the salty air of the Siren District, which had been known as Coronado in human times. It smelled of freedom.

Glass containers littered her storefront from floor to ceiling with who knew what kind of ingredients, and I didn't ask. Ignorance was bliss, and I didn't want to know if I had Phoenix eyeballs or Zombie entrails in whatever she gave me.

"Sup?" I said, plopping onto a stool at the end of the table she worked at.

She narrowed her eyes at me. "I expected you last night. I stayed up well past my bedtime, and you never showed."

"Funny story, grandma," I jested. But when I saw the look in her eyes, my lips sealed shut. Right, Kyla wasn't a friend I could poke fun at but a powerful witch. One who had a lot of dirt on me and could hex me sideways while blindfolded. Definitely not someone I wanted to mess with.

"Whatever it is, it better be good. I have a ton of orders to fill." She pinched a black herb and threw it into the pot. Sparks rained over the side, and I shifted away so none touched me.

Unsure where to begin, I spewed out information, recapping what I wore, those three demon jerks on the street, the terrible whiskey...

"Get to the point!" Kyla slammed her hand on the table.

"So, there's good news and bad news," I said. My fingers twisted together in my lap. "Which do you want to hear first?"

Kyla drummed her fingers on the table with a sigh. "I don't care, just tell me."

"Good news, I found him, and you were right! He totally cheated on you. With Gia, no less."

"I knew it! That bitch lied right to my face." She turned and shuffled through a cupboard before pulling out some kind of doll with strawberry blonde hair that looked just like Gia's. "She's totally going to pay."

I've learned it's better not to ask.

"Oh, and he's dead," I added.

The doll dropped from her hand onto the counter. Her

mouth hung open as she stared at me in wide-eyed shock. "What? Holy crap. Darius is dead? I know you said there was bad news, but I thought him cheating on me *was* the bad news."

"Oh, that's not the bad news either."

"Then what's the bad news?" she hollered.

"He died while I was talking to him. I got caught by the Demon Lord and had to tell him I was working with you so he would know I only gave him a truth serum. The only way he wouldn't kill me was if I made a pact with him," I blurted it all out in one breath, and by the end, Kyla's face was ghost white. Or maybe more of a ghoul because there was definitely a green tinge to it. "It was just a truth serum, right?" I clarified.

"Of course it was only a truth serum!" she snapped. "I wanted to know if he cheated on me, not kill him!" The glass shivered from the force of her voice, reminding me just how powerful she was.

"Alright, cool."

"Cool? Nothing about this is cool!" She shifted uneasily on her feet, eyes scanning her shop like demons were about to appear and slaughter her at any moment.

Not that I could blame her. It would've been a very demon-y thing to do. Thankfully, the main strip of the Magic District had a really strong protection charm. No non-witch Supe could pop up out of nowhere. They had to walk in, and when they passed the spell, security was notified right away. No one entered or left this district without it being known. It was the safest place in all of *Tenebris* and exactly why I chose to settle here and hide myself as one of them. Speaking of...

"Deep breaths," I reminded Kyla. "I've got it all under control. But I do need one teensie-weensie favor."

Kyla's eyebrows furrowed. "What?"

I gave her my best innocent smile. "I need you to make me appear to be an elemental witch."

"Are you kidding me?" She pinched the bridge of her nose.

"See, with this whole pact thing, I have a feeling I'll be around the demons a lot. They took my salt, so I need something more reliable," I explained.

"When do you need it by?"

I smiled again. "Well... I was hoping you could get it to me now?"

Her eyes closed with a deep inhale. Her jaw moved from side to side from grinding her teeth. "You are something else, Serena."

"I'll pay you," I cooed.

"No shit you'll pay me. Do you even have that much money? To make this so quickly, it'll use the last of my Ginkgo. It'll cost you double."

"Done."

She looked at me with surprise. "That's a lot of money. Are you sure you can pay?"

I pulled out the envelope at my back and placed it on the table. "Is this enough?"

Her eyebrows shot up. "Yup!" She leaned forward and snatched the cash away.

"Hey!"

She leveled me with a glare. "You're lucky I help you at all, especially with this mess. Think of the rest as a tip for the inconvenience and my silence."

I settled back into my seat. Damn, I should've asked the price first. "Fine."

She grabbed another pot from the back and threw ingredients into it until a soft orange bubbling liquid glowed inside. She was a flurry of movement I could barely keep track of.

"What kind of elemental witch do you want?" Kyla asked. "Being so close to the ocean, water would be good. However, air would be the easiest to manipulate and fake."

"Fire," I said without any hesitation.

"Fire? Seriously? You do want to keep staying hidden and not wave a sign that says 'Look at me! I'm not really a witch', right?"

"I'm in a pact with the Demon Lord himself," I explained. "I want fire."

I'd always been drawn to it; my apartment was littered with candles. It warmed me from the inside out, and I planned to fight fire with fire.

She shrugged. "Alright, whatever you say." She tossed in some more herbs, and the orange glow turned as red as my hair. From a small drawer set on the counter behind her, she pulled out another charm. Using tongs, she dipped it into the potion and murmured a spell I couldn't make out.

Flames erupted at the top of the liquid and died down when she withdrew the metal.

"It'll be a little warm." She motioned for me to hold out my charm bracelet, and I complied.

I brought my wrist to my face when she was done attaching it to see the addition of a little silver flame. "A little on the nose, don't you think?"

She ignored my comment. "Let's start with something small. A finger flame."

I nodded. "What's the summoning word?"

"There is none," she stated.

"Wow." That was a first. "At least I got my money's worth," I mumbled.

"Close your eyes," she ordered, ignoring my remark with a roll of her eyes; I obliged. "I want you to envision your fingertips warming. See them getting red like molten glass, and then push the building power out of your body. Be sure to focus on whatever form you want it to take. Don't lose the form or you'll lose the magic."

"What if I lose control?" I murmured.

"You won't. You're not really an elemental witch, it'll just disappear if you lose concentration."

I did as she said, and when I forced the heated power out of my fingers, I imagined a little flame flickering on my pointer.

Her gasp had my eyes flipping open.

Across all my fingers flickered flames, like five lighters.

"I've never seen someone take to fire so easily before, not even a real fire witch," she breathed. Her awestruck stare followed the dancing flames.

Tension built between my shoulders. I cleared my mind, and the fire dispersed with my thoughts.

"And I can use this whenever?"

She nodded. "This spell should last you a year without any problems. If it becomes difficult to summon or the flames lessen at all, be sure to see me. If you use it often, it won't last as long."

"Thanks," I said.

The bells of the shop chimed when the door opened. A breeze swept into the shop, ruffling my hair and cooling the back of my neck. It brought with it a smoky flavor, and a warmth whispered down my spine.

My back straightened from my jarred nerves. I knew exactly who had walked in.

Fear crawled across me until gooseflesh rose on my arms at what he might have overheard.

CHAPTER
Five

LAZARUS

I FOLDED MY WINGS, BUT STILL BARELY FIT THROUGH the door. My gaze roamed over the small shop, the pale face of Kyla, and the stiff shoulders of Serena. My hands clenched at my sides.

"You should've stayed at the tower," I said.

Serena turned, her fierce stare burning me apart.

My breath hitched, and it took every ounce of me not to step forward to ensure she wasn't harmed. It seemed my night with the succubi did very little to satisfy me. What about this witch had me so entranced?

"Someone took my protection salt, I needed to resupply." Her arms folded over her chest.

Kyla pressed against the counter behind Serena.

"As it happens, I was hoping you'd lead me to the witch in question," I said while pulling at the cuff of my dress shirt. I already knew where the witch's shop was, and I was annoyed Serena found a way out of my tower, but I wouldn't let them know that. I continued, "I needed to swing by here to have a chat."

Serena stepped in front of Kyla, cutting off my line of sight. "She didn't do anything. It was only a truth serum. I already confirmed it."

My head tilted to the side. "Oh, did you?"

"Yes, so you can leave." Her eyes widened when a sly grin spread across my face.

"Not without you, pet. And if you are correct, that still leaves us with the problem of who *did* kill Darius and how."

"I'm no one's pet," she hissed. Her eyes narrowed into angry slits, and I couldn't stop the thrill traveling to my cock. "And I am correct, there is no if. Kyla isn't a killer, unlike some people."

I licked my lips, my predatory side enjoying the challenge. "I see. Either way, you're mine until we discover what happened."

Serena moved closer, and the air crackled between us. "Let's go then."

"Itching to get rid of me?" I cocked my eyebrow.

"You could say that." Her full lips pressed into a hard line.

"I can help!" Kyla piped up from the back, breaking the trance between the two of us.

"What?" Serena's voice was as shocked as her face.

Seems they weren't friends but merely had a professional relationship. Interesting.

"I can help with Darius," Kyla explained. "I want there to be no doubt that Serena and I are innocent in this. I can run some tests to help figure out what killed him."

"You'd do that for me?" Serena's eyebrows drew together in confusion.

My blackened heart pulled in my chest. Did she not trust people to watch her back? Even as the Demon Lord, I had a couple I could rely on.

"For us," Kyla corrected.

They both turned to me with questioning looks, waiting for me to decide, which drew out a satisfied smirk from me. The power I held over others could be exhausting, but there was always a level of satisfaction that came with it.

"I will have one of my own men confirm your findings," I added.

Kyla nodded. "I would expect nothing less."

"Good. Shall we?" I held out my hands for them to take.

They stared at them like they were made of poison.

"Shimmering there will be much quicker," I added.

"Demons can't shimmer in and out of the main Magic District." Kyla's face was stricken and then turned green when she saw the glint in my eyes.

"I'm not just any demon. Although, I do try to be respectful and not cause unnecessary unrest."

"Whatever. Let's just get this over with." Serena slipped her hand into mine, and heat bloomed between us. A small gasp escaped her lips, drawing my attention to them. When she saw me looking, she turned towards Kyla. "Let's go," she pushed.

Kyla murmured a spell, and a coating of magic encased her shop, locking it up from intruders.

"You're rather strong," I noted.

"No shit," she said, grabbing my hand.

"Take it away, Demon Lord," Serena prompted.

I peered down at her. "Careful, pet, I do not take well to people making demands of me."

While others would have withered under my stare, instead she tilted her head up to look me straight in the eyes.

Interesting, again.

Their hands held mine tighter when my shimmer took hold of us. It was nothing more than a light swoop in the stomach, but they pulled at my arms to regain their balance when we landed in the main foyer of my tower.

Kyla looked around with wide eyes, and Serena's hand gave a small squeeze.

"Follow me." I walked away without waiting, and they scurried after me like little ducklings.

Demons bowed to me as we passed even though I kept my eyes forward. Their curious glances caught on the women behind me, and I bristled. I knew no harm would come to the witches while they were under my care, but it didn't mean I liked other demons staring.

I wouldn't think twice about killing someone who crossed me, and they knew it.

We traveled to an underground level where I had cells and the morgue.

"What the fuck is this place?" Serena whispered to herself, but my sensitive hearing picked up on it.

"Sometimes, beings are dumb enough to think they can cross me. This is where I rectify that notion," I answered.

As if to emphasize my point, a perfectly timed scream echoed through the hall.

The two women's heartbeats sped at the sound. They had the right mind not to ask questions. I'm sure they wouldn't like the answers. We lived in a dog-eat-dog world, but I was a fucking lion. Bred and born to lead.

I opened a door to the morgue, and the fluorescent lights automatically turned on, giving the white space an obnoxious glare. It was too bright for me. All the rooms on this level were this color; it helped with cleaning up the blood.

"After you," I offered.

Kyla hesitated, but Serena walked inside with her head held high.

I shut the door behind us and walked over to the lonesome

table in the corner. When I pulled back the sheet, Kyla clutched her hand against her chest.

"Oh, Darius," the witch murmured. From what I understood, he had cheated on her, and yet the scent of sadness seeped from her.

Darius was a piece of shit to women. I never complained because it made him stronger, which I utilized. The broken face of the witch proved there must've been some good parts to him.

I wonder which side was his true self.

Serena moved around the table. Her hair was a stark contrast to the white of the room. The image of splaying her over a table, the red tendrils across the surface, had me hard. I shifted my stance to readjust myself and focused on Kyla.

Determination settled across her face, and she placed a small bag on the table beside his head. She rummaged inside and withdrew some bottles.

Gently, she rubbed substances across his mouth and eyelids, using a purple liquid to draw designs on his chest. When she was done, she put it all away. Placing her hands on his arm, she closed her eyes and murmured a spell.

I didn't bother to translate, although I was sure I could if I paid attention. While she prattled on, my gaze drifted over to Serena.

She leaned against the far wall, watching Kyla intently. Her fingers toyed with the charm bracelet on her left wrist. The moment she caught my eyes, her hands dropped, and she perched them behind her against the wall.

I meandered over and propped myself beside her with enough distance between us that my wings didn't touch her. "You shouldn't leave the premises without telling me."

"I'm also an adult and can go where I please," she retorted with a scowl.

"Is that so?" My wings shifted behind me.

Her attention riveted to them, and they fluttered. "Can you fly with those?"

"Why else would I have them?"

"I don't know." She shrugged. Inspecting the veins running through the membrane of my left wing, her interest got the best of her, and she reached out.

They retracted on instinct, and her hand halted.

"Sorry," she murmured. "That was rude."

"It was," I agreed. Wings were sensitive. They could bring me the greatest pleasure or greatest pain; I made sure no one ever got close enough to learn that. Whether it was pleasure or pain, satisfaction or agony, the result could be disastrous. Their lives were never safe around me.

A deep green glow emanated from Darius's body. I turned my attention from her outstretched hand with great effort.

Kyla stopped chanting and stepped back while Serena and I moved forward.

"Well?" Serena raised an eyebrow.

A frown crossed her face. "He was poisoned with vampire saliva, but there's no trace of who it came from." Her finger tapped her chin. "I didn't think vampire saliva could kill. I thought it was only a numbing agent on site and added pleasure into the bloodstream."

"It doesn't unless it's concentrated into extremely high doses, becoming a kind of potent venom," I said. "The only time I've heard of people dying from it are junkies."

Kyla gaped. "People do that?"

"Junkies do that." Serena stood on her tiptoes to trace over Darius's glowing form. "You need to get out more, Kyla."

Kyla pursed her lips. "Why get out more when people come to me?" She side-eyed me. "Also, why leave the safety of my coven?"

Serena rolled her eyes. "Not all of us have the money to stay where it's safe."

"Sometimes people need to pay to keep their safety. They should be lucky I'm willing to help," Kyla retorted.

Serena paused on her toes, her heart skipping a beat.

Neither of us looked at one another, acting too casual. She was worried about me, as she should have been because this only spiked my interest in the feisty woman beside me.

"So, he was killed by a vampire?" Serena reverted the conversation to the problem at hand.

"Yes?" Kyla said.

"You don't sound too sure," I added.

She huffed. "Vampire venom killed him, but there would be a trace of vampire on him if it was given to him by one. The reading is so fuzzy and convoluted that I can't say for sure who administered it."

"So, a witch could've easily given it to him?" I probed.

The two of them whirled on me.

"We didn't do it," Serena claimed again.

"I was pissed at the asshole, and revenge would've been nice. I was planning on making him bald or something. I'm no killer." Kyla's voice raised an octave with her distress.

I heard the truth of Kyla's words, could smell her anxiety over being blamed, not from being caught. "I believe you."

"We're free to go?" Kyla asked. "I'm in the clear?"

"Yes," I said with a nod. "You are."

The glow on Darius's body died down, and Kyla snagged her bag from the table.

"Thank the fates," she said, heading for the door.

Serena was right on her heels.

"Not you," I demanded.

The pact locked in place, magic fusing Serena's feet to the floor.

Her head swirled, hair flying, as she penetrated me with an angry glare. "We had a deal. We didn't do it."

"Yes, we had a deal you would help me find out who did

kill him. We know it wasn't you two, but by no means have we found who *did* murder him."

Her jaw dropped. "You've got to be shitting me!"

"I don't... shit people," I drawled.

She turned to Kyla, who waited at the door. "It's fine. Go."

Kyla gave her one last worried look, but the fact that they weren't actually friends was evident again because a moment later, she raced out the door.

"You can release me," Serena grumbled. "Clearly, I'm not going anywhere."

As I breathed out, the magic loosened its hold.

She spun around to face me fully. "Where to next? I want to get this over with."

"The only clear path,"—a smirk pulled the corner of my mouth—"is to talk to some vampires."

CHAPTER
Six

SERENA

I TUGGED AT THE BOTTOM OF THE SILVERY DRESS, IF
you could even call it that, to ensure it covered my ass. It did.
Barely.

Lazarus leaned towards me, his wings ruffling close to my
back. "Stop messing with it. You look fine."

I glowered up at him and realized he chose a dress that
matched his eyes. I grimaced despite the flutter in my core.
"I'm not worried I don't look good," I hissed. "You couldn't
have chosen something a little... classier?" I frowned at the
sweeping neckline, which showed off the girls, and with the
stilettos it took all my balancing ability to stay standing.

A smirk pulled at the corner of his lips, and a flush of heat
ran through me. "We are going to a vampire club to get information. It's easier to do that if there's a delicious looking
distraction in front of them."

*Did he just call me delicious? No, not the point, Serena! Get
your head in the game.*

His hand fell to my lower back, nothing more than a wisp of a touch, but it was all I could focus on as we walked up to the bouncer. A thrill developed where his hand grazed my skin, a sensation I still wasn't used to when it came to Supes. It was strange for there not only to be no pain but for there to be pleasure. It took everything I had not to lean into it. I yearned for the hug of a loved one. Or to feel the ecstasy being screamed from the apartments around me at night.

The vampire bouncer grunted, drawing my attention. He was burly and wore all black, very stereotypical. Nothing screamed vampire. They could look like any other human, blend in with the crowd. At least, they could when humans were still on Earth... that was until they got hungry or ran at super speed. Appearing human was an evolutionary trait to gain their prey's trust and not raise suspicion. They were one of the oldest supernatural races on Earth because of it.

Humans and angels were like a delicacy for Supes, their favorite dessert, and for the past four hundred years, they'd been living off their equivalent of broccoli. This only made vampires and other Supes hungrier, constantly seeking out the high they once received when humans were their main food source.

The bouncer bowed his head at Lazarus. He wasn't their leader, but as the Demon Lord, he garnered respect wherever he went. Respect or complete fear. I was fairly certain a few people in line peed themselves a little when they saw him.

However, the girls who pushed forward, their eyes on him with keen interest, had my blood boiling. When I caught myself shooting daggers at them, I shook my head to clear it.

What the hell was that? Probably the damn pact.

A girl in the front of the line who was wearing what I could only describe as red lingerie reached for Laz. He stiffened. His dark gaze landed on her, and she paled before taking a step back in line.

A smug grin pulled at my lips as we continued onward.

"Were you jealous, pet?" Lazarus asked me with mirth in his silver gaze.

"Hell no," I scoffed. "I'd let a vamp suck my blood before that would ever happen, Laz."

He raised an eyebrow at me. "Laz?"

"It was that or Lazzy-poo. I haven't decided yet."

He leaned down to whisper in my ear, sending shivers down my spine, "Careful, pet, or I might just let these vamps get a taste of you."

"They could try," I retorted.

He pulled away with a deep chuckle. Stepping forward, he opened the door to the club. "After you."

I tilted my head while comparing his wings to the massive crowd inside. "Will you fit in there?"

He peered inside, seeing the menagerie for himself. Closing his eyes, his dark power seeped out, prickling against my skin, and his wings disappeared.

"What the?" I stared, open mouthed. "If you could do that, why don't you get rid of your wings more often?"

He rolled his shoulders while stretching his neck side to side. "Why would I want to do that?"

"Because it would make life easier?" I shrugged. Wasn't that obvious?

His eyes pierced me, skyrocketing my heart rate. "My wings are a part of me, a blessing. I do not conceal myself or my nature unless I must."

His words hit a cord inside of me. An ache developed in my chest, and I quickly pushed it away.

"Let's do this," I said. With the best sway of my hips, I sauntered past him straight into a club filled with blood-suckers.

Somehow the club toed the line between dangerous and opulent. Red booths lined the walls, which were roped off for high paying customers. It didn't have the tang of vomit and booze I expected, but smelled like roses and sex. The main lights were off, and strobe lights sparked from the DJ booth, reflecting off the crystals of a huge chandelier in the middle of the dance floor.

Laz stuck close to my back; the hot humidity of the club was nothing to the burning sensation of his nearness. At the bar, he ordered a shot of whiskey for himself. When he looked to me, I shook my head. I needed to keep my wits about me in a place like this.

The bass thumped in my chest. Bare skin was everywhere. There were plenty of vampires looking for a good meal and plenty of willing Supes ready to supply. Apparently, it was one of the most sensual feelings a person could have, hooking up with a vampire. Along the dark walls, people ground together, and not even simply couples. In one of the booths, there was a large group of six coalescing, grinding, licking, and, of course, biting. The club had very few rules. 'Don't kill' was essentially all because the moment you walked through those doors you consented to the debauchery.

As I grew accustomed to the floral scent, an underlying metallic smell of blood seeped through. My stomach roiled at it.

A vampire came up behind me, pressing himself against my back. His hand landed on my hip, and he licked the curve of my ear. "Hello, darling. Fancy a good time?" His voice was low with a seductive drawl that sent a thrill down my spine.

I gasped as my nerves were electrified. The touch of the vampire flush against me had every cell in my body revolting, and the pain was excruciating. I choked on my words, unable to utter for him to stop with the pain ricocheting through my body. Fear spiked through me.

More vampires closed in around me with a predatory slink.

"Don't worry," the vamp murmured. "I'll make sure it feels good for you. No need to be scared." His nose traced the side of my neck, inhaling me deeply.

"Get the fuck off her." Laz's wings were back in full force, and when he spread them open, vampires were thrown to the side.

The vampire squeezed my hip, making the pain worse. "She came in here willingly. It's within my rights to take a little bit of her. I'm sure you can share."

Lazarus stepped closer until he towered over the both of us, his silver eyes flashed red. "I do not share."

The warning was clear in his tone, and the vampire had enough sense to take half a step back.

"I'm sure I'll see you later, darling," he said with promise. The vamp disappeared into the club, off to find his next victim.

My tightened chest relaxed enough to where I could suck in a breath. My entire body trembled.

Laz inched closer, his wings wrapping around either side of me to block me from the view of the crowd. "Are you hurt?" He didn't touch me, allowing me time to regain myself.

The stinging in my muscles became a dull ache, the energy draining from my limbs.

"Yeah," I breathed.

"You can't show weakness. Not in a den of predators," he said while scouring the crowd for any potential threats. There was a tick in his jaw, and when he inhaled, his body pressed against mine, warming me and soothing my raw nerves.

"I know. Just give me a second." I took three steadying breaths. In through my nose, out through my mouth. When the feeling of the vampire was gone, I was able to stand up straight, even if I was ready to sleep for three days.

"Lazarus," a sultry female voice said on the other side of his wing. "To what do I owe the pleasure?"

"Alina." Lazarus's wings pulled back to reveal a woman with curly brown hair and dark eyes that matched her skin. She was more dressed than everyone else, wearing a red bralette and a black pencil skirt to perfectly accentuate her curves.

"Shall we find a more comfortable place to talk?" She arced a manicured brow.

"Please." Lazarus nodded at her.

She turned and headed to a hallway in the back. The crowd parted for Alina, people's eyes widening when they saw Laz. He motioned for me to follow, so he could take the rear. Everyone took an extra step back as we passed.

Inside the dark hall were more vampires and other Supes going at it. They seemed to be in a queue not for the bathroom but private rooms that lined the hallway where an assortment of cries echoed from. It was hard to tell if it was from pleasure or pain... or both. At the very end, Alina opened a door to a comfortable office.

There was a desk cleared of all contents except a piece of paper and pen. A filing cabinet sat in the corner obscured by a sheer drape. Two loveseats were on one wall, and on another was a long couch with an end table filled with candles, bottles of lube, and a few other toys. This room was meant for both business and pleasure.

"Have a seat," Alina offered.

Lazarus took the loveseat close to the desk, positioning himself so his back was to the corner and he could see the room.

I sat on the opposite couch, my butt on the very edge of the soft cushion. I didn't even want to think about what had happened on it. Gross.

Alina relaxed into the chair behind her desk. "It's rare for the Demon Lord to come to our neck of the woods. What can I do for you?"

"One of my men died recently," Lazarus cut right to the point.

Alina folded her hands on her desk. "Yes, I heard. I'm sorry to hear that, but I don't understand what that has to do with us."

Lazarus leaned forward, resting his elbows on his knees, watching Alina's expression carefully. "I had a witch do a spell on how he died. It was vampire saliva. One of my own men confirmed it later."

Alina leaned back and studied him. "Dying from vampire saliva is rare but not unheard of. I fail to see why your underling being a saliva junkie is our problem."

"Darius wasn't a junkie," he refuted. "The saliva had been concentrated into a venom. He would never lower himself to something like that."

Alina flashed an elongated canine with a snarl. "Careful, Demon Lord. I may not be able to do anything, but my Queen wouldn't be pleased to hear you speak so ill of us."

He gave a stiff nod. "I meant no disrespect. I simply want answers."

Alina drummed her fingers on her arm. "I may know something," she admitted.

Oh, come on. It was obvious by the sly grin that she was failing to hide that she knew something. She was just playing games, and Laz was letting her. Give me five minutes, and I'd get the information we needed. To each their own, I guess.

Lazarus's back straightened with interest.

"I assume you have payment?" Alina's gaze roamed over my body. A smile curled her lip. "She will do."

Wait, what? My stomach plummeted. Oh, hell no.

Before I could protest, Lazarus rose, drawing back the vampire's attention. "Serena is not for payment." His wings flexed behind him, something I was beginning to understand as a sign of agitation or warning. "Whatever payment you require, I will pay it."

I stiffened in surprise. Was he talking about his blood? Money? Or was it sex? My hands fisted at my sides at the vision of her crawling into his lap, legs astride him, his head rolling back.

No, he was loaded. He must have been talking about money, and any smart business owner would take him up on that. Right?

Alina trailed her manicured fingernail over her chin in thought. "Very well. Let us go to the business office to arrange payment."

Lazarus nodded.

How did he plan to pay? Was he really offering himself instead of me? Please, be only money.

Alina stood up, and so did I, ready to follow them out.

Lazarus shook his head. "You stay here. It'll only take a couple of minutes."

Alina frowned but didn't dispute me staying in her office.

I raised an eyebrow. "A couple of minutes for what exactly?" My blood heated at the thought of Alina having her way with him just a few doors down.

Laz smoothed the smirk threatening to take over his face. "Jealous, pet?" He leaned down to whisper in my ear. "Are you saying you want to join in?"

The tickle of his breath quickened my heart rate. "N-no!"

He pulled back with a twinkle in his eye, shoving his hands into his pockets. He inclined his head at Alina. "Shall we head to your business office so you can name your price?"

Alina sashayed towards the door. "You should be lucky that money is all I'm requesting."

I settled my shaking body back onto the couch.

Laz winked at me before closing the door behind them.

As soon as it clicked shut, I was out of my seat. Finding answers was my forte; that's why Kyla used me so much to get dirt. There was no way I wasn't going to pass up this opportunity.

The filing cabinet was boring, filled with payslips and invoices. Nothing caught my eye, and I didn't have enough time to look at every piece of paper. I crossed to the desk. One drawer held more condoms than anyone would need in a lifetime. Although, vampires were immortal, so I guess hundreds of condoms made sense. Another drawer held basic office needs: letter opener, tape, pens, paper. Nothing interesting. The final drawer was locked.

I searched for a key, running my hands along the bottom of the desk and under the chair; there was nothing.

Reaching back into the supply drawer I pulled out the letter opener and a paperclip. I had learned to open a lock without a key from a young age. It was necessary to survive, and the main reason I ate for many years. Luckily, this particular skill was what landed me my first paying job too, and I moved up from there.

The lock clicked, and I pulled the drawer open. Inside were handwritten notes, one in particular that caught my eye. A transaction for five-time concentrated vampire saliva the night before Darius died. A vial bought with cash, and by the wolves no less.

A normal dose of vampire venom would only have effects for twenty-four hours before the potency burned off. This concentrated, no one could survive. Their lungs would constrict, and their heart would freeze within minutes, if not seconds.

What would the wolves want with this? Wasn't the alpha a cougar? Did this purchase involve all shifters? They weren't known drug users, preferring brawls to get their adrenaline going.

If this was a normal transaction, it would've been in the filing cabinet, not hidden away.

Steps shuffled outside the door.

I snagged the paper, shoving it into the strap of my thong. I replaced everything else as fast as possible and shoved the drawers shut.

I was almost back at my seat when the door flew open.

In sauntered four vampires. The two in the back wore leather jackets with no shirt. One of them had a man bun and the other's head was shaved. In the middle was a stockier man who had red blood stains across his white shirt and tight blue jeans. The vampire in front was a pretty boy with bright blue eyes, a sharp jawline, and a tight shirt to show off his lithe muscles.

The vamp in front smiled, showing his fangs when he saw me. "Hello, darling."

My limbs froze. I recognized his voice; it was the vamp from earlier who had gotten too friendly.

"I told you I would see you later." Blondie licked his lips as his eyes traced over me.

They shut the door behind them and spread around the room. All their attention was riveted on me.

I backed up until I knocked into the desk.

With inhuman speed, the shaved head darted beside me and grabbed my arm. "You're right, Luke, she smells amazing." His nose grazed the inside of my wrist.

"Get away from me." The words rasped against my throat as shooting pain radiated across my skin from his touch.

The stockier one moved to my left side. He pushed my red hair over my shoulder to expose my neck.

I need to get out of this. I need to get away.

Clearing my mind, doing my best to ignore the pain, I concentrated on my charm bracelet. I focused on the elemental magic and envisioned a flame to call on the power just as Kyla taught me.

In my hand, a fireball burst to life.

The vampires jumped back.

"I said, get the fuck away!" I spat.

Blondie laughed. "Oh, you're going to be fun."

All at once, they came at me.

Pure instinct took over. I hadn't survived on my own for the past twelve years for nothing!

I weaved out of the clutches of Shaved Head while throwing the fireball at the stockier vamp.

He instantly caught fire, and his screams filled the room while he turned to ash.

The others stared in shock for a single heartbeat before turning to me with renewed interest, one that held a promise of pain.

"You'll pay for that," Blondie said with murder in his eyes.

"We're going to suck you dry," Manbun added.

I raced for the door, but Shaved Head rammed my side. I flew across the room, slamming into a mirror above the couch and landing in a heap. Shards littered the floor, my skin lacerated with cuts and mouth filled with my blood.

My scent hit the vampires.

Instead of angry sentients, they were now reduced to their base instincts, nothing but mindless predators. Their eyes had turned black, and saliva dripped from their fangs.

A scream tore from me as they came at me in a frenzy. I didn't have time to call up another fireball, and they were too fast. This was it. There was no way I wasn't going down without a fight.

Manbun got to me first, and I punched him clear across the face. I kicked Shaved Head in his balls, and he doubled over clutching them.

Blondie fisted my hair and whipped my head back. His

saliva dripped onto my cheek. "You smell so fucking good. What are you?" His lilting voice was guttural, barely containing his nature to kill me.

The door blew open, splinters flying everywhere.

Lazarus stepped inside, searching the room until his eyes landed on me. His silver eyes turned red for a split second. He spun in a circle, and the claw tip of his wing sliced Blondie's head clean off.

The decapitated body pinned me to the couch, and his cold blood seeped over me.

The rotting stench hit my nose. Bile rose in my throat as I scrambled to get it off me.

Manbun ran straight for Lazarus, dodging his wings with unprecedented speed.

He needed help.

I gave another shove to get the headless vampire off me. He slid off with a thunk as Manbun bared his teeth at Laz. My bloodied fingers fumbled with my charm bracelet. I swallowed down my panic from splotches of a rising memory. This wasn't the first time I had been in a pool of blood, but by the fates, let it be the last.

Manbun attacked before I could call out a spell to help.

With a feral expression, Laz reached out and caught Manbun by the throat, lifting him into the air.

"Let this be a lesson to you and everyone else. No one touches what's mine," Laz hissed.

A swoop in my belly at his statement made me pause.

Flames licked up his arms, reflecting in the bottomless eyes of the vampire in his clutches.

What Lazarus didn't realize in his fit of rage was Shaved Head prowling up behind him. He was too focused as his fire enveloped Manbun.

Shaved Head crouched in preparation to pounce.

I flung my hand at him. A fireball I didn't realize I conjured leapt from my hand and hit him square in the face.

Together, Shaved Head and Manbun turned into dust.

Lazarus stalked over to me and helped me to my feet. His hand engulfed mine, and pleasure trickled my skin where we made contact.

"What the fuck?" Alina gaped in the doorway.

Laz ignored her outburst, eyes trained on the exit as he led me out.

"We have rules!" Alina screamed.

Laz paused, eyes shooting to her. "And your guests were just attacked in an office, not a play space." His voice was cold, emotionless, and held a note of warning.

Alina's mouth snapped shut.

"I'll send over some of my men to help with cleaning up," Lazarus said. "Be sure your queen knows of this proposal instead of asking for retribution for what has occurred."

"Yes, sir." Alina lowered her gaze.

Halfway to the door, my legs buckled beneath me. I never hit the ground. Laz scooped me up and cradled me in his arms, walking straight past Alina.

I leaned into his chest, resting my head on his shoulder. My body still hurt from all the contact with the Supes along with coming down from the adrenaline rush. Everywhere my body touched Laz's was like a soothing balm on a sunburn.

His arms tightened around me.

I didn't notice we had made it out of the club until the cool night air traced along my bare skin.

A shiver wracked through me. It was difficult to keep my eyes open. I was in the Demon Lord's arms, one of the most dangerous places I could be. I couldn't afford to let my guard down.

His eyes, having lost their red glint, raked over me, noting all the cuts and bruises on my body. His nostrils flared at my scent.

I froze, waiting to see what he would do.

His Adam's apple bobbed. "I'm going to shimmer now," he rasped.

"Okay." I closed my eyes with the sensation, blaming the swoop in my stomach from the shimmer and not the contact with him.

A soft bed replaced the bracket of his arms.

I peeled my eyelids open to see we had shimmered into my room.

"I will send for someone to care for your cuts." Lazarus's fingers clenched into fists at his sides, and his wings shifted behind him.

"K." My response was half muffled by the pillow.

He left the room without another word, and I fell into a dreamless sleep.

CHAPTER
Seven

LAZARUS

ALINA HAD GIVEN ME A SINGLE NAME: BALTIC.

It meant nothing to me, too low ranking for him to be on my radar. I had scrounged up a few pieces of intel on him but nothing noteworthy. I had spent thirty-thousand dollars, and for what? Five-fucking-thousand dollars per letter. What a joke. Luckily, money was something I didn't lack. I was more annoyed about the insufficient information rather than the bad business deal.

I pressed the heels of my palms into my eyes. They had only turned back to their usual silver color a half an hour ago. The smell of her blood clung to me even though I changed my clothes. Her essence was like nothing I had ever come across, and it made me hungry.

When I heard her panicked heart down the hall, it pierced through my soulless body. My rage took over—at the vampires who wanted her and at myself for not knowing she needed help sooner.

The little witch, if that's what she was, surprised me over and over again. She was fierce, already having killed one blood-sucker before I even got there despite numbers not being in her favor. Most wouldn't have lasted ten seconds against four vampires. Not only that, she also saved me.

My anger had me so blinded, so focused, I hadn't heard the vamp sneaking up behind me. She could've let him take me down, or at least try to. He wouldn't have stood a chance. However, if something happened to me, our pact would have been broken, and she would have been free.

I would merely manifest back in hell; only an angel's blade could kill me for good. It would take me centuries to reach the surface again. Yet she threw a fireball like it was second nature to protect me.

With a groan, I dropped my hands to the file on my desk. Picking up the glass of whiskey, I took a swig and stared at the paper.

Name: Serena Bishop
Age: 24 years old
Class: Witch

I scanned the information my underlings dug up for me. I wouldn't say there was necessarily anything out of the ordinary. No red marks on her record, but what was odd was that her record only began at eighteen years old when she rented her own room. She had no cellphone and paid for everything in cash. She had no known friends, only clients. I tried looking into family history, but there was none.

I sent out some of my most trusted demons to find more information. They came back to tell me she had been homeless before that. The only way she could have survived was by steal-ing. It was no wonder Kyla hired her. A clean record like this meant she never got caught. No one could find anything prior to twelve years old. Half of her life was missing, and I wanted to know why. What I did know was for the past six years she'd worked as a spy of sorts, being paid to gather information.

My finger traced a photo of her taken at a bar a year ago. Her red hair hung low on her back, her full lips pressing together as she stared hard at someone across the bar. I assumed it was a mark.

Desire coursed through me.

Shutting the folder, I slipped it into a side drawer and finished off my whiskey. I pulled my cell phone out of my jeans pocket and dialed a number.

"Lavinia speaking," a smooth female voice picked up on the other end.

"I'll need five of your best girls tonight. Whoever has the strongest essence, and with two others to help feed the girls to replenish them. I don't want to suck them dry," I ordered.

"Certainly," she replied. "Any specific requests?"

My teeth ground together. "Redheads."

"I'll be sure they're ready for you, master." Lavinia ran my most prestigious succubi house in Demon District. It had the best, and I made sure of it by paying the women well.

Reaching over, I uncorked the bottle of whiskey and poured myself another glass.

The door to my office swung open.

"Save some for the rest of us." A lithe woman, dressed in leather pants and a silk top, waltzed inside. Her lips were painted apple red to juxtapose her cropped black hair and silver and gold eyes. Her black feathered wings slung over the back of the chair when she plopped down.

"Neferia," I grumbled. "Did you lose all sense of manners while you were away?"

"I tried to stop her." Azazel, my best friend who was more like a brother, shut the door. He shoved his hands into his jean's pockets, causing his biceps to push against his black shirt. Brown hair curled around two black horns twisting up six inches from his head.

"Family doesn't need to knock." Neferia leaned back and propped her feet onto the end of my desk.

I leaned forward and gently shoved them off. "Family most certainly needs to knock."

"I'm your sister! Not some lackey," she scoffed.

Azazel's blue eyes sparkled with amusement. "Is that why a non-lackey agreed to take on a mission for the Demon Lord?"

I frowned. I hated when he referred to me like that. He was fucking with Neferia, per usual, but these were the only two beings in the universe whom I could truly relax around instead of always having to be the heir of Lucifer. No decisions, no underlings, just... me.

Neferia folded her arms over her chest. "I took on the mission from the goodness of my heart. Plus, I was able to get out of this hell hole for a bit."

"Goodness? You?" I quipped. "Is this a new development?"

Neferia swiped the whiskey bottle off my desk and took a swig, eyes narrowed on the two of us the whole time.

Azazel and I exchanged a look, and smirks broke across our faces. In these moments, it was like we were the same kids who grew up together.

"No teaming up! That's not fair," she whined.

"No hogging the whiskey." Azazel snagged the bottle from her hand and took a few gulps.

She folded her arms across her chest with a pout.

"I think I liked it better when you two were away," I groaned. There were parts of this country less... civilized... than *Tenebris*, and they helped scout areas I may need to intervene and take control of if it got too bad. This allowed for cities of order spattering across the wasteland, but it was by no means what it was pre-apocalypse. Their return brought good news, having taken care of the unrest themselves, and welcomed assistance to keep me focused on my current predicament, not Serena.

"Liar," Azazel chortled.

"What has been going on while we've been away?" Neferia asked, head cocking to the side. Her astute gaze took me in and widened a few seconds later. "What happened?"

This drew Azazel's attention, his focus snapping to me with renewed intent.

Neferia always had a knack for looking deeper into people. She could somehow sense what others often kept hidden under the surface. She was by no means psychic; it was more of a wavelength she picked up on. At least, that's how I understood it every time she tried to explain.

My shoulders relaxed. I could always count on them to help, and with no complaints, too. Well, none from Azazel.

"Darius is dead," I said.

"Good. He was a scumbag anyways," Azazel commented.

Neferia narrowed her silver and gold sunburst eyes on me. "It's more than that." She sniffed the air, scenting it like a bloodhound for the truth of my turmoil, and to my displeasure, she did. "What's that smell?" She all but drooled, licking her lips like her favorite dessert had been placed in front of her.

Azazel moved closer, taking a whiff himself. His blue eyes turned black for a split second. "Indeed. It smells delectable. Are there leftovers?"

My hand clenched my whiskey glass so tight that a crack formed on the side. I set it down before I broke it completely. "She is not a meal," I said with a flat tone.

"*She*?" Neferia quirked an eyebrow.

"It's a business arrangement. A pact to find out who killed Darius and why," I explained.

"Right." Neferia crossed her legs, not pushing further; but

from long experience, I knew her calculating gaze meant she didn't believe me.

"I have work to do," I retorted. On my phone, I opened a text to Lavinia and typed to her that I would be there soon. I hunched over the device, spreading my wings to create a curtain between me and them.

"We'll leave you to it." Azazel nodded at Neferia, who begrudgingly rose from her seat.

"See you tomorrow?" she asked.

"Yes, I have some leads I would appreciate your assistance with." I may regret getting their help, but there were no two people I trusted more in the world. With their help, I'd find who'd killed Darius by tomorrow night, and I could be rid of the witch and whatever she stirred in me.

"Anything I can work on tonight?" Azazel offered.

I wanted to be there for the interrogation, but finding the vampire Alina told me about after I paid her a large sum of money was something Azazel could easily do.

I wrote down the information on a piece of paper—the vampire's name, where he was often found, and who he hung out with.

"Here." I held out the paper for Azazel to take.

Neferia stood on her tiptoes to lean over his shoulder to read the contents. "Ew." Her nose wrinkled like she smelled bad fish.

"You know him?" I asked.

"Yeah, he's a total low life. All he cares about is blood, sex, and money," she said.

"So, like most vampires," Azazel noted.

She grimaced. "Worse. He's taken underage girls, forced them into things. He's turned them into junkies and blood bags. It's disgusting."

My canines elongated and pricked my lip. "Why haven't

the vamps taken care of him? He should be dead for doing that," I sneered.

"The Vampire Queen has him wrapped around her little finger. He's a total rat for her. Tells her everything and does whatever she wants."

"How do you know him?" Azazel's sharp eyes bored into her, the clench of his jaw a dead giveaway how much he didn't approve.

Is that jealousy I smell?

Neferia pursed her lips. "For fate's sake, calm down, Az. Or should I say Azz?"

The 'z' sound sliding into an 's' only deepened Azazel's furrow.

She was astute as ever and completely unperturbed by him. Jealousy may not be the right word; Neferia would never settle down, and we both knew it, but it didn't stop him from bristling when Neferia made poor life decisions.

Neferia continued, "I've run into him a few times in bars around town. It's never been a pleasant experience. One time, I caught him in an alley with some sixteen-year-old shifter girls. He got away before I could end him, but I've kept tabs on him ever since." She shook her head. "I'm not surprised if he's involved."

"Can I trust you two to bring him in discreetly?" I asked.

"We should be offended that you need to ask!" Neferia placed her hand on her chest in mock affront.

"We'll have him by morning," Azazel assured me.

I nodded to them.

As they left, they discussed the best places to check first and fell silent the moment they were outside my office. I trusted those two for a reason. Nothing ever leaked from them. I couldn't say that about everyone, even with the threat of death for betrayal. Risk was something most Supes enjoyed a little too much.

I sighed, leaning back into my chairs. My back was stiff, which made the muscles in my wings hurt too.

We had a lead, and I was happy my trusted circle was back together, but my thoughts drifted to Serena. The cuts on her body from the vampire's attack, the stench of fear that clung to her skin, how she fell asleep the moment I left. I fought the urge to check on her. I needed to feed or else I might do something stupid. I needed her gone, though I balked at the idea.

This could be over in twenty-four hours. Did I want it to be? Would I be able to let her go when the pact was complete?

CHAPTER
Eight

SERENA

I WOKE UP EARLY.

The sky was a light grey, the sun not having fully risen yet.

I frowned at the smears of bloodstains on my sheets, quickly followed by relief when I saw my cuts had scabbed over during the night. Some were already beginning to heal. I considered taking my charm bracelet off, letting myself heal faster without the magic blocking the process, but I didn't want to be caught without it in this place.

My stomach let out a rumble, and I rubbed it. I needed food, and with my body demanding resources to heal and the adrenaline from last night, I was starving.

There was no food in the kitchen; there must be a communal area somewhere. The tower was a gathering place for demons, they'd need a place to congregate.

I cleaned myself up, throwing the ripped, dirty dress into the corner. In the closet, which had been stocked with clothes at some point, I found a fresh pair of jeans, and I paired it with my ass-kickers and a shirt that said "Witch, Please" from my backpack.

The elevator door wasn't locked this time. Up was the Demon Lord, so down it was. I pressed the button to summon the elevator. Tapping my foot, I watched the numbers change above the elevator, and when it reached my floor, it dinged.

I jumped back when the doors opened to reveal a woman inside. Her black-feathered wings took up half the space.

Her silver-gold gaze devoured me, and her blood red lips pulled into a grin. "Going down?" she asked with a honeyed voice, suggesting something else entirely.

"Yes." I swallowed and stepped inside with my head held high, putting as much space as I could between myself and the beautiful demon inside the small box.

"What floor?" she asked.

"Um..." I had absolutely no idea.

She sniffed the air, and her blazing gaze dropped to my wounds. "You must be Serena."

I stiffened before nodding my head.

"I'm Neferia." She dropped her hand from the buttons and took a step toward me.

Instead of cowering, I rolled my shoulders back and braced myself. My fingers flexed, ready to call a fireball.

She studied me, and the ruffling of her black wings caused the feathers to catch the light. A metallic blue shined off them. "I can see why my brother is interested in you."

I cocked my head. "Your brother?"

"Lazarus, the Demon Lord, Lucifer's son, Mr. High-and-Mighty... Or should I say Low-and-Annoying?"

A snort escaped me at the last bit, and Neferia's grin widened.

"I didn't know he had a sister," I said.

She huffed. "Most don't. Our dad sleeping with an angel isn't something we boast about."

My jaw dropped so hard it could've dislocated. "What? I thought nephalems were fictitious."

"First,"—she held up a pointer finger—"what about this world is fictitious anymore? Second, I'm not just a nephalem, I am *the* nephalem."

My mouth made an 'oh', and then I whispered, "That's kind of cool."

Her wings flexed at the compliment. "I am pretty cool, huh? There's a few demons you could help me remind." She winked.

A smile tugged at the corner of my mouth from the playful gesture. "Let me guess, Lazarus is one of them."

She chuckled. "You catch on quick."

"You have to be in order to survive this world."

I was captured by her intriguing eyes, and I now realized that the silver swirls were a clear indication of her lineage, or half of it. She studied me in turn. "I like you," she stated like a fact and less like a cat playing with a mouse from a few seconds ago.

My body relaxed. "You might be the first."

"I have a sneaking suspicion that's not true."

My eyebrows rose. I mean, no one outright hated me. Well, at least not if I did my job right. Still, there was something in her voice that made me think she was talking about someone specific.

"Where were you headed?" Neferia asked again, turning back to the buttons of the elevator.

"To find food," I said.

She smacked her palm against her forehead in exasperation. "Did Laz not put food in your place?"

Ha! I knew he went by Laz!

I shook my head.

"Demons don't eat normal food. The idiot probably forgot there's plenty of other races that still require it."

My eyes widened at her calling the Demon Lord an idiot, but I didn't say anything. "What do they eat?" I asked.

"Blood, souls, a person's essence which can be amplified during sex. It depends on the demon." Her lips pressed into a hard line before she hit the button for the thirteenth floor. "Let's go get you some food."

I blanched. "If demons eat what you say, I doubt the Demon Lord's suite will have anything to my liking."

"Probably not," she agreed. "You better believe we're going to make sure he stocks your place ASAP, even if I have to drag him to do it myself."

"We?" It wasn't even six in the morning, and she was waltzing into his place like it was nothing!

The elevator pinged, and the doors slid open after scanning Neferia of her biological markers. At least she was allowed here.

"LAZ!" she hollered, stepping into the apartment.

The short hallway led to an expansive open floor plan. The kitchen sat to the left with a long, tempered-glass table with six chairs just past it. Along the far wall was a line of floor-to-ceiling windows with a set of double doors in the center. I was unable to see outside them since the windows had their dark mode on, not that the view would be much different from my own. An L-shaped, grey couch sat atop a burgundy carpet, giving a pop of color against the various grey tones making up the walls, cabinets, and marble floor. A fire crackled opposite the sofa, and above it sat... was that *The* Starry Night?!

"Laz! Get out here!" Neferia shouted.

"What the fuck, Nef?" Lazarus stumbled from what I assumed was his bedroom. His hair was messy from sleep, and my eyes traced down the smooth skin of his broad shoulders along his muscular torso to a dark happy trail leading into a pair of black boxer briefs.

I dragged my eyes away from the bulge in material before either of them noticed.

He froze when he saw me. Narrowing his eyes, he trained his annoyance at his sister. "What the hell is this?"

"You forgot to feed the witch." She hitched a thumb in my direction.

His eyes widened. "Shit." He combed his fingers through his hair. "I'll take care of it. Give me a moment."

Neferia threw a victorious smile at me, and I couldn't help but return it with a short chuckle.

A few seconds later, he returned with his phone pressed against his ear. "Is there anything you don't like? Or prefer? Or can't eat? Or—"

"He's trying to ask what kind of food you want," Neferia interjected.

"I'll eat anything," I said.

Laz's mouth pursed, his eyes raking over me. They caught onto my cuts, some now turning pink with new skin. "I'm glad my healer saw to you. I was unsure if he would if you were asleep."

I didn't argue. Who knew? Maybe someone *had* seen to my wounds.

Someone picked up on the other end, and Lazarus ordered every type of food I could ever dream of. My mouth water even though I was unsure how to cook half of it. I would figure it out.

His enormous wings didn't make him look small with a broad chest, chiseled abs, and a delicious V at the bottom. Muscles corded his body. Lethal beauty was what came to mind when I looked at him.

"See something you like?" Neferia sidled up to me.

"I'm guessing it's not every day someone sees the Demon Lord in his underwear," I noted.

She threw her head back with a laugh. "At least not in his home. I promise you there are plenty of succubi who've seen more of his skin than you're seeing right now."

My stomach twisted with her words, and the tightness in my chest could only be defined as jealousy. The feeling surprised me, and my thoughts turned. I envisioned his fingers trailing along my skin, leaving lines of pleasure he brought to me every time we touched. The growls he gave the vampires in warning turned into rumbles of delight. His arms bulging around me as he scrapes sharp canines along my...

Goosebumps rose to the surface of my skin as I took a shaking breath, cutting off my train of thought. I interlaced my hands behind my back, hoping they couldn't scent where my mind had been headed.

I peeked over at Neferia, who watched me with amusement alighting her face. She swiped at the corner of her mouth, indicating I had drool there.

I didn't. My face heated.

When he got off the phone, he gave a curt nod. "It'll be delivered within the hour."

"Thanks," I mumbled.

His attention transitioned back to his sister. "I assume you found him?"

"Yup," she said. "We brought him in about an hour ago. I was on my way to see him when I ran into Serena."

"Who?" I asked.

"A vamp whose name I was given at the club. We think he was involved in Darius's death," he said.

Neferia raised an eyebrow at him.

Lazarus gave her a hard look as he explained, "The pact is for her to help me find out why Darius died. It's strictly business."

"Can we go talk to him now?" I questioned, my hunger instantly forgotten with a new lead.

Lazarus frowned, and Neferia avoided my eye contact.

I looked between them in confusion. "What?"

"There won't be a lot of talking," Laz said.

"At least, not at first," Neferia added. "We will need to do some convincing before he breaks."

Ah. They were going to torture him for the information.

I folded my arms in front of me and widened my stance. "I want to be there."

Neferia smiled with a ravenous look, turning to Laz with an approving gleam in her eye.

He studied me, and I could have sworn I saw heat flash in his eyes. "Are you sure?"

"Like you said, it's part of the pact. I want to help figure out who killed Darius, and if this guy is a part of it then I want to be there." I clenched my jaw, unmoving in my conviction.

Lazarus gave a brief nod. "Fine, give me a second to get dressed."

CHAPTER
Nine

LAZARUS

WE WEAVED THROUGH THE HALLS OF THE LOWEST floor, which was a hundred feet below ground level. The space was reserved for safety in case of any fall out, but there were special rooms for captives.

Serena's presence pressed against me with her timid breaths pounding in my ears. The sight of her in my living quarters, hair mussed from sleep and in a pair of tight jeans that made her ass look amazing, was burned into my brain. Was she part siren with this lure she seemed to have over me?

Last night, I fed on the essence of willing succubi, but with her cinnamon scent wrapping around me, my hunger returned like an angry beast hunting its prey. If I wasn't careful, that was exactly what she'd become. I hadn't lost control in centuries. I wasn't some young demon anymore. Yet one little witch had me constantly fighting my every instinct.

A part of me wanted to give in. To taste her and get it out of my system. However, I feared that once I started, I wouldn't be able to stop. I would kill when necessary, but killing when feeding was bad form. Plus, for whatever reason, my innards retracted at the thought of permanent damage to her. I wanted to protect her, from myself above all else.

My ears picked up on the muffled cries of the vampire behind the door at the end of the hall. I stalked forward, putting space between myself and the witch at my back.

Azazel was already inside sharpening a blade when we entered. He looked up from his perch leaning on a counter on the far side. He grinned when he saw me, which fell from his face when his attention dropped to Serena.

I hadn't realized I shifted in front of her until he looked at me with his eyebrows reaching into his hairline. Smothering any more reactions, I appraised the vampire. He was a good-looking man, as many vampires were. His sandy blond hair was cut so it swept perfectly across his forehead to the side, and his ice-blue eyes were alluring. Despite these attractive features, he had a weasley look about him, like his rat-like tendencies couldn't help but manifest outwardly.

I waltzed forward, keeping my form between his line of sight and Serena, and pulled out the gag. "Hello, Baltic," I purred. "I hear you've been doing some naughty business."

"That's putting it lightly," Neferia scoffed.

I glared over my shoulder at her for interrupting.

Her lips sealed shut.

Serena sidled up next to Neferia against the far wall, her eyes saucer-wide as they took in the vampire hanging with his hands chained above his head.

His shoulders were probably sore from the position; that would be the least of his worries today.

Azazel brought the edge of the metal to Baltic's neck. It seared against his skin—silver.

Baltic screamed in pain, and sweat beaded on his forehead.

When Azazel pulled the knife away, his head dropped

slightly. "What do you want? I've done nothing to your kind," he claimed.

"Oh?" I cocked my head to the side. My right wing bent; the talon on top poised to pierce into his chest.

"You think I'm stupid enough to kill a demon?" he spat.

Azazel lashed out and sliced a line clear across his cheek. The silver blade didn't allow his healing to kick in, so his blood ran freely down his skin.

There was a small gasp behind me.

When I looked over, Serena gripped her own arm with them folded over her chest. Her eyes were surprised, intrigued, but not horrified. There seemed to be a glint of vengeance.

Something the equivalent of pride pulled at my chest. Living on the streets, she had probably seen the scum of this city. She recognized it in him as much as the rest of us, and I could only imagine what this man represented to her.

"I'll tell you whatever you want," Baltic pleaded.

I frowned at him, disgusted by how easily he caved. He was worthless, and I had no doubt he would give us information. The only problem was I now knew of his other crimes because of Neferia, turning innocent girls into mere blood bags. Disgusting. This was too easy. I wasn't satisfied.

I called upon my flames, and their heat licked up my arm at their response. Bringing my flaming hand to his skin, I hissed, "Tell me what you've done."

He had the audacity to look confused.

I released my flames against his skin.

His wails turned to shrieks as his skin turned red and then bubbled.

I pulled away before the pain made him pass out. "Do not act innocent," I commanded. "Admit what you've done."

"Th-that's too broad. Ask me a question, and I'll answer," he stuttered.

This time I let my flames burn away his clothes, leaving him naked and exposed with fresh burns covering his body.

Azazel's own magic zipped out and snuffed out the flames before it consumed him.

I chanced another glance at Serena, and now mortification did cover her face, but the brave little witch didn't look away.

"Tell me!" I demanded. I could feel when my eyes shifted red with my anger surfacing. I refused to have him make me look like the monster here merely because he wouldn't speak.

Neferia stepped beside me, sensing my losing battle with my demon self.

The last time he was let loose, I blacked out, only coming to later with nothing except death surrounding me. I had earned my reputation, and I upheld it and would do what was necessary to protect my people, but I never wanted to be a mindless murderer again. The innocent lives that were lost haunted my dreams to this day.

Neferia and Azazel were the only ones privy to how much it destroyed me.

My sister placed a hand on my shoulder, and her fiery gaze pierced the vampire, matching the hatred in her voice. "Is it true you make vamp venom with your saliva?"

"Yes," Baltic rasped through blistered lips.

"Is it true you sell venom to junkies?" she continued with a harder question.

"Yes."

"Is it true you have taken underage girls, gotten them hooked on the venom, and either killed, sold, or turned them into blood bags for other vampires?"

Baltic lifted his shocked face. "How did you—?"

"Answer the question," I growled.

"Y-yes." His fear oozed into the room, choking out any other scent. Even the delicious zest of Serena, because I should've noticed when she moved closer, yet I only knew when she spoke up.

"He what?" Serena's small voice peeped from between Neferia and myself.

Everyone looked at her with mild surprise. Most would run screaming from what was happening, and yet she had stepped forward.

Her eyes were hard, unyielding. "What did you just say?"

Baltic shook his head.

I growled and brought my talon to his neck.

Azazel stiffened, thinking I was about to kill him before we got answers. I knew better than that.

"Answer her," I demanded.

"I...I... I make vamp serum and get young girls addicted to it," he said between shaking breaths.

To my surprise, a fireball erupted in the elemental witch's hand.

"Why?" she hissed, bringing it close to his crispy cock.

Neferia laughed at how brazen this little minx was, and pure satisfaction coursed through me. Azazel watched her with curiosity.

"They're the easiest," Baltic stammered. His wide eyes watched the flame, too scared to move in case he actually swung closer to it.

"Keep going," she snapped.

"They are the easiest to convince to try the drug, to get addicted, and their blood—" He cut himself off by pressing his lips thinly together.

"Their blood?" Serena tilted her head to the side, more animal than witch.

The tip of my talon pressed into his jugular.

"It's delicious, okay?" he hollered. "Is that what you want me to say? Especially if they're a virgin, it's fucking divine. To taste their sweet, young blood, to feel their life drain away or know I have full control over what happens to them is fucking addicting, and I've loved every moment of it!"

All of our jaws dropped at the admission. Mortification at his words swept through me. This low-life had everything he deserved coming for him.

"Fucking scumbag," Serena leered. "You ruined young girls' lives! Innocent lives! I hope you fucking rot in hell." Her fireball went out, and she pulled back as though she couldn't be in the vicinity of this vile creature any longer.

I winced at her using my homeland as a place for a curse. "Rot in *Tartarus*," I corrected. "Only the worst for someone like you."

"I'll do anything!" Baltic screamed.

"Tell me," I said. "Why kill Darius?"

"Darius?" His browless skin tightened in a confused scowl.

"The warlock. My warlock," I explained.

Dawning realization crossed his face. "I didn't kill him!"

"You gave the serum to someone who did?" Azazel confirmed.

He nodded frantically. "But I didn't know! I didn't do it!"

"Who did you give it to?" I asked.

"It was the wolves! The wolves bought it from me!"

Serena jumped beside me. There was something in her that snapped in place. She noticed my questioning look because she volunteered her thoughts without prompting. "I found a note in the desk at the club. I forgot all about it after the attack."

"Snooping were we, little witch?" I smirked down at her.

"There was a transaction in a locked drawer, not kept with the other files. One in cash with the vampires. I thought it was odd, so I took it," she explained.

Neferia's eyes swirled with mirth. "*Locked* drawer?"

Serena shrugged. "I'm decent with locks, and it's a good

thing too. I have it up in my room. His story checks out with what I found."

I nodded in agreement. It did, except once again we had yet to find the person who killed Darius and why. One more piece had fallen into place, bringing us closer to answers, but it was one more lead with something that should've been solved already. Annoyance clenched my jaw. I felt like I was on a wild goose chase trying to solve Darius's murder.

"Anything else?" Neferia eyed the vamp greedily.

I shook my head. "I think we've found all of our answers."

"What're you going to do with him now? Kill him?" Serena asked. Again, there was no fear, only acceptance in her eyes as she inspected the vampire. She was curious, and I couldn't help the smile from crossing my face.

Neferia gasped, covering her mouth in fake disbelief. "We can't waste a perfectly good essence. It'll be delicious when he tries to fight it. I wonder what horrid sounds will gurgle from his putrid mouth." She laughed when Serena took a stuttering step back. "Do you think he doesn't deserve it?"

Serena studied the vampire, his charred body hanging limply from the chains. His eyes begged her for mercy, but she showed none.

She shook her head. "If anything, he deserves enough pain for every young girl's life he destroyed."

Azazel stiffened at the claim. Witches didn't talk like this, although I wasn't surprised with her upbringing if she felt this way. In fact, I wanted names of every person who ever did or tried to do her harm so I could kill them all. Perhaps I would send Azazel to do just that.

"Let's go," I murmured to Serena. I placed my hand on her lower back, and the thrill of touching her gave me a heady sensation.

She was merciless when she needed to be, and knew this

man deserved what was about to happen, but it didn't mean she had to be here to see it.

To my surprise, she leaned into my touch as we left the room. The muscles in her shoulders relaxed, and a relieved sigh wisped from between her lips.

The elevator doors closed as the screams began.

CHAPTER
Ten

SERENA

THE BURNT STENCH FROM THE VAMPIRE'S SKIN STILL assaulted my senses. I rubbed my nose in an attempt to dislodge it. I jumped when the elevator dinged at the arrival to my suite.

Lazarus frowned down at me, a worried furrow between his brows. "Let's get some food in you."

At the reminder, my stomach grumbled, and I gave him a stiff nod.

With his hand on my lower back, he led me into my apartment. Tingles radiated from the contact, helping to release the tension in my body. I allowed myself to relish in it. Spending my life avoiding being touched could get pretty damn lonely.

I wasn't surprised at what had occurred downstairs. Worse things happened in this world. But the reminder of my past, of the times I'd been left helpless and almost lost parts of me because of it, was a lot to process. Baltic represented everything I hated in this world and why I never felt bad about stealing or screwing people over. Morals didn't seem to exist anymore. People only cared about money, sex, and power. Love, trust, and safety left with the humans almost four hundred years ago.

I peered at Lazarus through the corner of my eye. What had surprised me most was how pissed off he had seemed by Baltic's actions too. I knew why I was upset; however, for the Demon Lord to be angry was intriguing to say the least.

He caught me looking at him, and I quickly turned away, but I still saw the small smile he gave from my peripherals.

"I need to grab something," I murmured, slipping away to the bedroom to grab the crumpled piece of paper.

Reentering the kitchen, Laz pulled out a stool at the island for me to sit down.

I folded my arms over my chest. "It's hard for me to get food if I'm sitting."

"Please, have a seat." A heated challenge sparked in his eyes, daring me to not listen.

I obliged, even though it felt really freaking weird to be catered to. Seriously, who pulled out chairs anymore? It was more common to have offers to go screw behind a dumpster.

He circled the island to the fridge and pulled out ingredients: eggs, butter, cheese, and some vegetables.

My face contorted at the fresh spinach in his hands.

"It's good for you," he said.

"You don't need to torture me too by forcing me to eat something that tastes like dirt. I haven't done anything wrong." I held my hands over my heart to help prove my innocence.

A smirk pulled at the corner of his mouth. "Odd. I didn't realize thievery, breaking and entering, selling secrets to the highest bidder, and arson weren't offenses."

My jaw dropped. "How do you know about that? I was

fifteen when the arson happened, and it was an accident! I didn't know vampire blood caught on fire so easily!"

"I have my sources." He chuckled as he threw chopped vegetables and bacon into a pan.

"Extra bacon! Less veggies," I commanded.

"I'm sorry, who's the chef here?" With a spatula, he expertly sifted the contents around so nothing burned. "And you will eat your veggies. They're good for you."

I rolled my eyes. "How do you know how to cook anyways? You don't eat this stuff."

"I have lived for hundreds of years and am in charge of demons everywhere, yet you think I can't pick up a basic skill?" He cracked some eggs into the pan one handed and whisked everything into a scramble.

"Well, when you put it that way..." I trailed off. With nimble fingers, I pushed the slip of paper across the table.

With one hand still stirring, he picked up the receipt and scoured over it. "This is quite a potent batch of venom," he noted.

"Those were my thoughts exactly," I agreed. "A deadly batch is what? Three times concentration?"

He nodded, folding the piece of paper to tuck into his pants' pocket.

"If it really is the shifters, we should consider talking to their alpha, Knox. However, the slip of paper specifically said wolves, so maybe we should do some investigation ourselves to figure out the shifter's involvement." My fingers tap on the anger as I think through the information. "Shifters usually work as a pack, even if they're still grouped together, so it'd be weird if the alpha doesn't know."

Laz paused in making food to arc an eyebrow at me.

"What?" I shrugged. "This is what I do."

"So it seems." He lowered the heat on the stove, allowing the residual heat in the pan to continue cooking the food.

Wow, he really did know what he was doing. "I will send someone to investigate."

"Like hell you will." I leaned back and folded my arms.

His nostrils flared, and his power warped through the air. "There is no need to take my home in vain."

"Fine, but there's no need to ignore my capabilities. You will send someone to investigate? As in someone else? It's literally what I do for a living!"

"And it's a shock to me you have been so good at it based on how much trouble you seem to stir along the way. I need someone a little more subtle."

"I can do subtle," I scoffed.

"I haven't seen proof of that."

"You didn't know of my existence until recently. I'd say that means I'm pretty good at staying under the radar," I retorted.

A smile tugged at his lips.

"At least tell me your plan," I demanded. "That way I can tell you if it's a good one or not." The amused look he gave me only irritated me, like he was placating a child. I was damn good at what I did, and I'd be sure to prove that to him.

"I will send Azazel to talk with some shifters. He has some connections."

I couldn't stop my surprise. Connections with the shifters? They were the group of Supes least likely to turn on their own. "And your backup plan? You should always have a backup plan in case there is no intel."

"I'll go speak with Knox myself."

"And you think *I'm* not subtle," I scoffed. "If you need to talk to Knox, don't go to him, and don't summon him here either. Both situations will draw too much attention, not just for yourselves but to the other leaders of the districts. They'll talk about why you two are meeting, and depending on how deep this goes, we want it as quiet as possible. Send Azazel to give him a letter and meet privately in neutral territory."

"Giving me orders, pet? Careful or I may have to punish you." I could hear the jest in his voice, proven by his small smirk, and a thrill still went through my stomach. "Nonetheless, that is a very good suggestion. I can see why people hired you."

Pride swelled within me. Little did he know, I planned on showing him just how good I was at my job. While Azazel was digging up dirt, I would too, and I'd do it right under the Demon Lord's nose. This way when I came back with information, he would have no choice but to praise me.

Laz loaded everything onto a plate, including some toast which he used a small flame from his fingers to brown, and placed it in front of me. "Eat," he ordered.

My mouth watered at the food, the smell intoxicating. I really loved breakfast. I picked up the fork and pulled out pieces of spinach to pile off to the side.

"Eat all of it," he warned. His silver eyes trained on me, and a shiver ran up my spine like he'd discipline me if I didn't obey.

"Fine." I mixed the spinach back in, scooped up a huge bite, and stuck it in my mouth. Flavor erupted over my tongue.

The eggs were fresh and light. The vegetables, including the spinach, gave it an earthy aroma while the bacon brought a smoky flavor to it. It was freaking divine.

A moan escaped me as I chewed, my eyes fluttering shut.

When I opened them, Laz's attention watched my mouth like he was ready to take a bite himself.

I held out my fork with another bite already prepared. "You want some?" I offered.

He blinked, as though coming back from a reverie, and

shook his head. "That is not what I have an appetite for at this moment."

I shrugged. More for me! And shoved another mouthful into me. "Okay," I admitted, "spinach isn't *that* bad. At least not when you make it."

Pride expanded his wings as he stood straighter. They gave a little flap when a smile graced his face. "I'm glad you like it."

I continued to eat, and he continued to watch me with rapt attention. Normally, if it was any other Supe, I'd be kicking their ass for being creepy, except it didn't bother me with him. It was like he was savoring every bite as much as me. Maybe he wanted to eat and enjoy the food but couldn't.

He leaned his arms on the counter. "I do have a question."

I pointed my fork at him. "Ha! I knew this was an interrogation!" I piled some egg onto a piece of the bread. "Being good cop by making me breakfast is totally working though. Go for it."

"What happened to you before the age of twelve?"

I froze, the toast held mid-air towards my mouth.

My reaction clearly only made him more curious. "Working with someone as closely as I am with you, I have to be careful."

I leaned back in my seat. "You dug up dirt on me? Why not ask?"

He cocked his head to the side. "I just did, and you have yet to answer."

I threw the bread into my mouth and chewed slowly, giving myself time to think.

It's not like I really had anything to hide. Well, I definitely had something to hide. Thankfully, I didn't think he'd figure it out with a background check. I was in more danger by sitting here across from him. I didn't like the idea of someone poking around in my past, but perhaps with his resources...

"I don't know," I said.

His lips thinned. "I do not appreciate someone lying to me. I'm not asking for your darkest secret, at least not yet. Start with telling me a memory from your childhood."

Yeah, probably because from a single memory he could find out the rest with his connections; there was still one problem.

"It's not that." I hung my head, too nervous to look at him. "I don't remember anything from before I was twelve."

He was so deathly quiet that I chanced a glance up wondering if he had shimmered out. Instead, his mouth was downturned, and eyes creased with sorrow.

God, I hated that look.

I sighed. "It's not a big deal."

"You don't remember half of your life, sounds like a big deal to me." He supported his chin with the palm of his hand like we were two besties gossiping. "What do you remember?"

I pinched the bridge of my nose, squeezing my eyes shut. I didn't like remembering because it only reminded me of everything I lost, or felt I lost. I knew there was something missing in my head, but I didn't know what. My only clue was my secret, and I would take that to a grave. Hopefully, a very late grave because if anyone found out sooner... I shuddered at the thought of what would happen to me.

"Sorry," he said. "I don't mean to stir up bad memories."

"No," I shook my head. "My past is just not the most fun thing to reminisce about."

"I can understand that." His eyes burned with memories of his own past until pain etched his face. Despite his power and place in society, the Demon Lord seemed to have his own dark history haunting him.

"I'll tell you mine if you tell me yours," I said.

He stood abruptly, forehead wrinkling with a scowl. "I am the Demon Lord. My secrets are mine and for me alone."

"What?" I jumped up from my chair, fists balling at my

sides. "Seriously? You can probe into my history like it's nothing, which you already know plenty about, but it's absolutely absurd for me to do the same?"

"I am not some weak witch. I am Lucifer's son!" His eyes flashed red, and his wings outstretched. The boom in his voice shot into my chest. "Do not think we are on equal footing!"

I called a fireball into my hand. "Don't call me weak. I didn't survive all this time by myself because I'm weak. I don't have hordes of demons to do my bidding and wait on me hand and foot. I've survived by myself! Without anyone's help!"

"Yet I could kill you before you even blinked," he threatened.

"Fuck you," I sneered. With a twist of my hand, I lodged the fireball at his face.

He shimmered out of the path, and the fireball singed the wall.

"We have a pact," his voice echoed around me, though I couldn't see him. "Don't make me kill you."

"You can fucking try!" I screamed into the empty apartment.

He didn't respond. His presence, his power, was gone; I could feel the emptiness within the suite. It was only me and my fury.

My shoulder blades itched, and I twirled around, glaring at the empty room.

That's right, run away like a scared little puppy. In the end, I was a survivor, and I would do whatever I must to do just that.

I frowned down at the food, too pissed to finish it. Picking up the dish, I walked over to the trash can, which opened from a motion sensor. I threw it all in the waste—plate and everything. I'm sure he could replace it with the piles of money he probably slept on. It was still satisfying when I heard the thump at the bottom.

I marched over to the cupboards and trifled through them until I found what I was looking for. The merlot wine bottle gave a satisfying pop when I uncorked it. I stared at the wine glass in my hand. With a shrug, I threw that in the trash as well, the high pitched crash of glass drawing a smile to my lips.

I took three deep swigs of red wine straight from the bottle, ending with a sigh. I held the bottle into the air. "Cheers, bitches!" My fake-gleeful voice echoed through the empty apartment.

Alone, as always.

I brought the bottle back to my lips.

CHAPTER
Eleven

"What the fuck are you doing?" Azazel's stern voice ricocheted around the room as he burst inside the VIP room at The Succubi Lounge.

"Knock much?" I squeezed my eyes shut. I couldn't throw my arm over them because it was occupied by last night's meal. "Did you learn something from the shifters?" News must be the reason why he'd disturb me right now.

Azazel tiptoed around the rest of my dinner, all seven of them to be exact. "Did you leave any for the customers?"

"I was hungry," I growled. "What did you learn, Az?"

"They didn't know anything. All they talked about was some internal drama at the latest full moon event, nothing useful. I figured I would swing by to pick up the note for Knox, but I'm guessing you don't have that ready yet."

To my annoyance, he was right. I didn't have the note available; I was too wound up to write one last night before coming here.

Azazel crouched down and sniffed Emi, one of the best girls here. She was beautiful with her long raven hair and brown skin, which was on full display right now. However, the reason she was a customer favorite was because her energy tasted like the blossoming flowers of springtime. "She's half dead. You do realize they'll need to feed three times the amount to replenish themselves, right?" he asked. His dark eyes scanned the room, taking in the feathers from ripped pillows, piles of blankets turned into makeshift beds across the floor, and the circular bed I currently occupied with three ladies surrounding me.

"They'll live," I said.

"What the hell is going on with you?" Azazel's face twisted into disgust, and he shoved his hands into his jean pockets like he might catch something in here.

Luckily, demons didn't have to worry about catching anything. That was a human problem, and pregnancy only happened when we wanted it to, when we allowed it to, and even then, it didn't always take. It was one of the reasons my father didn't merely mass breed an army to take over the world.

"Nothing is wrong with me." My teeth grated together.

"Save the lies for one of your lackeys, Laz."

"Is there something you need?" I hissed between my teeth, my irritation getting the best of me. I'd been asleep probably only one or two hours before getting bugged by this asshole. I couldn't admit it to him, or maybe I didn't want to admit it to myself, but I fed all night, too pent up from my fight with Serena.

I came to blow off steam, to feed off a couple succubi, to find my appetite had been insatiable. If I hadn't asked for more ladies to be sent up, I would've killed them. I almost didn't have the control to stop at all. It's only when one of them had whimpered, on the cusp of death, reminding of the sound Serena had made in the vampire club. The memory broke through the haze enough to where I was able to cut myself off from feeding and ground out the word "more."

That's all I had said, and the woman had fled within seconds from my grasp in search of help. As their Demon Lord, and the co-owner of the business, they ran only to meet my demands. If they hadn't, there's no telling what I would've done.

"Get up," Azazel demanded.

I sneered at him.

"I said get up!" He yanked on my arm, dislodging a still sleeping succubus. She didn't even respond to his jostling.

Whoops, maybe I had taken it too far.

"Fine!" I pulled my wrist from his grasp. "Stop! I'm up, I'm up." I twisted out from underneath the tangle of limbs, and seeing the room from a new perspective, I understood Azazel's concern. It wasn't how they merely slept, but the pallor skin and bags under their eyes. They looked to be on death's door, which they kind of were, and it was my fault.

Damn.

I ran my hands through my hair and jolted when my fingers grazed two small peaks of my horns.

"What is it?" Azazel watched me with hard eyes.

"Nothing." I shook my head, my stomach remaining sour. It had been centuries since I felt those, and last time they had led to nothing good. I needed to get a handle on myself, and fast. I summoned myself some clothes, jeans and a fitted t-shirt, something nondescript to hide my walk of shame, and threw them on.

We weaved our way through the room, careful not to disturb any of the succubi.

The long, dimly lit hall lined with doors was quiet, which was a first. Whether it was day or night, some kind of cries of pain or pleasure, often going hand in hand, could be heard from a few rooms.

Azazel waltzed ahead, leading the way to the stairs at the end of the hall on the opposite side. The stairs curved downwards to the first floor, passing the second floor where there was a set of doors to one giant room for those with more exhibitionist interests.

On the ground floor, the entrance area was inviting, filled with sultry colors such as plum and maroon. Candlelight warmed the space, and supple couches lined one wall for patrons to wait for their desired succubus. Lavinia, the co-owner, looked up from her spot behind the glass desk. Her long, auburn hair cascaded over her shoulders, giving extra coverage to the revealing beige halter top she wore, which gave the appearance of wearing nothing at all. A long skirt fitted her hips with a high slit that showed off her milky upper thigh.

"You're up early," I noted.

"You stayed late," she purred.

I sauntered over to the desk, summoned a wad of cash, and handed it to her.

Her red manicured nails trailed the back of my hand when she took it. Interest alighted her hazel eyes. "What's this? Usually, I'm the one who gives you half our profits."

"For your troubles," I said. "I'll send some of my men over to help replenish your girls."

Lavinia gave me one of her notable sly smiles. "I look forward to seeing them.'

I nodded at her once before departing through the red front door.

"We aren't shimmering back?" Azazel picked up his pace until we walked side by side.

"It's a nice day, and I could use the fresh air."

The sun was out, and to my surprise, so were some demons. Granted, the streets were still quiet, and the demons milling about were most likely headed home after a night of debauchery, too drunk or low class to shimmer themselves.

"So, the girl," Azazel started.

"What girl?" There had been so many girls in that room, I didn't know which one he was referring to.

"Serena," he added.

I sucked in a breath and shut the lid on my powers so fast it was like extinguishing a flame before it became a forest fire. To think a single name could have such an impact, and hearing another male speak it... it made me see red. But this was Azazel, not just anyone, and I was the Demon Lord. I couldn't let some witch rile me up so much.

Azazel whistled his surprise. We had been through too much together for him not to notice my subtle tells.

"Shut up," I barked.

A pit demon, identified by their reddish skin tone and pointed tail, stumbled past us on the street, bumping into Azazel's shoulder. "Watch it!" he yelled, raising his face to meet my friend's. His yellow eyes widened in horror. When they bounced over to me, he took two bumbling steps backward. "I'm so sorry, my Lord." He lowered his head immediately. "I didn't realize where I was going. Please don't send me back to hell. I have a family here. I'll never see them again. I'll—"

I raised my hand to stop his spew of words. "Leave."

"Thank you, sir. Thank you, thank you. I'm so sorry. Again, my apologies. Thank you." He bowed at the waist repeatedly as he scrambled past us.

Azazel watched him go, a smirk peeking out from the corner of his mouth. "It's been a while since we walked the streets, especially during the daytime. It's a good reminder for them, and for us."

"Mm," I grunted, continuing on my way, carefully stepping around the stains on the sidewalk that could be blood, urine, vomit, or lord only knew what else. I didn't care to take a sniff to find out. "We need to clean this district up," I commented flatly.

Azazel snorted. "How do you plan to do that?"

I said nothing. There was plenty I could do, and we both knew it. Most involved force, and even if I scared the shit out of enough demons to clean up the place, it would only last for so long.

"Maybe a witch could help out, at least glamour it away so it seems nice," Azazel offered.

I nodded. That was a brilliant idea and one of the many reasons Azazel had my ear where others did not.

"I'll search around, see if there's someone powerful enough," he said.

"Kyla, find Kyla."

"Who?" His head cocked to the side.

"Serena's witch friend," I explained.

Azazel waggled his eyebrows, much to my annoyance. "Serena's friend, eh?"

My lips pressed into a thin line. "I met her briefly, but the depth of her powers were impressive and immediately obvious. Although, I don't believe she has realized her potential yet. She may be the strongest witch presently alive. If anyone can do it, it's her."

"Are you sure there aren't any other ulterior motives?" Azazel jested, but his smile dropped when I leveled a glare at him. "Jeez, Laz, you're really wound up. Seriously, what's going on?"

"Nothing."

Azazel stepped in front of me, halting us in our tracks. "It's me. And I'm worried. The last time you were this way, you killed—"

"I know," I cut him off. He didn't need to say it aloud; it was already bad enough to recall it myself. "I know, but I've got it under control."

"Do you?" Azazel shifted on his feet. "You nearly killed half of Lavinia's staff last night. And every time I say Serena's name, it looks like you're a hair away from ripping my head from my neck with your bare hands. See!" He pointed at my face. "Your face is turning an alarming shade of red."

Anger boiled within me. This was the third time he'd said her name, and he was wrong. I didn't want to rip his head off, I wanted to swipe his mouth right off his face. "Just don't say her name," I said from between gritted teeth.

He held up his hands in a placating gesture. "Okay, okay, I won't. But clearly there's something going on, and we need to take care of it before you get consumed and go on another killing spree."

I winced. It was both a blessing and a curse I couldn't remember much from that time, but the aftermath was horrendous. I think the fact I had no memory was the only reason Neferia forgave me for what I had done, although it didn't mean I forgave myself, and it was something I would never allow to happen again. Losing control wasn't an option.

"I'll be fine," I repeated.

"You don't need to go through this alone. You're not alone, and you're not under your father's control anymore," Azazel reminded me. Based on the worry in his eyes, it was a reminder for himself too.

"If I'm worried I'm going to break, you'll be the first I come to."

Azazel studied me. "You fucking better."

"I fucking will." I playfully punched his shoulder to lighten the mood, and within a second, a smile broke across his face. "Go check in on the witch. The thought of walking home in this stench..."

Azazel rolled his eyes. "You can just shimmer."

I took a mock offense. "And miss the chance of scaring lesser demons?"

He chortled. "Yeah, that is pretty funny."

"Indeed." I grinned back. "I'll see you back at the tower."

Azazel nodded. Before shimmering away, he looked at me, his blue eyes hard. "Seriously, come to me if you need."

"I will." The problem was that it was not a promise I could keep.

CHAPTER
Twelve

SERENA

I PACED MY APARTMENT FOR THE BAZILLIONTH TIME, half expecting a worn-down trail to appear in the marble floor.

No one had bothered me for twenty-four hours, which was nice, and for once I didn't need to look over my shoulder every second of every day. But I was bored out of my mind, and I wanted to go check out the wolves. Clearly, they did it, or knew something. So why the hell hadn't Lazarus come for me to go knocking on their door yet?

With fidgety hands, I braided my long red hair.

Screw this. I was a professional. People literally paid me to infiltrate and get information. I didn't need Laz's help. We made a pact to clear my name, and that's exactly what I planned to do.

I threw on my leather jacket over my tank top and marched to the elevator, slapping the down button.

The doors slid open with a ding, and I was thankful to see no one inside. It would be a lot easier if I didn't need to explain to anyone what I was doing. Although, I was a grown ass woman, so I shouldn't have to explain myself anyways.

I crossed my arms over my chest and tapped my foot impatiently as the shaft worked its way down to the ground floor. When it landed, I slipped out quickly. Keeping my head down, I beelined for the front door.

A few demons milled about; none tried to stop me. Many of them were caught up in their own conversations about a new club in town or one of the underground battles, which were technically illegal, but no one stopped them since all Supes took part.

I was three feet from the door when someone sidestepped in front of me.

"Whatchya doin?" Neferia smirked down at me. She was dressed in her usual black leather outfit. Her halter top had an open back to account for the dark wings posed behind her.

"Going for a walk," I said.

She tilted her head, and her swirling eyes assessed me like a predator with its prey. "I'm the queen of sneaking out. You're going to have to try a lot better than that."

I stared at her without comment; she stared right back. When her dark eyebrow raised, I caved. "I'm going to the Shifter District," I murmured.

"Oo!" She clapped her hands in excitement. "I want to come!"

"I think it would be better if I went alone."

She narrowed her eyes. "We can double check with Laz—"

"No!" I interrupted. "No," I smoothed into a casual tone. "It's fine. You can come."

She threw her arm around me with a smile. "That's what I thought."

I stiffened, waiting for the pain, and to my surprise, nothing came. It didn't feel bad like most Supes, and neither did it feel good. I didn't remember the last time I was touched without any kind of visceral reaction. It was like I could finally breathe easy.

More demons loitered in the front courtyard. They turned when they saw us, their eyes quickly falling when their attention landed on Neferia beside me. A few even redirected their path to give us a wide berth as we left the tower.

I snorted. "Seems like you have a bit of a reputation."

"One I would like to uphold." Neferia winked at me. "If you could give a little blush or squirm, it would really help me out."

"A blush?"

She gave a knowing smile. "I'm escorting you off the grounds, so clearly you're not one of my victims, which only leaves being one of my conquests."

"Ah." I tried to hold back my chuckle. "I'm guessing you have yet to find your mate?" I questioned in a teasing tone.

Neferia's teasing grin fell away, and instantly guilt twisted my gut. I leaned into her, hoping to distract her, and encircled my arm around her waist while being careful of her wings. Giving her my best doe-eyed look, I said, "Can we do this again sometime?"

The glint in her eyes and massive grin on her face were quickly smothered into a sultry gaze. "Don't you worry, honey. I'll call you."

"Promise?" I bit my lip with a soft smile. "You were..." I nuzzled closer for a loud whisper, "... the best I've ever had."

Neferia pressed her lips into a hard line, trying her damndest not to laugh. When she contained herself, she replied, "Let me leave you with a reminder of my promise."

With me still holding tightly to her, I felt her magic envelop me, and we shimmered away.

We popped back into existence less than a second later in an alley a few blocks away. Pulling apart, we both doubled over in laughter.

"Holy hell," Neferia said as she wiped away the tears from her eyes. "I'm pretty sure we just gave them gossip for the rest of the day. You were way too good at that."

I clutched my stomach from the pain of laughing so hard. "I couldn't help myself. Playing characters is one of my fortes for my business," I wheezed.

"I can see why people hire you with that kind of talent," Neferia chuckled. "Do you want to shimmer into the Shifter District? Unless you can secretly fly too."

My face fell with nerves twisting through me. When I saw the twinkle in Neferia's eye, I relaxed. "Nope. No flying here. Just fire." To prove my point, I summoned a flame to the tip of my pointer finger.

She nodded. "I remember. For a second, I thought you were going to kill the vamp with your powers before we got a chance to get any more information out of him."

I frowned. I had let my temper get the best of me. My tactics were usually more subtle and less brute force. I didn't know what had come over me. Whether it was redemption for my past. The thing was, I could've done revenge killings plenty of times before. The difference this time was it wasn't me against everyone else. In this situation, I had others to back me up, which was a first for me.

I knew this would have to come to an end. We were only on the same side because of a bargain. Nothing else.

"We can take a cab," I answered. "It'll be less conspicuous."

"You sure? I could take us to the outskirts," Neferia offered.

I nodded. "I'm sure. A cab will help us scope out the place a little bit too."

"Good point," she agreed. "Wolves are a little unpredictable. You never really know where you're going to find them or what kind of situation they'll be in."

My thoughts exactly. The Shifter District encompassed what was once North Park and Balboa Park. They could be found partying it up, fighting, or fucking at different bars in North Park, or running wild through the nature of Balboa Park. Taking a cab through the area would give us the best place to see where the wolves were at, along with a sense of their mood. If they were doing a pack run, there was no way to infiltrate without being unnoticed. Conversely, if they were getting drunk at a bar, it was what I would call "easy money."

"Cab it is," I said.

Stepping out of the cab, it was like many districts, and yet it wasn't at the same time. Yes, there was still a dangerous energy to the atmosphere, like something bad could happen at any minute, but there was an elegance to the Shifter District that was uncommon in the others. Despite the underlying risk, it felt more controlled.

"What's that face for?" Neferia leaned forward to peer at me.

"I don't know how to explain it..." My voice trailed off as I scanned the area, trying to identify how to put this feeling into words.

Shifters of all kinds strolled through the streets—wolves, cougars, foxes, and hawks. Most in small packs, which was to be expected. I often tried to avoid this district, and maybe I had the bad luck of frequenting the bad parts of the area because, much to my surprise, there was no fighting, fucking, or frothing mouths of wild animals. Their clothes weren't shredded. Hell, they weren't even rumpled. No one fought or got angry, instead a lot seemed focused on their next destination while others laughed. Either way, I knew what they were capable of.

Neferia followed my gaze and nodded. "You don't come out here much, do you?"

I shook my head. "Not really."

I didn't want to tell her I avoided this district like the plague. Not only because I avoided Supes for a reason I didn't want her to know, but because of a memory I was actively shoving back down.

"Don't be fooled," Neferia said, strolling forward with a confident sway of her hips.

I stifled a grin when some interested looks turned her way.

She continued, "Their alpha has them locked down. He doesn't want the other leaders to view them as a bunch of animals. Trust me when I say, it only makes them more unpredictable, thus ten times more dangerous than most other districts."

"You don't have to tell me," I mumbled to myself.

A glinting fang, sharp claws, and ravenous eyes flashed through my mind, my memories assaulting me until I squeezed my eyes shut to make it go away. I avoided shifters for a reason. Mostly wolves for a reason. It wasn't soon after I had woken up, my memory gone, that I had been attacked by a couple shifters. They had attacked a little girl in their crazed state, and it was something I kept repressed, being here made that difficult though.

"Make a right up ahead," I directed Neferia, who was a few steps in front due to her long strides.

She smirked over her shoulder. "Someone knows what they want. I like that in a girl."

"I'm a woman, thank you very much," I retorted.

"Noted." She winked.

I repressed my smile. "Not interested."

"We'll see about that," Neferia snickered. "It's okay. I don't like sharing."

I narrowed my eyes at her. "What's that supposed to mean?"

She grinned but didn't answer. "Where to, boss?"

"There." I pointed to a forest-green building nestled amongst the row of shops along the street.

"I thought you didn't come here much," she said.

"I don't. However, it's my job to know where to find information in this city."

We were about to pass the small side alley filled with large garbage cans used by the establishment when I stopped short.

"What?" Neferia was instantly on high alert, scouring the area for danger.

I stared at her—full red lips, tight leather outfit, and black wings shuffling behind her with every turn of her head. "You can't come in," I said.

"Excuse you? I'm a mother fucking nephalem, I can take care of myself."

I hushed her, snagging her upper arm and dragging her into the alley for some privacy. "Careful, there are eyes and ears everywhere."

"Yeah, you would know," she snorted.

"Seriously. You can't come in," I repeated. "The fact you're a nephalem is exactly why. You'll draw too much attention, and no one will open up." Shifters rarely trusted non-pack members, especially when it came to demons. It was an uneasy alliance, probably because they felt threatened by Laz. The egocentric nature of shifters didn't help.

Neferia's lips pulled into a hard line.

"Unless you're able to make your wings disappear like your brother?" I wondered.

Her brows furrowed. "No," she sighed, "I can't." She

pressed her finger into her temple. "Fine. I'll stay here, but be careful. If anything happens to you, Laz will kill me."

"I'm sure." I didn't lessen the sarcasm coating my voice.

"Really. He'll already be pissed I let you leave. I figured I could work it in my favor if I explained you were going to find a way to leave no matter what, and I was protecting you. That goes out the window if you get hurt."

"Ah, yes. Gotta protect yourself." The ugly twist in my gut made me frown. For a moment, I nearly forgot the world I lived in. For a heartbeat, it was like I had a friend.

"Don't throw me under the bus," Neferia snapped. "It's a harsh world, especially in this district. Don't judge me for looking after myself when you would do exactly the same thing."

My fists clenched at my sides. "Correction, I *have* to do the same. I don't have a pretty tower I can go stay safe in when things get messy."

"Correction," Neferia mimicked. "You do now."

My lips parted in surprise. "Not by choice," I argued. "And once I get the information from inside, the deal is done."

Neferia scoffed. "Impressive that you really think my brother, the Demon Lord and son of Lucifer, would let something like you go."

I stiffened, my heartrate picking up. Shit, what did she know? Oh crap, oh crap.

"He lost his best warlock, and you fell into his lap. I know he's intrigued by you, and he needs a new witch. Plus, you've proven useful with getting information, and you aren't afraid of how we get ours either. When the deal is up, I'm sure he will think of something else to keep you around."

My shoulders relaxed. "Right. Well, I better get going. Hold this." I shimmied off my jacket, leaving me in nothing except my form-fitting shirt, and passed it to Neferia. "Stay here." I shuffled past her, the adrenaline of thinking I had been caught still coursing through my system. Good, they still thought I was a witch. I needed to get away, clear my head a little.

"Be safe!" Neferia hissed after me.

When I turned the corner, I glimpsed her leaning casually against the wall, and to my surprise, what looked like worry creased her flawless face.

This only ratcheted up my own concern. I didn't have the best history with shifters, and this wasn't ideal. It was necessary to clear my name. I shook out my hands to clear out the rest of my spiked adrenaline and get in character.

The door swung open without even as much as a creak, still, all eyes turned to me when I entered.

I held myself tall, walking through the joint like I owned it, and headed straight for the smooth bar off to the side. I scanned the place to see it was a true sausage party, and there wasn't a beer mug in sight.

The wooden floor was polished, not sticky or worn. Plush leather seats and booths surrounded solid wood tables. Dart boards lined one wall beside a set of pool tables. The men were dressed nicely. Not a suit and tie, but there were no rips and stains. They held tumblers in one hand and cigars in the other. It was like a country club and dive bar had a baby.

"I'll take a scotch," I told the bartender. "Make it neat."

"Coming right up." He gave me a wink before flinging a white rag over his shoulder. Flipping around, I braced my elbows on the bar and waited for my drink.

Shifters no longer outright ogled me, instead choosing to side glance at a man near the pool table in the back. It wasn't the alpha of the shifters; I made a point to know the leaders of all the districts on sight. He was probably one of the betas.

With every second that passed, everyone relaxed, and their conversations started up once more.

"Here ya go." The bartender placed my drink on the counter.

I swiped my hair over my shoulder and gave him my award-winning smile. "Thanks."

His eyes batted in a bit of surprise, a small blush creeping up under his beard. "No problem."

Ha. Still got it.

Snagging my drink, I waltzed straight to the beta and two other men holding cue sticks in their hands. "Any of you fancy losing a few bucks?"

I may avoid shifters, but that didn't mean I didn't know exactly what made them tick. Even though they may be on their best behavior, they were competitive by nature.

The beta had dark green eyes, matching the exterior of the building, and his light brown hair had been highlighted blond from hours spent in the sun. The V-neck of his fitted shirt gave me a glimpse of chest hair, and jeans hugged him in all the right places.

For a shifter, he was hot.

When he flashed his grin, I was reminded of the complete opposite of a sexy woodsman. No, he was the wolf ready to eat grandma. I actively suppressed a rising shudder.

"Never seen you before," he said, tone wary.

I shrugged and took a long swig of my drink. "I heard this was the best place in town to play pool. I was hoping for some real competition. If you don't think you're up for it..." I trailed off and turned on my heel, ready to walk away.

"Now, kitten, I never said that," he retorted.

Like putty in my hand. Men were too easy.

I spun around. "I'll break."

"Not so fast." He stepped closer to me. "What's the bet?"

"Money?" I pulled out a wad of cash. I had swiped it from a dish at the entrance of Laz's suite when Neferia had taken me up there. Old habits die hard, and with Kyla having taken everything else, I needed a way to replenish my stash. Until I could work a paying job, stealing would have to do. I had been surprised neither him nor Neferia had noticed, or if they did, they hadn't said anything.

"I can think of something else better than money." He ran a fingertip along my bare arm, and it fucking burned.

I bit my lip to keep from crying out, which he mistook for me enjoying his touch.

His eyes flashed yellow with thoughts I would rather not know.

I moved away at a casual stroll and re-racked the balls to get the hell away from him. The further I got, the easier I could breathe. Pain lingered, but it was nothing I couldn't handle. "I'm passing through on travel, I could use the money," I said.

"If you're passing through, you may need a bed," he suggested.

I crossed my arms, pushing my breasts even higher and drawing his attention. "Hmm... no, thanks. I've got a place. I'd rather take your money."

The man threw his head back and guffawed. "Spunky. Alright, kitten, play hard to get. Maybe when I win, I can change your mind."

I held my hand out to the shifter against the wall. "May I?" I pointed to the cue in his hand.

His eyes shifted to the beta, who gave him a nod, and he handed it over to me.

"I'll break," I stated again.

"Be my guest."

I lined up my shot and was about to shoot when I stopped and peered up at the beta across the table. "Wanna make this fun?"

"If it involves you, absolutely."

"For every ball I sink, you answer a question."

"What do I get when I make a shot?"

"What do you want?"

His eyes roved over my body. "Strip pool?"

I pretended to think it over.

"I'll strip my soul if you strip your clothes," he offered.

Heads perked up across the joint at this, and all the eyes trained on me widened in shock when one word slipped from my mouth.

"Deal."

CHAPTER
Thirteen

LAZARUS

I leaned back in the leather chair at my desk, steepling my fingers against my mouth.

A pile of papers sat in front of me, calling for my attention. I needed to go through the budget of the district and ensure everyone was paying their rental fees and property taxes. There was an accord I needed to review for the districts too. Other Supes were always vying to claim more land. It was an exhausting yearly battle, and frankly, I was over it.

Work was work, and it needed to get done.

I picked up a pen to sign the documents needing more immediate attention.

Look at what you've become. Nothing more than a glorified secretary. Disgusting.

I froze as my father's voice rang through my head.

You were meant to be great, follow in my footsteps, and look at you now... paperwork.

The disgust of his voice was like oil burning atop the

ocean. I could easily envision his red eyes closing as he shook his head. His disappointment would haunt me for eternity.

"Shut up," I growled. I knew he was dead, as I had confirmed it myself. I mean dead-dead, not merely back in Hell. Yet here he was in my head, tormenting me with the same criticisms I grew up hearing.

I wouldn't criticize you if you were stronger. But no, instead you smother your true self.

"This is my true self." I squeezed the pen so hard it snapped in half.

My father's slithering laugh mocked me. *This is not you. You are destruction. Death. Fire and brimstone. Right now, you are weak.*

"I'm not weak," I grumbled. Was I insane for talking to myself in the office? Yes. Was there no one here to see it? Also, yes.

It should've been your sister I bestowed my greatest gifts to. She would've accepted them, been by my side as we took over the world and destroyed the angels. That blasted Priya had to come along and ruin everything.

"Leave her out of this." My jaw was so tense that my teeth could crack. Neferia had found her matebond and had deserved all the happiness and fulfillment it had brought.

How many times had we had this conversation? How many times had I distracted him so he'd leave Neferia alone? Despite all my efforts, it was I, not my father, who had ruined her life, her chance at happiness.

You're pathetic. You've let yourself go soft. But it's not too late. You can still become the most powerful being to have ever lived, even beyond me. Take what you need from others, power yourself, and let your true nature out. You will be unstoppable. Magnificent. All you need to do is say yes.

"No," I choked as the power within me rose to the challenge, filling my chest with its heaviness, begging to be released.

Yes, that's it. Let go, son. You will transform into something greater than us all. It's all I ever wanted for you. You can rule this world, any world that you want.

My powers raced into my fingertips, burning along the way, and fire erupted in my palms. I cleared my mind, snuffing out the flames. My muscles knotted with the strain of holding it down. "I don't want it," I whispered. "You are dead. This is me. I am enough." I repeated the words over and over until I felt my power recede back into my center.

Coward. Weakling. You are no son of mine. You are an embarrassment. Had I known that this is who you would've become, I would've killed you while you were still in your mother's womb.

I swallowed down my rising stomach. My mother, Lilith, died giving birth to me. My power was too great even against her own. My magic had absorbed hers, making me stronger while also weakening her until she died.

My father praised me for it throughout childhood. He was so proud I could steal energy so easily, even from the strongest female demon to ever exist. And I did it as a baby.

I thought it was disgusting, I was a monster. My father... he thought I'd be his biggest accomplishment. He didn't realize I had no desire to follow in his footsteps until it was too late. When he did find out, it wasn't good. He took something from me, something I'd never get back, and because of it I was destined to be alone for eternity. What was worse, it made someone else, someone who could've been more to me, doomed to be alone too.

Even with dampening my powers so they weren't all-consuming, I couldn't avoid leadership. I'd stick with *Tenebris,* the little corner in the world I carved out for myself and shared with other supernatural leaders. I wouldn't rule over everything like my father had planned.

I should've killed you and taken all your powers. This world could've been great, would've been nothing like anyone had ever seen before. Now it's become a waste. You should leave it and return home. Let it rot.

"No," I said, fisting my hands in my hair. I felt for the bumps, the protrusion of horns, and to my relief, they weren't there. "I'm still in control," I reminded myself.

Earth was my home, and my father would've turned it to dust. If anything, I should thank Archangel Michael for taking him out, even though it meant he had to die in the process too. The two of them left everything in chaos, in limbo, a true in-between of Heaven and Hell. At least, until the angels and humans left, then it really became Hell on Earth. Granted, there was more space, and the air was cleaner, and there was more free will with my father not ruling over everyone.

Free will is a lie. You think you've run from your past, escaped what you are. It's only building, and when it's released, this version of you will be gone forever. What happened centuries ago was a mere fraction of what you will become, what you are capable of. Everyone will bow at your feet, and those who don't will cower at them. Just you wait; he is coming. It was your destiny.

"No!" My arm swept, knocking everything off my desk. A glass flew across the room and smashed against the wall, papers littered the ground, and pens bounced across the red carpet.

Yes. Just you wait. His voice faded with these final words.

I blew out a breath. He was gone.

No. He had been gone for a long time, and 'it' wouldn't happen again. I wouldn't allow it. I would kill myself before ever permitting that to happen again.

CHAPTER
Fourteen

SERENA

WITH THE FIRST FEW BALLS I SANK, I LEARNED HIS name was Liam and he was, in fact, third beta to the Alpha of the shifters. He was twenty-eight years old and had been beta for the past three years.

There were the wolf shifters, fox shifters, hawk shifters, and cougar shifters. The Alpha had one beta from each set of shifters, a system they set up hundreds of years ago. Before that it had been all blood and fights; honestly, what wasn't back in the day? The whole world was one huge battleground until the angels and humans left, seeking a better home after this one was destroyed. There was only so much livable space, especially after Lucifer and Michael took out half the globe when they killed one another. A hundred years after, The Great Genocide occurred, which was the last straw for the angels, wiping out tens of thousands of lives within a mere blink.

That was in the past, the distant past for most. Right now,

I needed to learn more about the shifter training his eyes on me.

I pointed to the corner pocket, lined up my shot, and the solid red ball sank right where I claimed.

The others gave a small laugh until their beta shot them a menacing glare, which shut them right the hell up.

"What kind of shifter are you?" I snagged the chalk off the corner and covered the tip of the stick in its blue powder.

"Wolf." There was a mild growl in his throat.

Shit, he was getting worked up with me kicking his ass. I broke the balls and had yet to miss, so he hadn't gotten a single chance. Little did he know I had no plan to let him because there was no fucking way I was ending up in my panties around a wolf shifter. Never again would I let my guard down around one. It seemed he was my intended target, though, because everything pointed to the wolves, not the shifters in general.

I needed to lighten him up.

I held up two fingers towards the bartender. "Another round for me and my friend," I hollered.

The bartender gave a single nod.

"Friend?" Liam raised a thick brow, his tone already happier.

"You could be, if you want." I winked.

The flirting did the trick, and when two glasses of scotch were brought over, he relaxed against the wall, downing half the glass in one go.

He was a wolf, and I knew the current Alpha was a cougar. Alphas were often closer to the beta from their own pack. Wolves were formidable, tactical, and chances were whatever had happened, Liam knew about it, especially if it came from his own pack.

I took my time leaning forward for the next shot, one I chose specifically to angle my cleavage in his sight.

His eyes trained exactly where I wanted, but his distraction was cut short when I didn't miss... again.

I gave him a sly smile, making promises with my eyes I didn't plan to keep, like I was showing off for him.

He ate it up.

"Keep it up, and I may need a rematch in a different kind of game," he said.

My stomach twisted at the game I was sure was on his mind. "Have you heard about the Demon Lord's guy who died?"

He stiffened, and when I walked past him, I made sure to rub myself against him to get to my drink.

Yes, it fucking hurt like a bitch, but a girl's gotta do what a girl's gotta do.

"Who hasn't heard about the warlock?" One of the guys off to the side snorted. "It's the talk of the district."

"Oh?" I cocked my head to the side. "Yeah, I was really surprised to hear about it when I first arrived. I thought this area was safe. Well,"—I gave a bashful smile—"I heard the shifter district was."

All their chests puffed with the compliment.

It was an utter lie. This district was only safe for their own kind... sometimes. I had a part to play, and the innocent out-of-towner was getting the job done.

I turned around, jutting out my ass, and hit another shot into the pocket. "I heard he was a bad guy, deserved it, but that he was powerful. I bet only the strongest could take him down." I scratched my chin. "So, maybe the vampires?"

The second man laughed. "As if! Only a shifter could take down a strong magic-user like him."

"Yeah, we are the best of the best," the first guy agreed.

I nodded along, my eyes wide with mock innocence. "Wow, I didn't know I was around such powerful men." I leaned into the beta. "Are you powerful enough to take him down?"

His lips twisted into a grimace, and I had a moment of worry before I realized it was not about me. "I could have," he mumbled, "but instead it was entrusted to a stupid bird-brain."

Another hole in one. A bird shifter did it. This was almost so easy, I felt bad for them.

I spun around and sank the eight ball before anyone had a moment to comprehend a thing. "I win," I quipped, gulping down the rest of my drink. I threw a few bills beside the empty glass, enough to take care of the rounds of drinks I bought.

Liam smirked, unbothered by me winning with the promise of his own soon-to-be victory with me as his conquest shining in his eyes.

I stepped away. "Well, I'd better be off. Thanks for the game!"

"What?" He stopped short. His surprised look turned to anger within a heartbeat. "What do you mean?"

"I have a friend I have to meet in another district. I had fun, though, keep your money." I turned to head for the front door when Liam's hand shot out and grabbed my wrist.

A hiss slipped from my lips from the sudden pain. His grip was tight, but the electricity shooting up my arm from his contact was a thousand times worse.

"Let go," I said through clenched teeth.

"You promised—"

I ripped my hand from him. "I did no such thing."

His eyes flashed yellow. "Who the fuck are you and what exactly are you doing here?"

The entire bar went still, and a few shifters got up from their seats to move closer.

"I was just a girl looking to blow off some steam," I retorted.

"One problem, kitten," Liam growled while his gaze burned into me, "I don't believe you."

It was deathly silent for one breath. A single breath was all I had to prepare myself.

The man to Liam's right lunged at me. I already had a fireball headed for his chest. When it hit him, he flew backwards with a howl and crashed against the pool table.

"Get her!" Liam yelled.

I ducked between one set of arms only for them to then surround me. I didn't hesitate. I broke a pool stick over my knee and slammed it into the shoulder of one and smacked another in the side of the head. It broke again on impact. Now useless to me, I tossed it aside and called two fireballs. I caught one shifter in the side of the face, and another's clothes caught on fire. Howls erupted from him as he burned.

There was an opening.

I dove towards the front, Neferia's name on my lips, when pain like I've never felt before exploded on my backside.

I fell to the ground in a heap. An unwanted scream spilled out of me. My back was on fire, and it was undoubtedly the worst thing I'd ever felt. It was as though someone was pouring molten lava all over my skin while fileting me with a knife.

A clawed hand turned me over, and another cry ripped out of me as the wounds on my back slammed into the hardwood floor.

Liam stood above me, his hand having transformed into claws with my blood dripping off of them. He could barely talk with the canines in his mouth. "You're going to regret this."

"Like hell she will."

I careened my head back, seeing a person standing behind me. With them looking upside down to me, and my vision blurred from the pain, it took a moment for me to realize it was Neferia.

Her wings were splayed out, and menace darkened her face. Red instead of silver now mixed with the gold of her eyes. The nephalem had come out to play.

I closed my eyes when the screams started, doing my best to stay conscious. I jumped when arms slipped under me.

"I've got you," Neferia whispered. "Just hold on."

"Ikandt." It was supposed to be a full sentence, but it came out in a gibberish jumble. I was dying. Whatever was happening to me, I could feel it spreading through me, and the pain just kept getting worse.

"I told you not to get hurt," Neferia chided before shimmering us away, which I only knew happened when more light pierced through my eyelids, and a new voice joined us.

"What the fuck happened!" Laz was there in a split second, pulling me from Neferia's arms.

The moment he touched me, the pain eased enough that I could open my eyes.

I blinked up into silver eyes. "Hi," I croaked. "A bird..." I coughed. "A bird did it." I couldn't summon any more words.

His eyebrows drew together in confusion on what the hell I was talking about.

"What the fuck happened?" he asked again, eyes fully turning red as he trained them on Neferia.

She took a step back, a moment of alarm flashing across her face.

I leaned my head against his chest, and a little more pain ebbed. When I patted his chest, even more subsided. The more of him I touched, the easier it was. With my head a little clearer now, I interjected. "It wasn't her fault. She saved me." I pressed further into him, like I could sink into his skin.

His grip tightened.

"I've never seen anyone react this way to a shifter scratch before," Neferia breathed.

"You went to the shifters?" Lazarus hollered.

Neferia leveled him a glare. "Can we not right now? I understand the mistake, but we have more pressing issues, like figuring out what the hell is going on with Serena!"

"Kyla," I said. "I need Kyla."

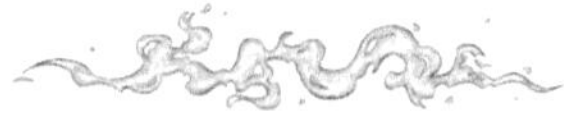

"Where is she?" Kyla's crazed voice broke through the haze.

Laz stroked my hair, my head in his lap on the couch in his living room. "She's here."

Kyla's jaw dropped when she rounded the corner and saw my back. "You need to move so I can tend to her."

"Not gonna happen," Laz stated.

"I can't diagnose her without you moving." Kyla dumped her bag of supplies onto the coffee table.

"The only time she's not writhing in agony is with Laz nearby," Neferia added.

Kyla's eyes jumped between me and the Demon Lord whose lap I occupied.

My body shook with agony. At least I no longer felt like I was on the verge of death. When he touched me, whatever poison was spreading through my body seemed to slow down.

"Her back is ripped to shreds and is at risk of infection. Either way, I need her lying on her stomach to clean it, and I can't do it like this." Kyla crossed her arms over her chest, not budging.

"It's fine," I rasped.

Laz hesitated before begrudgingly shifting out from underneath me. The world blurred.

The second my body wasn't touching his, a strangled cry pried from my raw throat. He dropped to his knees, pulling my hand into his grasp.

"I'm right here," he reassured me.

I sucked in small gasps of air as the pain lessened.

"Interesting," Kyla mumbled. She opened her bag and rummaged through it, pulling out random elixirs, sometimes shaking her head to put one back in and take another out.

She sat on the edge of the couch and carefully peeled away the strips of material from the open wounds on my back. "This is going to hurt."

I nodded, and I hadn't realized I had squeezed Laz's hand tighter until he gripped mine back. I peered into his molten eyes. They swirled with anger, concern, and something I couldn't quite place my finger on.

"Ready?" Kyla asked.

"Wait," I said. I bit the corner of the pillow, never taking my eyes off Laz, and nodded.

A single drop, one tiny drop of whatever Kyla had, and tears streamed down my face. My hand shook with how hard I grabbed Laz's hand; he never complained. Instead, he held onto me like he was trying to absorb some of the pain. No such luck.

When the next concoction came, the screams began. I was burning from the inside out, being stitched back together to be torn apart all over again. Every time I nearly blacked out, Kyla would reach for a new bottle, giving me a moment's reprieve, and then the torture started all over again.

"That should do it," Kyla said, stepping back.

I panted as I moved sweaty strands of hair off my face.

Laz pulled back, and I buckled.

My back arched as another spasm of agony spliced through me.

His hand engulfed mine a second later, and it dulled to an intense throb.

"I thought you said you fixed it." His face was murderous when he looked at Kyla, like she had inflicted this upon me herself.

She shook her head, eyebrows furrowed. "I don't understand. This should've worked. Unless…" Her words trailed off and when her eyes met mine, I froze.

"Leave," I choked.

"You heard her," Laz spat. "You can go now."

"Not her," I cried. "You." The fear of what I would feel when he did almost had me changing my mind, but it'd be worse if he stayed.

Laz's jaw ticked. "You aren't thinking clearly."

"I need to talk to Kyla alone." It was difficult to talk, my throat shredded from screaming. I met his eyes, and I was surprised to see hurt that mirrored my own. "Please."

Neferia dropped her hand on his shoulder. "Come on, Laz. Give them a minute." She gave me a sorrowful smile.

Laz took his time with letting my hand go.

When the torment ratcheted up, I bit my tongue to keep myself from reacting. I bit it so hard I tasted blood. Laz would've been able to smell it if it weren't for my blood-soaked clothes.

He gave me one last apprehensive look before Neferia dragged him out of the room to give us privacy.

When I heard the door shut, I turned my head towards Kyla.

"It should've worked," she insisted, and then she waited for me to respond, but I didn't. "Having an extreme reaction to the poison from a shifter's claws is rare. I did everything by the book, plus some. It should've worked… for any Supe."

I swallowed but didn't object.

Dawning lit her face, and she looked at me like someone had slapped her. My stomach dropped despite understanding the truth had to come out if I had any chance of her helping me.

"You're human," she stated, still gaping as all the pieces fit together, and I didn't correct her.

"You can't tell anyone," I said.

She ran her hand through her hair, surprise widening her eyes. "Holy shit. Holy shit. Holy shit. What? How did I not see it before? I just thought you were weak, or a mixed breed, hiding from your old coven. With the charms, and the work, and the..."

"Am I going to die?" I interrupted her tirade. "Or...turn into a shifter?"

Kyla paused and gave me a hard look. "You owe me."

"I know." My vision blurred with tears from the pain assaulting every nerve in my body. "Am I going to live?"

Kyla sighed. "No. Or you shouldn't. Well, I don't think so."

I focused on breathing, three seconds in, two seconds out. It was getting harder and harder to concentrate.

"What I gave you should work, but it needs time to take effect. At this rate, your body will shut down before the elixirs acclimate to you and fight off the toxin," Kyla explained.

At the mention, trembles grew through my body until I was sure it was about to turn into full blown a seizure.

"Please, help me," I pleaded.

"There's one thing that may give you time," Kyla thought aloud.

"Anything." It was the last word I uttered before blacking out.

CHAPTER
Fifteen

I PACED MY SCANT BEDROOM. "WHAT THE HELL happened?" I whirled on Neferia, who lounged at the end of my bed, one leg crossed over the other with her foot swinging. How dare she sit so casually while Serena was on the verge of death.

Neferia looked up from her nails, lips pressed into a hard line. "She'll be fine."

My wings expanded out, pulling my back muscles taught. "What the fuck happened?" I growled through my teeth.

Neferia stood, her eyes swirling as she went head-to-head with me. "Calm down, Laz."

"Don't tell me to calm down!" Spittle flew from my mouth, and my powers surged. I clenched my hands into fists to keep it at bay.

Neferia took a steadying breath but didn't step away from me despite the scent of fear now lacing the air around her.

"Laz," she said calmly, "you need to calm down before she dies because of you, before anyone dies because of you."

I winced. With the way Neferia assessed me, I sobered up, and my powers receded enough to where I got a better handle on them.

With a sigh, I sat on the edge of the bed and hung my head into the palms of my hands. "I'm sorry."

The bed dipped beside me.

"I know," Neferia whispered.

"It won't happen again."

Neferia stiffened beside me; I couldn't even hear her breathing. "Don't make promises you can't keep."

I straightened and eyed her.

She sat, looking forward, staring off into a past we never talked about. The pain in her eyes, the way they glistened with unshed tears was the giveaway where her thoughts were. Her usual swagger was gone, as was the curl of her lip in a playful smile that always made it seem like she had a secret. All the layers she threw up against the world didn't exist at this moment. Her layers were peeled away, leaving my broken sister before me. What's worse was I was the cause of it.

"It was a long time ago," she uttered, unblinking.

"It still hurts like it was yesterday," I said. Not that I would know. I had the luxury of no memories. Instead, I was haunted with the aftermath, of the pieces of people from my destruction, both literally and figuratively. "Why don't you hate me?" I asked.

Neferia looked at me, eyes wide and lips parted. It was a question I never had the guts to ask before, too afraid of what her answer would be, and it was never information she offered. Denial, ignorance, it had been our way of living for centuries.

My fingers dug into my thigh. "I killed her."

Neferia blinked, and a tear fell. "I know," she breathed.

"I killed Priya, your mate, and yet you forgave me," I said.

She turned her head to stare at the wall again. "Who said I forgave you?"

"You're still here."

"You're my brother. You're my family, my only family." Her bottom lip trembled despite the evenness of her voice. Her eyes dropped to her lap, where her hands twisted together. "I will never forgive you for killing the love of my life. I will make damn sure you never lose yourself again, that you never inflict that damage, that amount of death and pain ever again. I stay because you're my family, and because I will kill you before I ever allow that to happen again."

She would. I didn't know if she could kill me, and sometimes I wondered if I could die. No more angel blades existed on Earth anymore; I had checked. If anyone could pull it off, it would be her, and I would let her, I would want her to before losing myself to the true demon within me once more. I barely came back last time, and there was zero doubt that if he ever took over again, I would be lost forever, and then the world truly would be doomed.

"Promise?" I asked.

She met my gaze, and there was nothing except pure determination. "Promise."

I nodded. "Good."

Neferia reached over and placed her hand on my knee. "I may never forgive you for that, and am willing to kill you if I must, but that doesn't mean I want to or that I don't love you. This world would have burned a long time ago if it wasn't for you."

I snorted. "It's still just ashes."

My sister shook her head in defiance. "There are rules, cities, areas for Supes to call home instead of complete chaos because of you. It's no longer monsters ravaging the land and dying along the way. It's not perfect, but it's a hell of a lot better than what we were left with."

She had a point. What I had never voiced was that making this world better, livable, had started out more as an act of redemption. I admit, over the years, a new hope dawned in me. To reverse the damage in other parts of the world, make the entire thing habitable again. It had once been beautiful, only for debris and ash to overtake the greenery and life. I would spend the rest of my life correcting what my father and I did.

"I don't know what's going on with you," Neferia chimed in, "but I think the witch is good for you. You are so afraid to feel, to lose control, but maybe repressing so much of yourself is exactly the problem. I don't know if it means much, but I like her. I hope she doesn't die."

I couldn't say I agreed with her, as keeping myself on lock-down was the only way to ensure everyone's safety. My sister's input did mean a great deal to me, though, not that I'd ever admit it to her, and I didn't want Serena to die either.

"I need you to take this to Azazel," I said, handing her a piece of fabric.

She pulled the blood-stained rag from my eyes. Her nostrils flared from the scent of Serena.

"Have him take it for analysis. If Kyla can't help her, I want to see if there's another way," I admitted.

Neferia nodded. "I'll get this right to him." She stood, pocketing the torn piece of shirt, and paused. "Try letting someone in for once, Laz. Everyone deserves a little happiness." Then she shimmered away.

I sighed, my shoulders sagging under the weight of the world. Little did she know that happiness, especially with a mate, wasn't in the cards for me.

"I need you!" Kyla called from the other room.

I was up in an instant and raced into the living room.

Serena laid on the couch, Kyla kneeling beside her with

panicked eyes and controlled breaths as she tried to contain her fear. Under all the blood, Serena's skin had turned grey.

I couldn't hear a heartbeat.

Kyla looked at me, eyebrows furrowed. "If you want her to survive, she needs your help."

CHAPTER
Sixteen

COMING TO, MY BODY WAS OVERWHELMED WITH raw nerves simmering over an open flame. I gasped from the invasion of agony.

"Shh, I'm right here."

I turned my head on a fluffy pillow to see Laz lying pressed against my side. I scanned the bare room.

We were lying on a huge walnut-frame, California king bed with smoky satin sheets. The floor-to-ceiling windows were darkened to a black, and I didn't know whether that was from technology or the time of day. How long had I been out for?

A fire crackled on the wall with a single reading chair in front of it. Surrounding the fire were built in bookshelves packed with books. Other than those shelves, there was barely anything.

"Kyla," I rasped.

"She went home. Neferia will shimmer to her if she's

needed. Kyla gave her a special charm directly to her shop to forgo the Magic District's protection charms," he finished. His silver eyes were no longer mixed with the red fires of Hell, but their intensity stole my breath, nonetheless.

"She said... I need..." Words were hard to form.

His lips thinned as a darkness crossed his face.

Did he know? Did she tell him?

I made a move to shift away, and found I couldn't. Not because Laz stopped me but because I physically couldn't. I was too weak.

"Your body is weakening with every second. Kyla warned me if we didn't lessen your pain, it would give out," Laz explained.

I swallowed, clutching onto the reasonable part of my brain. "She said there may be a way." And then she left. She fucking left me to die.

"There is." Laz's wings shuffled behind him.

"What?"

"We have found only one way to dull the pain." He paused. "Me." As if to prove a point, his cool finger trailed down my arm, and its wake left a sensation of peace.

I pushed closer, searching for more reprieve; it only did so much. What more could be done?

"May I try something?" he asked, moving a strand of my hair behind my ear.

I nodded, unable to speak, too overcome by his touch.

He cupped the side of my jaw and slowly lowered his lips to mine. The kiss was soft, like he was scared to hurt me.

It did the opposite.

A heady sensation spread outwards, absorbing the pain. Tingling pleasure spread in its place. I pushed my lips against his, demanding more.

He tasted of smoke and spiced cider.

My tongue swiped at his lower lip.

He moaned against my mouth, opening up for me. Our tongues toyed with one another, and when my hand reached up to run through his hair, it was like something snapped within him.

His kiss became bruising, and the tips of fangs that weren't there before nipped at my lower lip. His hands roamed down my side, over my ass, and pulled my leg over him.

The more he touched, the more pleasure he gave, and the better I felt.

He pulled away, squeezing his red eyes shut with a shudder. "Give me a moment."

My body shook with a sudden onslaught of pain, and my nails dug into his shoulder.

His head snapped to me; I didn't have time to suppress my pained face. "Kyla was right," he said.

"Right about what?" I whispered.

"I can get rid of your pain. Give your body the abatement it needs to heal."

"By kissing?"

A sly smile crossed his face. "To start."

Oh... Ohhhh. He meant... right?

I searched his hungry gaze, only need and dominance resided there. I should be scared, the way he seemed more like a beast with prey in his grasp. Instead, heat pooled in my core.

His nostrils flared, and his face darkened even more.

"Is there another way?" I mumbled, ignoring the thrill of the prospect of him.

A wall slammed into place at my question, and I could only assume he took it as a rejection.

"It's not that," I admitted. "I've never... not that I haven't wanted to!" I couldn't tell him I essentially couldn't unless I wanted to be in writhing agony. I could barely handle grazing a Supe, let alone sleeping with one.

"I see." He gave nothing away.

I couldn't read him; I didn't know if he wanted this. When he shifted and his hardness pressed against me, I had my answer.

"I will stop whenever you want. All you have to do is ask." His fingertip swirled designs on my shoulder. "I'll be honest," —he licked his lips—"it may be difficult for me to hold back."

"And if we don't..."

"Your heart will most likely give out," he confirmed.

I chewed on my bottom lip. "You'll stop when I say?"

Laz's eyes flashed red as he watched my mouth. "If I make it worse, and you don't want it, say the word 'lollipop'."

I smirked. "Lollipop? What if I say, 'I want to suck your lollipop'?"

His chest rumbled, and wings shot out. "Careful what you say, pet, or I might lose control even sooner." He cleared his throat. "What word do you suggest?"

I mulled it over. "Cantaloupe."

He pulled back to arc an eyebrow at me. "Cantaloupe?"

I shrugged, which elicited another wave of pain. "I doubt it'll be said otherwise."

"Fine."

"Alright."

"Okay."

We stared at one another, waiting, seeing who would make the first move. When my back seized in agony, I flew to his mouth. Instantly, pleasure spread in its place.

My hands moved under his shirt to his chiseled stomach. He moaned against my mouth, and my core throbbed at the sound.

"More," I demanded.

A rush of his power swooped over us, tingles releasing all over my body. When I looked down, we were in our under-wear. I stared in shock before stammering at the hard length clear as day underneath his boxer briefs. He was huge.

Laz distracted me by trailing kisses down my jaw, throat, and spiraling the tip of his tongue on the vein of my neck.

My eyes rolled back into my head, and I pulled him towards me. We rotated together so he could be above me; I hissed in pain when my back hit the mattress.

Laz pulled away, worry creasing his forehead, and understanding lit his face. "Get on top."

"What?" I gulped.

"Get on top. You take control."

"O-okay."

We turned until I straddled him. When his hard length pressed against my soaked panties, a moan slipped out.

His fingers dug into my hips, eyes devouring me, when he directed me to move slowly. I followed his hands, rubbing our most sensitive areas together.

I braced myself against his chest, my head hanging back as pleasure built higher inside of me. "Laz, I'm gonna—"

He pushed up against me, hitting the ball of nerves, and I burst.

A muffled cry of ecstasy, not pain, spilled out of me, along with other things. I moved to get off when his hands gripped my legs.

"We're not done yet." His eyes were stark red with nothing except desire shining through. "Kyla said your body would potentially need an hour of reprieve, and I plan to give you exactly that."

I nodded, and my stomach fluttered with both nerves and excitement. I'd given myself plenty of orgasms, rubbing the right spot just like what happened, but... more? And with Laz, no less? I wanted him. I wanted him in a way I didn't know I could, in a way only a lover could. I wanted to feel every curve of muscle, wanted his power to help me orgasm, to wrap myself around him like a bow on a present. Yes, I wanted more, and I wanted it with Laz.

I bit my lip at the anticipation and his gaze locked onto the movement.

He *tsked,* a fierce gleam in his eyes that spoke of a dark promise if I didn't stop. "Pet, the only one who should be biting you is me."

Another wave of power came, and the thin film of fabric separating us disappeared. The warmth of his skin pressed against the sensitive spots of mine, and I dripped with need.

His attention shot to between my legs, and a cruel smile crossed his face. "I want to taste you."

My legs clenched with desire while I sat there, unsure what to do or say.

Again, he directed me.

I lifted my hips and scooted forward. He shifted his wings so I didn't crush them. My knees landed on either side of his head. "Now, what?" I breathed.

"Sit down and come for me."

Sit? Like just sit down?

I lowered myself closer to him, hovering, too nervous to sit down.

He lifted his head off the mattress and swiped my core with one languid lick.

My hands grasped the headboard as I bowed forward from the pleasure.

His tongue swirled around my nub until my legs were shaking from how good it felt. His large hands grasped my hips and pulled me down, and he relaxed his head on the pillow to more easily devour me.

When I was flush against his face, he sucked.

A gasp whipped out of me as my core tightened.

He dipped two fingers inside me with ease. His tongue stroked the perfect spot, moving in unison with his fingers.

The knot in my core built up until I tightened around his fingers and another orgasm blasted through me. A scream lifted from me as I held onto the bed to keep from collapsing onto him.

When I caught my breath, I moved back.

Almost lazily, with desire flaring in his eyes, Laz licked my juices off his fingers and lips, making me want him even more. He never took his eyes off me as I straddled his lower waist. His eyes watched as I grasped his hard length, something my fingers almost couldn't fit around, and pressed the tip to my entrance.

I sank down onto him, and a thrill went through my chest when Laz's head fell back with a groan. To my surprise, it didn't hurt. He filled me, and once I had adjusted to his size, I lifted myself up and came back down.

This time we both let out a moan.

I began to move faster, spinning my hips in a circle every time our skin met. When I reached out to touch myself, Laz cursed.

"Fuck, you're going to be the end of me," he growled, his gaze watching every single movement I made.

I tightened around his hard length as I got closer to climaxing, his already large cock getting bigger with each passing second. With one last swipe of my finger and slamming myself back down, I came with a cry.

Hunching forward, my palm landed on Laz's chest as I lost myself to pleasure. As I came down from the high, I peeked at him, and quickly realized my mistake.

Salacious intent flickered in his red eyes. The corner of his lips turned up. "My turn." And he flipped us.

I braced myself for the pain to ram into my back—nothing happened. Instead, I was met with the fizzing of Laz's power, supporting me a foot above the bed. His magic caressed my bare skin. Another round of pleasure coursed through me, and I was already dripping with need at the feel of him and his power.

"Not yet, pet," he warned. His wings beat gently behind him, helping to keep us aloft and providing gentle movement in and out of me.

I bit back a groan.

"Remember our safe word?" he asked.

I nodded dumbly.

"Good." He pulled himself out slowly, as if savoring every single feel of my wetness, before slamming back into me —hard.

I gasped as pain mixed with pleasure. Not the pain of the poison but at the brutality of the movement.

His power seeped further, and what seemed to be the tips of horns appeared within his black hair.

He rammed into me again.

I had nothing to grasp onto, so I reached up to grasp my bouncing breasts. This only seemed to make him more frenzied.

He bent down and pulled one of my nipples into his mouth as he continued to pound into me. He twirled his tongue around the peak, then bit down. The flash of pain was quickly soothed by the gentle lick of his tongue. His power coursing against me seemed to darken, as though trying to pull something from me. When his intense red eyes found mine, he bit me again, harder, until there was only pain.

I sucked in a breath. "Stop!" I grasped his shoulders, trying to move him away; he didn't budge. A whimper escaped my throat. There was too much pain, and a flood of memories shoved into my head of the last time a Supe lost control around me.

A snarl reverberated in his chest. He trailed his canines up my skin, one pricking the top of my breast, drawing a bead of blood.

Panic seized my chest, making it hard to breathe, and I pushed at his chest before he could lick at it. He couldn't taste me. I didn't want that. What if he loses control and kills me? He's a demon after all, the top demon. Already, he wasn't listening to me, or rather was so far gone it was as though he couldn't hear me at all. I whimpered. I didn't like this.

His red eyes, without a single hint of silver, watched my chest rise and fall, and his mouth opened, saliva dripped from a fang. He was going to kill me!

"Cantaloupe!" I cried out.

As though I'd thrown a bucket of ice water on him, he drew back, leaving cold air in his wake. Blinking rapidly, the red cleared back to their usual silver. "Are you alright?" he asked, peering down. Comprehension turned his eyes serious. "I'm sorry," he murmured.

I bit my lip, hard, refusing to let the unshed tears fall.

He ran his hand through his hair, worry creasing his face. His magic lowered us to the bed until we were curled side by side. He was careful of my back and kept minimal contact so I wasn't wracked with pain.

"I'm sorry," he repeated as he searched my face. "What can I do?"

I shook my head, either refusing or unable to speak, I couldn't tell.

"Pet." His soothing voice stretched towards me as his hands stroked the side of my face. "I want to help, but I need you to talk to me. You did the right thing. You used the safe word. You did well."

He had stopped as soon as I said it. He had warned me he might lose control, and when he started to and I got scared, he backed off immediately, just as he said he would. I didn't want to stop, but I didn't know if I was ready for... that.

"No blood," I whispered. It was too triggering to be covered in blood while vulnerable, and I found it difficult to speak that aloud.

He nodded without hesitation, completely respecting my decision. "No blood," he agreed. "Anything else?"

I didn't know. I had no experience, so I didn't know what I liked and didn't like.

"I don't know," I whispered, cheeks heating with embarrassment. "I'm sorry."

A small growl rippled from him, and I froze. "Never be sorry for your boundaries, Serena. This is mutual, and I want to provide what you want and avoid what you don't."

My shoulders relaxed, and Laz seemed to mirror me with an exhale.

"I don't want too much pain. The biting with the licking was fine, but when you bit too hard..." I trailed off.

He nodded again. "You need the soothing more immediately rather than after the session. I understand."

I picked at the sheet between us. "Is there anything you don't want?"

A smirk pulled at the corner of his lips, and my core heated all over again at my wanton thoughts of what his mouth did to me. "None that I know of yet. How about we explore together? This time with you in control," he purred.

A throb between my legs screamed 'yes', but the word left me as no more than a breath.

Before I could think better of it, I threw my leg over him, straddling him until I was slick against him.

"Tell me what you want," he said, eyes trailing down my naked form while his hands hovered above my hips.

"Pinch my nipples," I said.

He obliged, pinching then releasing, then repeated.

I grabbed his hard cock and slipped it back inside me.

His eyes closed with a groan, and when they opened again, they were still silver. Relief washed through me.

My hips moved slowly, and as my wetness grew, so did my

need to feel him deeper inside of me. Soon, I grinded on top of him while his hands massaged my breasts.

"Bite me," I exhaled between moans.

Abs flexing under my hands and he sat upright, putting his chest flush against mine. My arms wrapped around his shoulders as he brought his mouth to my shoulder. He bit down gently, the sting of his fang followed by a chaste kiss.

I moved faster and faster with every nip he gave me. Soon, I slammed onto him, driving us both closer to oblivion. My head lolled back. "Grab me, hold my hands." It was hard to form coherent sentences as my brain was overcome with the feel of him. Thankfully, he needed little prompting to comply with what I wanted.

His hands encased my wrists, trapping them behind my back. The drag of my shoulders angled me backwards until his cock was hitting the perfect spot. I mewled with delight, which was answered by a rumbling from Laz.

I pulled against the restraints of his hand, righting myself, and he dropped his hold instantly. I shoved into his chest, and he fell back down onto the bed.

The red engulfed the silver of his irises, but his wide-eyed surprise almost had me laughing instead of afraid. *Let's see if I can shock him a little more.*

I leaned down to whisper in his ear. "Fuck me, hard."

With a growl, he flipped us, pounding into me along the way. His power kept us above the mattress once more, and my head fell back as he filled me with every thrust.

The sensitive nub between my legs throbbed with need, and like a siren calling its prey, Laz's thumb found it. He switched between rubbing the perfect spot and pinching it lightly, never enough to hurt but just enough to cause a crash of new feeling through my body.

Everything he did to me was a mix of pleasure and pain,

just like this entire experience, the way it started. What I didn't expect was... I enjoyed it.

His pace picked up, and his wings flapped harder to keep us floating above the bed. His magic pushed into my back, lifting my hips until they were angled for him. Somehow, this made what I thought was blissful even better.

My body tightened, and my breaths came faster.

"Not yet," he said. His fingers twisted in my hair and pulled my head back. His mouth found my neck, and he sucked and kissed and licked.

The pleasure built inside me until I thought I was going to explode at any moment.

His cock somehow grew bigger until it was rock hard. He filled me, stretched me, until I couldn't take anything more. "Now."

With the demand, his mouth found mine, and we both exploded together in a moment filled with so much ecstasy that I could barely see.

He pumped into me, releasing every seed he had, and prolonging my orgasm until I thought my body would give out.

We twisted in mid-air and landed on the bed with me on top.

His chest rose with deep breaths that matched my own.

Shocks of pleasure continued to wrack through me. It didn't stop my surprise when his hand trailed down my back and there was no pain.

"You should sleep," he said. A moment later, he slipped out from underneath me.

The bed already felt emptier and colder. For the first time in hours, I wasn't in agony when not touching him.

I was going to be okay.

"Where are you going?" I leaned up.

"I have something I need to take care of." He was already buckling a belt on a pair of dark jeans. He gave me a sad smile.

Did I do something? Was he okay? He probably had business to take care of now that I was better.

I hid my disappointment with my hair, falling back into the bed. I didn't need my first time filled with cuddles, plus he was the Demon Lord. He was simply trying to save my life, and it was silly of me to expect anything else.

"I'll go back to my place," I offered as I searched for clothes instead of looking at him.

"Stay. Sleep."

I was tired, and I didn't see my clothes. There was no way I was traipsing through this tower wrapped in a sheet.

"Thanks," I retorted, nestling into the pillow and trying to ignore how it smelled like him.

He didn't say anything. The only way I knew he left was from the click of the bedroom door being shut.

How was it I almost died earlier, but for some reason this moment felt worse?

CHAPTER
Seventeen

LAZARUS

I landed in the middle of the bar and released my power. Tables, chairs, and shifters alike went flying in all directions. I scanned the area, and a piece of pride lit inside me from the singed marks on the wood.

My little minx put up quite a fight.

A scent hit my nose, and my power nearly consumed me.

I followed the smell to a red patch on the floor. The bastards didn't even have the decency to clean up her blood.

"Who the fuck do you think you are?" a shifter beside me yelled.

In a flash, my claws dug into his throat—a cougar by the smell of him. Not the guy Neferia told me about. It was a wolf shifter who hurt Serena.

"Where is he?" I ground out for the room to hear. No one chose to answer.

A sting pierced my back. I dropped the man into a heap on the floor and spun around.

The bartender, also not a wolf, had another throwing knife at the ready.

I reached my hand over my shoulder and pulled the blade out. With flames licking my fingers, I burned off my blood. I couldn't risk a witch getting a hold of that, and when the metal was glowing red, I flung it into his thigh.

The bartender fell to his knees, dropping the other knife in order to cling to his new wound.

"Don't make me repeat myself," I warned. "Where is your beta?"

"Which one?" the bartender asked between clenched teeth.

I stepped forward until I loomed over him, nothing more than a bug I could squash under my boot. "I said, don't make me repeat myself." I roundhouse kicked him in the face, and he went flying. The crunch of the bones in the face matched the sound of the splintering wood of the side of the bar when he hit it.

Throwing my arms out to the side, I turned in a slow circle.

"Does anyone here feel like answering? Or do I need to beat the shit out of all of you?"

They would pay; every last one of them. Every one that tried to lay a hand on her, that took a swipe or merely sat there and watched as their beta attacked her.

"What the hell is going on here?" Silhouetted in the doorway was a shifter. The power he exuded electrified the space.

I pulled his scent in. Wolf.

He stepped further inside, taking stock of the damage to his precious bar. Not a single hair on him was misplaced, yet Serena had spent hours in agony. She had almost died. It was the first time in the centuries where I had felt useless, and I never wanted to feel that way again.

When his eyes landed on me, they widened, and he took a staggering step back.

"Good," I sneered. "You know who I am."

"W-what are you doing here? W-we haven't done anything to you." The wolf beta retreated another step towards the exit.

What a fucking coward. No wonder he wasn't alpha, and acting like this he never would be, especially after I talked to Knox about his piece of shit beta.

"You,"—I moved forward—"are in a lot of trouble."

His face hardened, and he squared his shoulders. Some of the shifters had come to and were now making their way to their leader's side.

"Ah, ah, ah." I wagged my finger at them. "I wouldn't suggest that if I were you."

The beta narrowed his eyes. "This is our turf. It's you who is overstepping."

The air crackled with the shifters calling on their power to transform into their animal counterparts.

They forgot one thing. I was the fucking son of Lucifer.

I called on my own power: the darkness, the fire, the smoke... the death. It all swirled within me, and when I released it, where men once stood was nothing more than falling ash.

I was no longer a kid, though. My intended target still stood, horror morphing his face as he took in the death of his brethren.

Finally, he seemed to grow some balls because when he looked at me, his eyes sparked with anger. Nothing like a need for revenge to fuel bloodlust. Maybe I'd have a good fight for once. It was rare I got to let this side of me out to play.

In fact, it had been so long that my beast was asleep. Wrapped up so deep inside of me, he had been in a coma for centuries. I didn't want to lose myself to him again. I wanted to find other ways, better ways to live in this world, but when

Serena was lying there dying, I could do nothing. When her little gasps of pleasure escaped her and she shone with a brightness I didn't know could exist in this world anymore, he awoke.

He wanted to make these fuckers pay, and for the first time in nearly half a millennia, I didn't want to stop him.

The beta shifted, his wolf ripping through his skin in a blink of an eye. He was large, and his grey coat matched the color of the ashes of his compatriots. His lip pulled back with a growl, and he launched toward me.

Spreading my wings, I leapt at him. This piece of shit would pay, and I didn't care about the repercussions. No one hurt what was under my protection!

We collided in mid-air. His teeth snapped at my neck, and to my surprise, I needed to use both hands to keep him at bay. He was stronger than I had anticipated.

We hit the ground with a thud and rolled away from one another. I jumped to my feet, his blur of movement already coming at me again. Damn, he was fast too. I now understood how he became beta.

I spun out of his path, and to my dismay, he anticipated it and moved with me. When I stopped, he did too and sank his teeth into my calf. I winced at the sudden pain. He shook his head, like a dog with his favorite toy, ripping more of my muscle into tiny shreds.

I stared in surprise as black blood leaked from my wound. My head dropped backwards, and I laughed. Stunned, the beta lost his grip.

I used the distraction to whip down and slammed him into the floor. My fingers transformed into claws, and he whimpered when they pierced the hide in his neck.

I leaned forward and whispered in his ear, "Transform back now or end up like your friends."

He was smart and didn't make me repeat myself. Naked

on the ground, the blood seeping from the wounds were easier to see. He smelled of fear, but his eyes were filled with hatred. "Fuck you," he spat.

"I'm sorry it has to be this way," I said, "but you shouldn't have touched her."

"When my Alpha finds out what you did, you're as good as dead!"

I sat back on my heels. Folding my arms across my chest, I studied him. He may be pack, but I had the ear of the Alpha whether he knew it or not. "When I talk to Knox, you'll already be dead."

His heart rate picked up at the threat, but it wasn't enough. I wanted him to hurt the way he made Serena hurt.

Closing my eyes, I concentrated on my connection to my brethren until I found the one I wanted. "Azazel," I summoned.

He appeared a second later, hands shoved in his pockets. He took stock of the place and let out a low whistle. "You've been busy."

"I need you to take the mutt," I commanded.

He cracked his knuckles, a hiss of excitement escaping him. "Want me to make it hurt?"

I felt the pent rage of my beast threatening to burst from my chest like an alien. It still wasn't enough.

"No," I said.

Azazel's eyebrows shot to his hairline. "You want it quick?"

I scoffed. "He doesn't deserve quick. And I want to be there... *need* to be there," I corrected.

Azazel pulled the shifter up by his neck.

The beta had no time to object before Azazel shimmered him away.

Rolling up my sleeves, I sauntered over to the bar and

reached over the edge for a rag and bucket. I drifted over to the stained wood that still smelled like Serena.

Bending onto my hands and knees, I got to work wiping her from this place.

I wanted no trace of her for others to find. She deserved better than to have her blood meaninglessly splattered across the ground. I got a whiff of her sweet, cinnamon essence from her blood.

My beast raged, remembering the taste of her, the tiny droplet. He wanted more, he wanted to devour her in every way he could, the world be damned.

I paled and scrubbed harder.

CHAPTER
Eighteen

ROLLING ONTO MY BACK, I STRETCHED MY LIMBS until my toes curled, ending it with a giant sigh. I blinked my eyes open and swung my legs over the side of the bed. Slipping out from under the covers, I padded across the room to a giant bathroom to freshen up.

In the mirror, I contorted my naked form to peer at my back. Red marks razed across it, slightly puffy from new skin.

"That'll leave a scar," I muttered to myself. *It's better than being dead.*

My skin still tingled with the feel of Laz, from his blazing touch and heated breath. I crossed my legs as I dampened at the thought.

I didn't know it could be good, not like that. But damn, that was brilliant. Even with the haze of pain and being near death, I was a panting mess. Fuck, what would it be like with him when I was in normal shape? I shook my head to clear it. I couldn't let my thoughts take me there. It was a one-time thing, and to save my life. It was the only reason he did it, and I doubted it would ever happen again.

No. I couldn't *let* it happen again. I couldn't risk him finding out what I was.

I tiptoed into his bedroom and frowned when I found the bloody remnants of what were once my clothes.

Those wouldn't do.

Opening a set of drawers of a mahogany wardrobe, I found a pair of black boxer-briefs and a navy-blue t-shirt. I threw them on, smelling Laz's smoky scent along the way. The shirt only hung to my upper thigh, so the boxers were definitely needed.

I ambled over to the kitchen. "Hello?" I called. "Anyone home?"

Silence greeted me.

My attention homed in on a fancy coffee maker. One of those where the coffee beans were already in it, you pushed a button, and voilà, you had a delicious cup of coffee.

I scanned the device and chose what looked like a cappuccino option. The machine whirred to life, and the first splash of espresso sent the smell of coffee into the kitchen.

"Fancy," I said with a little laugh to myself.

Cup in hand, I meandered Laz's apartment.

The glass dining table looked uninviting, and the fire near the grey couch was out. I grasped the double doors off the living room and yanked.

Wind whipped my hair as I stepped out onto a large balcony. The horizon was cotton-candy pink, dappled with sherbet-orange clouds. Direct above me, the sky was a darkening blue with two twinkling stars already showing.

How long was I asleep for? I needed to talk to Laz about what I had learned at the bar. It was one more piece in the puzzle, albeit a small piece, but it being a hawk shifter was important information we needed to look into.

A small metal table with two chairs were off to the right. I took another sip of my coffee, warming me from the inside out before placing it down.

Carefully, I edged to the side of the balcony. There were no railings, nothing to stop me from plummeting two hundred feet to the ground below.

I could see everything from up here. The buildings stretched into the distance, their brown and beige roofs speckling the landscape. Many were abandoned, not nearly enough beings to fill the city like when the humans were here. Those were obvious to pick out by their broken windows and holes in the roof. I had been great at spotting them before I got my own place, seeking some semblance of a roof to sleep under for the night. Thankfully, *Tenebris* never got too cold, but there were plenty of nights spent shivering. My arms instinctively wrapped around my middle, those times not always feeling like a distant past.

Times had definitely changed. I would have laughed if someone told me I'd be living in the Demon Lord's tower, sleeping in his bed. Even now, it was surreal and didn't sit right. I didn't know where I belonged. I used to dream of meadows, swimming in creeks, and sunbathing in the sun. I would pick wildflowers and have a warm bed to sleep in. I never saw any faces, but I was surrounded by love. Being woken up from such dreams to crashes, screams, and snarling Supes made it hard to sleep, and as I got older, the dreams came less and less until they stopped all together. It didn't matter where I was from now, or who may have been looking for me. They never found me, and maybe they didn't care enough to. I was nothing more than a street rat now.

In the area below, demons milled about. It was always busier at night. My toes squeezed over the edge as I looked down. The swoop in my belly was from excitement, not fear.

Oh, to fly, how amazing that would be.

The muscles around my shoulder blades pulled taut at the thought.

Another gust of wind had me teetering.

I sucked in a breath but held my place, relishing the moment of near freedom.

"You're up."

I screamed, wheeling around to face the person behind me. My right heel didn't land on the smooth balcony, rather the air past the edge. My eyes widened at Lazarus as gravity pulled me backwards. My lungs were frozen, unable to voice a need for help.

He was there less than a second later, arm wrapping around my waist, and pulled me back to safety.

My hands and cheek pressed against his chest while my breath caught up to me.

"Are you alright?" His voice was even, calm, like there wasn't a doubt in his mind I wouldn't have been okay. It settled me.

I nodded and withdrew from him, more careful of the edge this time. "Yeah, thanks."

His silver eyes caught mine for a split second before I was completely distracted by his clothes.

"Is that blood?" I shrieked, reaching out to it in the space between us. My heart pounded as I searched his body for wounds.

Red tinged the white fabric of his shirt and marred his hands. His shirt wasn't even rumpled, but there was a huge tear in the calf of the pant leg. Smooth skin peeked out from underneath, no scratch in sight. Black dried blood coated the jean fabric.

"What the hell happened?" I gaped.

"I had to take care of a few things," he uttered, shoving his dirty hands into his pockets.

My jaw rose and fell while I searched for the words. "You're okay though?" I verified.

He chuckled. "You should see the other guys."

I blinked up in surprise. Guys, as in plural? Shaking my head to help clear it, I refocused on something else. Images from last night, his wings flapping as he drove into me, flashed in my mind. Nope! Something else, anything else. I scrambled for another thought before he scented my desire.

"The bird!" I blurted.

Laz cocked his head. "What bird?"

"The wolves," I said, watching as Laz's face darkened at the mention of them. I continued, "The shifters told me that a hawk shifter distributed the venom."

"I see." His brows furrowed in thought. "You did mention the bird shifter earlier. Hmm ..."

"What is it?" I asked.

"This is getting messy, convoluted. I don't like it."

He was right. Every time we found a piece of the puzzle, it only brought more questions. The leads were shifting, making it more confusing than any typical job I've taken in the past. Usually, it was a lot more cut and dry than this, and it seemed that Laz thought this too.

"It's on purpose," I said. It was the only explanation that made sense. "Whoever is pulling the strings wants us chasing our tails and purposefully made it difficult to lead back to them."

Laz frowned. "That's an awful lot of trouble to cover up a murder. It's not unheard of for Supes to die. Why try so hard to hide their involvement?"

"Because usually it's not the right hand of the Demon Lord that dies."

There was an unnerved rumble from Laz's chest. "I don't like this."

I took a step toward him, drawing his attention. "We will figure this out."

His gaze raked over my form, red glinting in his eyes. A predatory smirk pulled at the corner of his mouth. "I think I have a new favorite shirt."

My hands shot down and pulled at the hem of it, like I could somehow cover up more of me, even though he had seen me naked. Something I was overly aware of right about now.

"My clothes were in worse condition than yours are right now," I replied.

He nodded, never taking his eyes off where my bare legs escaped his boxers.

I swallowed. "I should get going. Go find some clothes in my apartment. I mean your apartment," I corrected as I moved past him. "I mean your guest suite I've been staying in."

Holy hell, could I be any more awkward right now?

Laz shimmered in front of me, causing me to grind to a halt so I didn't knock right into his broad chest. "I want to show you something," he said.

"Oh?" My head cocked to the side. The Demon Lord wanted to share something with me? How could I say no to that? "I should change first," I replied, narrowing my eyes at his stained clothes, "and so should you."

He snapped his fingers, washing magic over the two of us. It crackled against my skin, warming it like I was sitting next to a fireplace. When it dissipated, he wore the navy shirt I had just been in over a pair of black jeans. He'd been dressing more casually recently compared to his usual suits from when I first met him.

I was decked out in my ass-kicker boots, black leather pants, and a black leather jacket. Underneath was a white t-shirt that read 'Not Your Basic Witch'. There was a flutter in my chest at the punny shirt. He had been paying attention.

They all hugged my curves perfectly, leaving very little to the imagination despite covering all my skin.

I tilted my head at him. "Really?"

He gave a devilish grin in reply.

I rolled my eyes and stifled the smile threatening to come out. "What exactly do I need so much leather for?"

His wings unfolded from behind him. The light from the living room displayed the intricate veins within the webbing. He stepped closer to me. "Do you trust me?"

"Not at all," I breathed.

His eyes sparked. "Good, you shouldn't."

"Although I've never been one to shy away from danger," I retorted, taking a step closer to him. Only six inches separated us, and the hum of his energy grazed me. Heat pooled between my legs.

His nostrils flared, and his eyes flashed red as he sensed my body's reaction to him. His arm encircled around me, pulling me against his chest.

A small gasp escaped my lips, and his attention drifted to my mouth.

He continued to press into me, the weight pushing me a few steps back. Bending his head, his breath tickled my ear. "Hold on tight," he whispered.

Then we were free falling.

My nails dug into his shoulder as I stared at the retreating balcony above us. A star twinkled in the night sky, and I screamed.

Lazarus's deep laugh reverberated against the side of my face.

We were halfway down the tower, and the reminder of the ground below had me clawing at Laz like he was a ladder.

His wings shot out, momentarily blocking the view of the darkening sky.

An *oof* left me from the jolt of my body against his banded arms when our plummeting ceased and turned into a graceful glide.

"You little shit," I growled.

Laz replied with another chortle. "Little?" His tone held mockery, and I'd pinch him if I wasn't worried he'd drop me right after.

His bat-like wings flapped, easily carrying us higher into the sky. Soon, buildings no longer blocked us, and over his shoulder, the ocean reflected the sherbet sky.

My jaw hung at the view. It was as though there had been something missing from my life, and I didn't know until right now.

"Dusk is one of my favorite times to fly, watching something that could be a painting turn into a speckled dark sheet." Laz swooped to the right, and a squeak popped out of me.

"Do you really need to do that?" I grumbled. "It's bad enough I'm hanging on here for dear life." I squeezed my legs that were wrapped around his waist for emphasis.

His arms tightened back, a silent reminder that I was safe. Half a breath later, his wings tucked, and we flipped.

I closed my eyes on instinct; it was over after a split second. Prying one eye open at a time, I realized he had changed our positions. I was still wrapped in his arms, except now his wings were splayed out beneath me, gliding us across the sky while I straddled his waist.

My grip loosened, no longer fearful of gravity taking hold of me with him underneath. I craned my neck back and was met with a small smirk.

"You're safe," he soothed.

Despite this being the deadliest man in the city—hell, probably the world—I knew even if I fell it wouldn't be for very long.

I slowly sat up, keeping my hands on his chest and legs locked around him to straddle him in mid-flight.

A hardened bulge met my core, and I looked down at him with a raised eyebrow. Someone was definitely enjoying this.

He gave me a little wink and rested his hands on my waist, helping me balance while the wind whipped around us.

My attention drifted to the world around us. Twinkling lights glittered the city below, mirroring the stars being unveiled as night descended. The city came alive at night, as most Supes preferred it, and up here, where there were no threats, I was able to appreciate its beauty. The way the inhabitants came out like the city was stretching its arms, and laughter, growls, and music started up like *Tenebris* was letting out a giant yawn. We soared over rooftops, and faces lifted up to watch us pass by. I waved at them to be greeted with gaping mouths.

A bubble of laughter burst out of me.

Laz's fingers pressed into my thigh, drawing my gaze to him with a bright smile.

His face was blank, shocked, and riveted to me like I was the only thing in the world.

I squirmed under his penetrating gaze, my laughter dying off.

He shook his head, refocusing, and pumped his wings in a backward motion to take us higher into the sky.

The people became dots, and the buildings and pavement became more like a carpet covering the Earth than a death trap if we fell. The air was cooler up here, refreshing. It cleared my head and rejuvenated me like nothing I had ever experienced.

I closed my eyes and brought my arms to my sides. I saw a photo once, of a woman doing this at the end of a huge ship. Up here, away from everything, it was better than I imagined. When my eyes opened, I stared ahead into the horizon, envisioning myself soaring into it.

I leaned a little to my left on instinct, and Laz followed my guidance without question. We banked left. I pulled a little to my right to straighten us back out, and he followed the movement again.

I wanted to do this forever.

With a devilish grin, I peered down at him. His gaze bored into me. I brought my hands down and pressed into his shoulders.

Understanding lit his face, drawing out his own playful smirk.

I leaned further down into him, and he tucked his wings, wrapping them around the two of us.

We spun downwards, like a bullet, racing towards the ground below. My stomach swooped for a second before catching up to me, and I squealed in delight. My high-pitched 'eeee' morphed into a bellowing laugh.

Laz joined in, his deep chuckle melding with my own. When his wings widened once more, he was on top.

I relaxed into his arms, sad it was over, almost wishing he'd drop me so I could feel the freedom of flying for a few more seconds before he'd undoubtedly save me. My heart calmed, like it knew what we had last night was more than just sex. My mind didn't know if it agreed, but for the first time in my life, I felt safe, and that was irreplaceable.

He banked right, heading towards the hills that were inland. Away from the city, away from the colorful ocean.

CHAPTER
Nineteen

My power thrummed with her body against mine, her cinnamon scent washing over me with the wind. My canines pricked my bottom lip.

I needed to get a hold of myself, which is exactly why I decided to bring her here. We both needed to face the truth. I killed, wiped out an entire bar of shifters, and I didn't even blink. She was all-consuming and muddling my attention from what was important. I had to remain in control, and with her around I didn't think that was possible. My beast was awake again. Even now, he slithered inside of me craving more bloodshed, to make the world burn. I couldn't allow this.

When we landed on the peak of a hill, my body blocked her view.

She slipped off of me, bright-red hair windblown and sexy as fuck.

I readjusted myself by shifting to my other foot. Didn't really help.

"That was amazing," she said, still a little breathless from the flight.

The spicy scent of adrenaline poured off her, only making her more intoxicating. I had expected her to cling to me, demand for me to put her down, and curse me out. Never in my wildest dreams had I expected her to unleash herself with such unadulterated joy, relishing in flight the same way I did. And the way she had taken control; steering me, riding me with the sway of her hips.

Fuck me. This desire, how the world faded away when I was around her, was exactly why this couldn't go any further. This only spurred me to do what I must.

I ran my hand through my hair, pausing at the feel of the tip of my horns. I needed to get this over with, sooner rather than later.

"I have something I need to show you." I kept my face blank, watching hers pinch with concern.

"Ah yes, the classic 'jumping off a balcony just to show someone something'." She nodded her head.

I smothered my smile at her acidic little tongue. The number of deaths I would've given to demons if they talked to me the way she did, but with her, it merely amused me. "Don't act like you didn't enjoy it, pet." I couldn't help but tease her right back.

"Let's get on with it." She waved her hand. "I've got a lot of wolfy-ass to kick."

She'd nearly died not even a day ago and she was already ready to pick up where she left off. This woman needed a healthy dose of concern for mortality or else she was going to get herself killed. Which made what I was about to do all that more important, not just for me, but for her.

She narrowed her eyes at me. "What's that look for?"

"What look?"

"Don't play dumb with me!" She poked her index finger into my chest. "I mentioned the shifters and you made a face."

I did? Damn, my guard was too lowered around her.

I grabbed her index finger. "Careful, pet, poke the beast and you might get bit."

A sultry smile replaced her annoyance. "Don't threaten me with a good time."

Fuck. Fuck. Fuck. *Okay, time to get this over with.*

"The shifters shouldn't be a problem. They've been thoroughly warned," I assured her.

Her eyes widened and dropped to my clean shirt as she put two and two together. "You... you..."

Yes, fear me. That will make this a whole lot easier. I could end you, and everyone else, in a second.

She blew out a breath. "Good, the piece of shit deserved it."

My wings ruffled behind me. Well, that was unexpected.

"What is it you wanted to show me?" Her eyebrows raised up, waiting.

There was no way to introduce this, so I simply stepped to the side.

Her arms dropped to her sides. She stepped past me and gaped at the scene beyond.

Black, everything was black. There were no trees, no grass, no houses. There wasn't even any dirt because it was buried under layers of dark soot and charcoaled bodies. It went for miles, well beyond what a mere witch could see. However, I could see it all, the destruction, all the lives lost.

"Wh-what happened?" she breathed, never taking her eyes off the scene, not shrinking away like anyone else would.

"Me."

This dragged her stricken face to my own. Her forehead crinkled with confusion, as though she was trying to piece together the man before her and the destruction below.

My fingers itched as I reached up, parting my hair to show the peeking horns. "I am the Demon Lord, son of Lucifer. There are things I have done, lives I have taken by the thousands..." I trailed off. There were no explanations, no excuses, and it was better off if she thought it was purposeful.

Her heart rate picked up, and a shiver ran through her. "I remember reading about this," she whispered.

Of course she read, an art lost over the centuries. Everyone was too preoccupied about fulfilling their base natures. I was pretty sure I alone had the largest library of preserved books in the world by this point. Not that she needed to read about it, everyone had heard of this destruction. Few saw it with their own eyes.

She continued, "The Great Genocide." I flinched at the words, and thankfully she didn't see it as she recapped. "Thousands died when a power was unleashed, nothing like anyone had seen since the fight between Michael and Lucifer. Even that fight took years to wipe out so much land and people. But this... this power wiped out miles, an entire civilization within seconds. It's what spurred the angels and humans leaving our world." She turned to me. "You did this?"

I nodded.

"I-it was four hundred years ago. How is there still..." Her arm swept across the view. "... this?"

"My power is insurmountable, some claim even more than my father's. It... I... was not made for this world. Earth cannot overcome the havoc I have wreaked."

"I don't understand. Why would you do this?" She hugged herself.

Fear scented the air. Good, what I was showing her was finally sinking in. I was a monster, and what I swore would never happen again was too close to the surface. She was a risk I couldn't take.

She shook her head, eyes dropping to the ground. "No, it couldn't have been you."

My nostrils flared as I inhaled. "It was me," I said with a stern tone. She needed to see. "I killed thousands. I killed Neferia's mate. One slip up, one emotion not carefully controlled, and I could destroy this entire planet and everyone on it."

"You wouldn't." She peered at me, searching my face for some secret truth.

I had none; this was it. I was a monster.

"You need to listen." I held her gaze, releasing a small bit of my true power until it washed over her.

It was obvious when it hit her. Her sharp intake of breath, her muscles tightening, the way she took a half step away from me.

"You are different. You are like no witch I have ever met," I began. I could hear her heart slamming against her ribcage. "Every moment I am with you, I get closer to losing a battle within myself that will destroy everything. What you see now is a mere fraction of what I am capable of. I lost myself to my true nature for seconds, and I destroyed everything I knew and loved. I would've destroyed more if it hadn't been for Azazel. It's a miracle he didn't die in the process. If it happens again, nothing will bring me back. Death is the only outcome for myself and everyone on Earth."

She bit her lower lip as she absorbed my words. I didn't want to hear her thoughts. I was not worthy of her acceptance, nor could I stand to hear her condemnation.

"You are free from our pact." As I said the words, a zip of power severed the magic tying us together. I felt emptier.

She blinked at me in surprise.

"I'm sorry for any inconveniences. You are cleared of Darius's murder, and I will ensure your rent is paid for the year for your time," I said.

She said nothing.

"Goodbye, Serena." I did not grab her nor wrap her in my arms like I craved to do. Instead, I lifted my hand, called upon my power, and snapped my fingers.

I shimmered her out of sight, leaving me alone with my past.

Alone was exactly what I was meant to be.

CHAPTER
Twenty

"KYLA! LET ME IN!" I POUNDED AGAINST THE SHOP door. Where the hell was she?

You are different. You are like no witch I have ever met, his voice echoed in my head.

"Kyla!" I hollered.

The door swung open, leaving my fist in mid-air.

"What the hell, Serena?" Kyla used her body to block the inside of her shop.

The side of me that used information to survive piqued, while the current frantic side smothered it down. "Let me in," I demanded.

"I'm with a customer, which is why my door was locked." Her grip tightened on the door. "If I wanted people barging in, I would've left it unlocked."

"This is urgent." My voice shook a little. I needed help. I wouldn't say I trusted Kyla, but she had held more secrets than anyone I knew, including about me. She hadn't concluded I was human until recently, but there were plenty of times I had gotten into trouble, and she didn't tell a soul of my involvement. The biggest intel she had on me was what I kept hidden in my apartment; it was the only way I ensured she gave me spells strong enough to mask it. Granted, I made her take a blood oath of silence before I showed her. I wasn't that stupid. Still, she knew where it was concealed, and that was information enough to keep me on edge. It had been years, though, and I learned to trust the silence. I could still recall her wide-eyed wonder and stuttering reaction. It was the only time I had ever seen Kyla truly uncomposed.

Her brown eyes roved over me. "Fine." She widened the door to allow me to pass.

Inside, a cedar incense burned, as well as a few candles around a small altar; nothing was out of the ordinary. There was no trace of anyone.

Whatever. What Kyla chose to do with her business wasn't any of my concern.

The door snicked shut behind me. Kyla turned on the lights to the shop, walked around to the other side of the center table, and blew out the candles.

"Are you going to tell me what's so urgent, or do I have to guess?" She folded her arms in front of her chest.

I paced, picking at my fingernails as I tried to figure out where to start. "Lazarus was the one behind The Great Genocide." When she didn't respond, I stopped and looked at her. Her face was calm, unperturbed. "You knew?!"

She shrugged. "It doesn't take a genius to figure that one out."

Great, so I was both in danger and an idiot.

"He's deadly," I murmured.

"He's the Demon Lord," she said.

"He's a murderer," I added.

"He's Lucifer's son."

"He's... He's..." I stuttered.

"Evil?" Kyla finished. "No freaking duh, Serena! He walks into a room and everyone pisses themselves. He did not acquire this reputation from baking cookies and picking daisies."

"I know that," I argued, my hands balling into fists. "But I thought he was... different."

Kyla chuffed. "With Lucifer and Michael dead, and all the other angels gone, he is the most powerful being in this world. Power corrupts people, I would know, and based on his family tree, there was only ever one path for him."

As she said it, I understood. On paper, it made sense. Yet when he told me what he had done, what he did to Neferia's mate, and hearing the pain in his voice, witnessing how Neferia was still loyal by his side, my heart told me otherwise. It still refused to fully believe what was laid out in front of me.

Nonetheless, that didn't change the situation. If he knew what I was, or found out, it didn't matter what I believed because he'd kill me. If not him, someone else would, if word got out.

"And..." I hesitated. "I think he knows about me or is at least onto me."

How many times had he told me I was different or how I smelled good? It was only a matter of time before he found out, and by then it would be too late.

Kyla's arms dropped to her sides. "What? How?"

"I don't know. He kept talking about how dangerous he was and how he couldn't be around me. He mentioned how I was different and then released me from my contract and sent me to the edge of the Magic District. I know he's looked into my past, and with what happened yesterday..." I fumbled through my words.

"This is bad," Kyla said.

"I know!" I threw my hands into the air. "That's why I

need your help." I waltzed over to the table, leaning into my hands against the edge. "Please, help me," I pleaded.

Kyla swung a golden medallion at the end of a necklace back and forth while she thought. "Are you sure he's onto what you are?"

"I don't know what else it could be." I shrugged.

Kyla nodded. "He's the Demon Lord. He'd try to learn anything he could about those he worked closely with, especially if they interested him." She sighed. "There is nowhere in this city you can go where you'll be safe. Your only option is to run. Honestly, I don't know if there's anywhere on this planet you can go where he won't eventually find you if he really wanted to. At least it's better than staying here."

Leave *Tenebris*? It was the only home I had ever known, or at least ever remembered. Was it the best place? No. But it was home.

"I-I don't know where to go." I chewed my bottom lip as my stomach squirmed. I was used to being on my own, fending for myself. When I was younger, I allowed my loneliness to get to me, to consume me as I cried myself to sleep at night. My heart pinched anytime I heard others speak of their loved ones. Kyla was the closest thing I had to a friend, and I wouldn't call what we had warm and filled with love. Respect? Sure. Not real friendship, though.

Her index finger tapped against her lips. "I have a cousin in the bay. The trek there is treacherous. After today, don't travel at night, and stop for no one. You'll need to make sure you are fully supplied with food and water between towns because it's been a wasteland since the war." As she spoke, she grabbed a backpack from inside a cupboard and began throwing potion bottles and dried herbs inside of it. "This will help with dehydration, this will stave off hunger in an emergency situation, this will help maintain body heat on cold nights, this is a one-time invisibility potion if you come across anything dangerous. It will even mask your sounds and scents."

The red bottle was warmth. Silver for hunger, blue for dehydration, green for invisibility. I tried to take mental notes as she continued to throw things in the bag while verbally throwing out their purpose. She was really loading me up.

I hoped they were labeled because there was no way I'd remember this.

"How much is this going to cost me?" A lot of these weren't cheap to make and took weeks to brew. A couple I was pretty sure she was the only witch in the entire city who had the capabilities of making them. There was no way I had enough money for this.

She paused and stepped closer to me. "You are the last of your kind in this world. I should've seen it sooner, the signs were there, and I'm glad I've helped you over the years. I only wish I had done more. I have no idea how you wound up here or how you exist, but I will do my best to ensure you keep living."

My throat tightened. To have someone care that much about me... I had no words. I didn't know how I ended up here either. My kind left a long time ago. I was an enigma, something that shouldn't exist in this place, yet here I was. I had spent the last decade fearing for my life, thinking I'd be killed or have my life sucked out of me the moment someone found out. Kyla knew I shouldn't be here, but she didn't view me as a prize, rather a rarity worth protecting.

"Now,"—she turned back to keep loading the backpack— "don't return to your apartment. Buy clothes on the road if you must."

My breath caught in my throat. Her logic was sound; my apartment would be the first place someone would look for me. Nonetheless, the idea of leaving it behind hurt. It was the first place that was mine that wasn't an alleyway or abandoned building. I wasn't materialistic, and I had my favorite boots on, but to leave *everything* behind? I swallowed through my tightening throat. My blade was well hidden, and I was sure I could ask Kyla to retrieve it, however it was the one thing that linked me to my mysterious past. I hoped one day I would figure out how or why I had it. The idea of leaving it behind didn't sit right with me. Hopefully, I could come back for it soon.

Kyla walked over to me, shoving the backpack into one hand and metal keys into another.

I stared at the dangling things in confusion.

"Keys to my car. It's just North of the district and has a full tank of gas. It should get you to the next town. There's money in the bag to help you the rest of the way. Once you're in the bay, look for Jocelyn. She's a powerful blood witch," Kyla explained.

"A car?" I muttered. I had never learned how to drive one.

Kyla noted my confused face. "Push the button of the stick in the middle and move it to the D. Right pedal is go, and left pedal is stop. The car moves the direction you turn the wheel."

"Okay," I breathed. My hands shook, rattling the keys.

Kyla placed her hands on my shoulders, drawing my attention. "You'll be fine. Everything you need is in the bag. I will send word to my cousin about your arrival. She will keep an eye out for you."

My mouth opened and closed, wanting to object.

"Don't worry, I won't tell her anything about you. That is your secret, and it should be kept that way," she reassured me.

I nodded. "Thank you."

She gave me a tight-lipped smile. "Leave now before he realizes the truth and comes for you."

"Thank you," I whispered again, and it was the last thing said before I left.

LAZARUS

"WHAT THE FUCK DID YOU DO?" NEFERIA'S SCREECH was so high she could've been mistaken for a banshee.

I leaned against the kitchen island, the marble cool against my hands, over a cup with one finger of whiskey left. I had already drunk the other three.

Neferia marched around the corner, Azazel right on her heels, and stopped at the entrance to the kitchen. "What. Did. You. Do!"

I sighed. "What was best for everyone."

"No, it's not best for everyone. What could possibly possess you to scare her away? Make her leave?" Neferia paced.

Azazel leaned against the wall, arms folded, watching my sister act like a child. Forever the calm and collected one, something I admired and appreciated about him.

"How do you even know?" I asked. It had only been a couple of hours since I released her, said goodbye to her, and I was well on my way to getting drunk in order to forget her.

"I always know," she scoffed. "Eyes and ears everywhere, bro."

I took another swig from my glass, letting the burn wash away everything. "Right."

Azazel piped in, "I've been watching the witch as you've asked, and I saw her."

"And you went to Neferia?" I frowned.

Azazel straightened. "I was worried. She looked scared. Kyla's shop is blocked with spells, so I couldn't hear what was said once they were inside, but when she left, she had a backpack on. I think she's leaving town. If she does…"

"I released her from her pact. She won't die," I cut in.

"I told you!" Neferia pointed at Azazel. She spun towards me. "I repeat, what the bloody hell happened?"

"I was losing myself." I paused and took another gulp of whiskey. "Hearing things, feeling things…"

Azazel stepped forward. "You need to let go of the past."

I shook my head. "I can't."

Neferia's lips thinned. "If anyone is going to condemn you, it should be me, not you."

I captured her gaze with my own. "I killed her. I killed Priya. Your mate is never coming back." I wanted her to hate me, scream at me, and leave me the fuck alone. It was better if everyone stayed away. It's how I was destined to be.

Without breaking eye contact, she inhaled, flaring her nostrils. "I know this better than anyone, except it wasn't you! Your powers took over, your true demon form came forward. It wasn't you," she repeated.

"Yeah, and if it wasn't for Azazel…" I murmured.

Azazel walked around the counter and dropped a hand on my shoulder. "That's what I'm here for. I will always have your back."

"You could've been killed," I retorted flatly.

"And?" He shrugged one shoulder. "Just because I'm a

demon doesn't mean I'm not willing to risk my life to save others."

"Ha!" Neferia's eyes lightened. "If only daddy dearest hadn't given all of us such a bad rep."

"For good reason," I mumbled.

Azazel gave my shoulder a squeeze before dropping his hand. "You never told us what happened, why you lost control, why you're so scared now of losing control. It can't just be the girl. Let us help you. We can't do that with only part of a story."

Could I admit the truth to them? They were the two closest beings to me, but it sounded insane even to me, and I was the one who had experienced it. If I couldn't trust these two, then who could I?

It was now or never, just open your mouth and speak the words. Just do it. What did I have to lose?

You can lose your friends, your family, and then you'll truly be alone. My father's voice echoed through my mind, ripping the air from my lungs.

Damnit. Alright, I can do this. I needed to do this.

"I hear him," I said. I kept my breathing even, staring at the white countertop to avoid seeing their reactions.

"Who?" Azazel asked from beside me.

"My father," I breathed.

There was silence.

Shit. I knew I shouldn't have admitted it to them. They thought I was crazy. I probably was. It would be the death of us all if I wasn't crazy.

"You hear him," Neferia repeated, processing my words.

I nodded.

"Like a lot?" Her tone sounded intrigued, not damning.

I chanced a look up, and her eyebrows were pulled together. She didn't look angry, and her eyes didn't scour over me like I was completely unhinged. It was more like she was working through a question, trying to find an answer to a complex math question.

"Not always." My hands shook. "But before my true demon form took over, I heard him."

"What did he say?" Azazel leaned onto the table.

"That I was worthless. That this world didn't deserve saving. That a clean slate would be best for everyone. That I was no son of his and nothing but a disappointment. That I had all this power and I smothered it instead of using it." It was only a fraction of the things I had heard his voice say to me. "He wouldn't stop, and it only got worse. I hadn't slept for four days before... it happened."

Neferia's eyes widened. "Four days? No wonder you lost it."

"Even in death, your dad's a real piece of shit," Azazel noted. He looked between the two of us. "Sorry."

Somehow, having someone speak so plainly about our father had Neferia and I bursting into laughter.

"Honestly!" She swiped away tears from laughing so hard. "He was a dick, and it's better he's dead."

"Yeah," I muttered, my chuckle dying off. He may be dead for everyone else, but everything I had spent my life hearing still haunted me. *He* still haunted me.

Neferia sobered. "Listen. Our father was literally the worst, and apparently the humans had an entire book on how terrible he was, but he's gone now."

"I know." And that was exactly why I hadn't told them. I realized I shouldn't let it get to me. He was gone. I had tried ignoring it, but it only got worse until I cracked. I couldn't let that happen again.

"I still don't understand what this has to do with releasing Serena." Azazel's inflection rose, turning his statement into a question.

"I heard him again a couple of days ago in my office," I confessed.

"We all have demons in our heads," Neferia said. "Telling us we are unworthy, not good enough, dumb, ugly, fat, and plenty of terrible things. Yours just happens to be voiced by the worst demon to ever exist."

I snorted. "That's an understatement."

"Don't listen to him," she said.

My wings shifted, straining the muscles in my shoulders. "I tried that, and it failed. With catastrophic problems."

"Then talk to us," Azazel added. "Don't hold it in. If you can't ignore it, come to us. That's why we're here. We're your family, and you should be able to rely on us."

I pulled my wings tight against my body, like I could curl in on myself and make it go away. "It's not just the words, but the feeling. My powers get stronger, unpredictable. Azazel, you've seen how much I've been feeding, and it's barely helped at all. I felt myself unraveling, and then I heard his voice. It's not a coincidence. It's a warning, and I listened." I couldn't admit to them that my beast stirred within me too. I hoped with Serena gone he would settle back down and I could forget this ever happened.

"I understand," Azazel sighed. "Still, you shouldn't have let her go."

"I had to," I insisted.

Neferia's eyes narrowed. "She made you feel. Really feel, probably for the first time ever. I thought you'd spend your life as a gargoyle, nothing more than stone. You finally allowed yourself to care, to worry. That's a gift, not a curse."

"That's exactly the problem. She made me feel too much," I retorted. "I can't risk it."

Neferia's nails tapped against her arm. "You're making a mistake. Priya was the best thing that ever happened to me. I wouldn't be the person I am today without her in my life, no matter if our time was cut short. If I hadn't met her, I'd probably have helped you destroy this world all those years ago, relished in it, and, unlike you, I would've done it by choice."

She was right; she would have gladly helped me destroy the world, which was why I had protected her against our father, why I stopped him from getting his claws in her. Priya had been her saving grace, and I took her away. If only I could find the happiness Priya had brought her.

Except I had no mate. My father made sure of that before he died. He magicked my matebond away, something sacred across all the supernatural races, in order to power himself up for his fight with Michael. Taking a matebond was something only a demon could perform, directly linked to our ability to make deals, and it was one of the worst things we could do to someone.

For that, I would spend my life alone.

CHAPTER
Twenty-Two

MY BOOTS SLAPPED ACROSS THE PAVEMENT AS I headed North with nothing more than the clothes on my back and the pack Kyla gave me. A shiver ran through me with the cooling night air.

"Red car at the corner of Seville and Evergreen," I repeated to myself. Most streets still had their signs, even if they were a bit rusty. We may have created new Districts, but it was still easier to have streets to follow, and why worry about making up new names when they already existed with handy little plaques?

My stomach flip-flopped with the anticipation of leaving. I could do this; I needed to do this. I was 99% sure Kyla wouldn't say anything to anyone. I mean, she had given me thousands of dollars' worth of potions and supplies in order to help me get away. However, I had witnessed Lazarus's torture techniques firsthand. Kyla was strong, but I doubted she was that strong.

This was for the best.

Despite the sentiment, a lump formed in my throat. I was alone. Again. I finally found a place where I could have belonged, a place I felt safe. Apparently, it had been all a lie. I swatted away a stray tear. No, I would not fucking cry over a man... a murderer... who dumped me as soon as he got some. And he made me feel like I belonged! Ha! A fucking *demon*. No, *the* demon.

My teeth ground together. I knew he was a murderer; he never tried to hide that. If anything, he tried to warn me, and I still wanted him. I still craved his delicious touch. He had killed tens of thousands within seconds, The Great Genocide was horrific, yet the look on his face wasn't that of a monster. It was someone repenting. I knew there was more to the story, more to him. Otherwise, my body would reject him like all the others... right? My heart squeezed in my chest. He should've given me a chance, heard me out, let me help him.

No. This needed to happen, for my safety, for my life. I got in too deep with him, and ripping off the band aid would be for the best. I just wished I didn't have to flee the city. I was never a runner, even when I was twelve and woke up alone on the streets of *Tenebris* with no memory of my past aside from what I was and my name. I had given up a long time ago on trying to find answers. I bought hexes, spells, even tried meditation, which was an utter fail. Nothing worked, no memories came back. At sixteen, I realized this was my life now, and there was no turning back.

Just like now. I needed to keep moving forward; that's what's kept me alive all these years, and I didn't plan on wasting how far I've come even if I had to leave the only home I've ever known.

My breathing became heavier as I climbed the hill at a brisk pace. The ridges on the keys dug into the palm of my hand, centering my mind and helping me stay focused.

Movement caught the corner of my eye.

I looked around without pausing; there was no one there. The Magic District made up the northern edge of *Tenebris*, and I was now outside the district line; even with all these abandoned buildings there was still plenty of room for some creeps.

There was a problem when a supernatural didn't belong to a community. They went a little feral. If the shifters had no alpha, the vampires with no queen, the demons with no lord, the witches with no high priestess, and the sirens with no highness, they went a little mad. They needed the guidance, the camaraderie, the connection of power to another being. Angels, humans, supernaturals, we were all meant to be social creatures, and when we lost that piece of us, it had dire effects.

Footsteps sounded behind me.

I sped up while listening closely, and heard nothing more.

Damn, I wish I had my charm for hearing, but I had used that on a job a year ago in order to get intel. Nah, it was worth it. The money from that gig paid for my apartment for five months.

I sighed. An apartment I would probably never see again. There was a pull in my chest urging me to go home, to return and stand my ground. I couldn't, not if I wanted to live. I knew it was for the best, but it still hurt. The one thing I had on me when I woke up, aside from clothes I outgrew years ago, I had to leave behind, hidden away in my apartment. If they searched the room and found it, they'd know. I hoped the spells I had to conceal the weapon would hold; they were the best of the best. One day I'd return, and hopefully it would still be there. I'd spent my life pretending to be other people, I could do this. Once things have died down, I'll come back and retrieve the one item connecting me to my past—an angel blade.

I have no idea how I got it or how to use it, but I knew

what it was. If it was ever found in my possession… I shuddered. This was why I was running; no matter how much I hated the fact that I had to.

Footsteps sounded behind me again, matching my pace to blend in; they were closer this time.

I shuffled my feet at random to confirm, and whoever it was couldn't keep up with the sudden change in movement and their shoe pounded the sidewalk once.

I stopped and spun to face the stalker head on.

A rugged-looking man with long, curly brown hair and an untrimmed beard froze twenty feet away. A streetlamp reflected off his eyes, giving them a reflective yellow.

Wolf shifter. Shit! I meant it when I said never again.

I turned and sprinted.

He growled before hauling after me.

I pumped my arms harder, running with everything inside me until my lungs burned. The bottles in my bag clanked together.

Please, don't break.

Who knew what kind of explosion would occur on my back if any of them mixed together?

A flash of blood-coated teeth assaulted my mind, and I stumbled.

Shit, please not right now. I had little memories when I first woke up behind a dumpster at twelve years old. Pieces speckled my mind, usually choosing to haunt me at night. Of course, they decided to surface at this moment.

The hairs on the back of my neck stood on end.

He was getting closer.

Another piercing memory muddled my vision. My screams as a feral shifter pounced on me, biting into my shoulder, and how I grabbed at the assaulter to get him off. Feathers flying everywhere. There was blood, so much blood. I didn't remember how I survived, nor what happened after that. It was like a fever dream. Pain, sweating, sleeping. I had woken up in a puddle of dried blood with a dead wolf shifter next to me. I had avoided them ever since.

"Get back here, witch!" His voice was directly behind me.

I caught the first charm from my bracelet I could inside my palm. It was the feather.

"*Fuga*," I breathed out the magical word. My shoulder blades twitched, and with every pound of my foot, I felt lighter. I gave a giant leap, and when I landed on my right foot, I pushed off the ground with all my force.

I rose into the air.

And rose.

And rose.

I was fifteen feet in the air and still rising; it wasn't enough.

The wolf shifter jumped up after me. His hand wrapped around my ankle, and he pulled.

My nerves electrified from his touch, mixing with my terror.

I swung down like a pendulum. My arms came up instinctually to protect my face from the concrete. My shoulder smacked into it, and I let out a cry as a popping reverberated through my torso.

The shifter picked me up by the foot again and flung me.

This time, I didn't have time to cover my head before it hit the side of a brick wall.

The rumbling of crashing waves hit my ears before the salty air. My head throbbed, but I was unable to bring my hands up to it. My shoulders hurt, one locked and the other nearly numb. Cool stone pressed against the side of my face.

My eyes finally pried open, and the light of a fire pierced through my skull. I winced.

"She's awake, sir," a male from beside me informed someone.

This time, I opened my eyes more slowly, avoiding the flames. Beside me stood the shifter from earlier. He didn't even chance a glance my way, too confident I wasn't going anywhere.

I sat up with a grunt. My hands were tied behind my back, and my ankles were as well. The rope from my feet trailed off to the side where it was attached to a cinder block. Were they worried I was going to hop away?

"Hello, little witch, you've caused quite a stir within my pack." Another male stepped forward, blocking the fire so he was a silhouette. I could still make out his bronzed skin, wide shoulders, and dark hair falling into his green eyes.

It was Knox, the Alpha of the shifters. I had never met him before, however, I made sure I knew of everyone in power in this town on sight.

"What the fuck?" I rasped. The sound of my voice bounced around inside my skull, and I bit my lower lip from the pain. Damn, I probably had a concussion.

Knox sauntered over, crouching in front of me. His rough fingers grabbed my chin and lifted my face to meet his eyes.

I bit my tongue to keep from crying out as his touch burned against my skin.

"Careful, love. I don't appreciate that kind of language," he chastised.

I spit in his face. "Fuck you. Let me go."

The shifter who had caught me snarled in warning.

Knox cut him off with a single look before refocusing on me. "You should be lucky I don't hit women."

"Maybe that's something you should teach the rest of your pack." I side-eyed the other shifter.

More growls erupted from behind Knox; they were blocked by his enormous body.

I stilled. Shit. How many of them were there?

"What do you want with me?" I asked as my stomach twisted. They must've figured it out somehow. I wasn't careful at the bar, and my blood was left behind. They must know about me.

"Who said we wanted *you*?" Knox cocked his head to the side. "Although, you put up quite a fight at one of my favorite bars, even took out a few of my shifters. I have every right to do whatever I want with you." His attention dipped to the right at my backpack lying on the ground. "And it seems no one will even realize you're gone."

"Th-they'll know," I said. It was a total lie, and I prayed I had sounded more convincing. No one knew where I was, and Laz had gotten rid of our pact so he could no longer find me through it. Hell, I didn't even know where I was.

I scanned the area, unable to turn my head as Knox still held my chin firmly. I was able to make out a cliff's edge, a beach off in the distance, and a couple of sea lion barks echoing into the night.

We were in Shipwreck Cove, a place once known as La Jolla, and one of the sirens' favorite places to hunt. We were far away from everything, especially the shifter territory. Even if someone managed to discover the shifters took me, they'd never think to search here. Which was probably exactly why we were here.

Shit.

"Let me go," I pleaded. I didn't care how pathetic I sounded. I needed to get away. "Take my backpack; it's filled with witch's potions and charms, the strongest in the entire city. Take it as payment for my deeds."

Knox clucked his tongues. "The lives of my shifters are not worth a few potions."

I narrowed my eyes at him, ignoring the unsettled shift of the wolf beside me. "They attacked me first."

"And that was worth the lives of twenty shifters? Including my beta?" Knox raised an eyebrow, fingers tightening on my jaw until I was sure I'd have bruises.

"What?" I blinked in surprise. "Twenty?" I killed maybe one or two, not twenty! Neferia may have taken some down, but she got me out of there too quickly to kill everyone. Even though the piece of shit beta deserved it, I didn't kill him.

"Ah," Knox chortled. "You don't know?"

"Know what?" I asked.

"The Demon Lord wiped out everyone in the bar, leaving nothing but dust." Knox dropped his hands when his claws sprang forward. He grimaced as pain flashed in his eyes.

What? Laz had *killed* them? I thought he just tortured them a bit, gave them a little taste of their own medicine.

A trickle of blood slipped down my throat from where his dew claw had pierced me. The poison from his claw burned but didn't incapacitate me like before. Whatever Kyla did for my back was still in my system.

My mouth opened and closed. I shook my head. "No. He didn't. I..." My voice trailed off. He had come back covered in blood, and then he took me to the place where he had taken thousands of lives. He... he killed because of me.

I took a steadying breath. "What're you going to do to me?"

"Isn't it obvious?" Knox stood, towering over me. "I'm going to kill you, at least not before he has a chance to see it."

To mine and everyone's surprise, I laughed. "S-sorry." My body shook as the shock continued to wear off. My dislocated shoulder was less numb now, and the throbbing mixed in with the pain of his touch and the lump on my head. Every scratch, every ache made itself known. I needed to focus on not passing out, especially around shifters. I sobered, my laughter dying off. "You did all this for nothing," I said. "We'll be waiting here a while."

They caught the wrong person. Laz let me go. He scared the crap out of me, then let me go. He had no idea where I was, or even that he should be looking for me, and if he was looking for me then that was bad news because it means he discovered what I am. This was all with the assumption he would even care, and he was the Demon Lord for heaven's sake. He wasn't coming. He wasn't coming, and a weird combination of sadness and satisfaction bloomed through me, mixing together like water and oil. I was glad the shifters wouldn't get the best of him, that Laz would be safe. I may not be, but he would be. Yet, a part of me secretly hoped he would come, despite knowing he wouldn't. I'd been alone for twelve years, and it was how it should be.

Knox's nostrils flared, eyes flashing a reflective green. "He will come. I made sure of it."

I stiffened. "What did you do?"

"I made sure he knew we had you, and where to find you," Knox replied. "Little does he know I have a pack waiting for him."

With the admittance, howls, yips, squawks, and roars cascaded into a symphony of sounds. Briefly letting the world know just how many of them there were. From the sounds of it, it could've been the entire shifter pack of *Tenebris.*

Knox held his fist in the air, and they cut off. "He's coming," he hissed.

The wolf shifter barreled over to me and lifted me up by my armpit. The movement wrenched my dislocated shoulder, and his touch seared my skin.

I screamed out in pain as my tendons pulled and burned.

Another shifter stepped from the shadows, one with

beady black eyes and a sharp nose, and picked up the cinder block at my feet.

The two of them hauled me backwards.

I kicked out my tied feet, trying to get the hawk shifter in the head or wrench myself out of the wolf shifter's grasp. They were too strong.

"Let go of me!" I screamed. My breath quickened from the effort, and the wolf shifter needed to use both hands to keep me under control. The wind whipped my hair around my face, but I could still make out Knox gazing at us with no remorse.

A buzz of power permeated the air a split second before Laz shimmered into the space between me and Knox. His back was to me.

My breath hitched. I had never seen such a beautiful sight. His wings were flared, the muscles bulging through his shirt. He was lethal, and it wasn't directed at me. Instead, his deathly dominance was focused on the shifters.

He had come for me. He learned I was in trouble and actually came! Hope burst through me, swelling me up like a balloon filled with helium. I could float away. I wasn't alone. I wouldn't die alone. He'd save me.

"Where is she?" he hollered.

He had no idea it was an ambush! He appeared right into the middle of their trap.

"La—!" I opened my mouth to warn him, but his name cut off, turning into a whoosh of air as I was thrown over the side of the cliff.

The last thing I saw were his red eyes before I fell to my death.

CHAPTER
Twenty~Three

LAZARUS

I PACED MY OFFICE, HANDS LOCKED BEHIND MY BACK with my shifting wings grazing against them. My demon beat against my ribcage, demanding we go get Serena. Walking over to my bookshelf, I brace myself against it with my elbows interlocking beside my ear as I hung my head with a deep exhale. The wooden shelves creaked with strain from underneath my tightened fingers.

For fate's sake, how did this woman have so much control over me? I sent her away to protect her, and I have regretted it ever since. It was taking all my effort to keep my demon at bay. What was it about her that woke so much inside of me? Was I wrong to let her go?

No. It was the right decision. It wasn't just a risk for her, but the entire world. If she stirred this much in me after such a short amount of time, after bedding her once...

I pinched my eyes shut with a huff. No, I could not go there. I needed to get her off my mind and forget that she ever existed. It was for the best, and I understood that, even if my demon didn't. If I burned the world, she'd burn with it, along with everyone else I loved and everything I had tried to build.

Speaking of, I shoved away from the stacked books and headed for my desk. Neferia and Azazel's report sat there about their expedition, or should I say Azazel's report. Neferia just signed her name at the bottom per usual. I picked up the page, and scanned the page, welcoming the distraction. Or at least tried to.

We tracked the ferals East by a thousand miles, but the terrain became less inhabitable. When we reached The Black Trench, we turned back. The cities 500 miles North and 1,000 miles Northeast of Tenebris are functioning and self-sustaining. Minor infractions by local demons were reported, but there has been mild unrest amongst the witches in the North. They claim they felt an influx of power, there are no readings to support this.

Influx of power could mean anything. From a ritual gone wrong to too much essence being produced due to an orgy. However, I would be sure to see to it as soon as everything was wrapped up here involving Darius. In fact, I needed to find a new witch of my own to replace his position. Kyla was a businesswoman, I could use her for contract work. It was clear she liked her solitude; I doubted she would sign on full time to work for me exclusively, even if I paid her a large sum. Perhaps the trip North could double as a recruiting mission. There was no one else in *Tenebris* of interest to me. Well... there was one red-headed witch, which was exactly why I planned to stay far from the Magic District for the next few decades.

A rattling sound came from the glass window behind my desk, like someone was throwing rocks at it.

It couldn't be.

With my heart rate skyrocketing, I fisted and released my fingers to ease some tension. Had she come back to me? I glided over the window, taking my time, when there was another tap. I attempted to stop myself from rushing over, determined to stay calm and collected, which slowed my pace. Finally reaching the window, I pulled the curtains to the side.

Intelligent golden eyes stared at me. The hawk fluttered his wings and gave the window another tap with its beak.

Bloody shifters. My teeth ground together. This bird made a poor mistake coming to my window instead of arranging an appointment. I should have ignored him, but I was too wound up, and I planned to make it clear to him how inappropriate this was by scorching off a few feathers. I unlatched the window and drew it open.

He bucked wildly, a feather flying as I made a grab for him. In his crazed state, an envelope dropped from his mouth. Flapping his wings, he brushed against my arm as he flew out of reach like his life depended on it, which it did. A flameball hovered above my hand, ready to be launched at the bastard. It would serve him right. I held back despite my annoyance. Seemed there were some Supes who were forgetting exactly who I was and what I was capable of; I would be sure to remind them in the near future. Relocking the window, I shut the curtains and bent over to pick up the envelope from the ground, where it had landed during the scuffle.

The cream-colored envelope was addressed to no one; it smelled like shifter. I ripped it open, not caring to use the letter opener Neferia had gifted me, and the edges jaggedly tore apart. I peered inside and froze.

Carefully, I turned the opening over, dumping the contents into my awaiting palm. Red hair, shining with strands of burgundy and caramel, fell into them. Hair I had grasped, had smelled, and had the pleasure of feeling fall across my chest. I didn't even need the cinnamon scent to trace along my senses to know who it belonged to.

My demon roared in my mind, drowning out the sounds of the real world.

The shifters had sent me a message. They had Serena.

My body was made of stone, unmoving as I stared at these pieces of her. She needed my help.

It felt like my demon grabbed my ribs and rattled them like the bars of a cage.

They took pieces of her. She would never have allowed that. She was in trouble. I needed to help her. My demon settled, although his burning fury heated my body. Or was it my own fury? It was hard to tell, hard to think. All I knew was we needed to get to her. Now.

I studied the contents, the envelope, looking for clues. Breathing in deep, there was an underlying scent of salt, and when I looked closely in my palm, blending in with the color of my skin were small grains. I picked some up between my thumb and forefinger and rolled the gritty substance between them.

Sand.

I knew exactly where they were.

Hair in hand, I shimmered out, not even stopping to get help because she needed me, and she needed me now.

The sound of her voice was like a pickaxe to my chest. Turning, putting my back to my enemies to follow the sound, I saw her. Then her head, hair matching the strands I squeezed in my hand, disappeared over the cliff's edge.

Serena!

My heart thundered in my chest. My power coursed

through my veins. My wings flared, readying to go after her. I didn't even get a chance to launch from the ground.

Knox, now in cougar form, hit my back while a dozen hawks rained down on me from above. Their talons sliced into my wings as I fell face first into the ground.

I bellowed at the searing pain, dots filling my vision. Dirt gritted against my teeth.

Knox's giant paw razored across my back, the impact cutting off my breath.

I pushed my hands under my chest to throw him off me.

I had to get to Serena. The snap of rope as the cinder block plummeted, taking her with it, would haunt me forever. I needed to get to her!

I roared, wings flaring. Two more bodies landed on the shredded membrane of my wings, jaws latching onto the bones. There was a crunch. My vision blurred as my bones broke. My blood pooled under me.

"Submit and I'll make it quick." Knox stood atop me, foot pressing into my spine.

I had no idea when he transformed back.

"Let me go!" I hollered, rage making my voice hoarse.

"Funny," Knox mused. "She said the same thing."

"Let me save her! This isn't her fight!" My fingers dug into the ground, the rock cracking underneath each pad.

"She made it her fight when she walked into my territory and stuck her nose into our business," Knox scoffed.

"She did it because of a pact with me. She would've never been there had she not been trying to clear her name of murder," I wheezed. He was a heavy bastard, and the blood loss from my wings wasn't helping.

"And while trying to clear her name of murder, she committed it against innocent members of my pack," Knox snarled.

"They attacked her!"

"That's a risk you take when you enter shifter territory without invitation. It's a risk walking into any territory that isn't your own," he retorted.

"She was under my protection," I snapped, and my chest constricted with the admittance. Yet I had put her life in danger time and time again, and when she needed me most, I wasn't there. I had to have a fucking bird shifter deliver me an envelope filled with her hair and a note to even know she was in danger. And now? How long had it been? If she didn't hit the rocks and die instantly, how long could she hold her breath? I had to get to her soon...

"Your protection is exactly why the witch lost her life. You killed my men, not even coming to me first. I plan to repay the favor," Knox said. "I don't know if I can kill you, but I can sure as hell kill her."

My body shook with adrenaline, power, and pain. I was pinned, but I'd never be helpless. I was an idiot, I should've gotten Neferia and Azazel, had them come with me. In my blind rage, I came straight here as soon as I read the note. Even if I was stuck here, they could've gone after her.

"Time?" Knox called out.

"Seven minutes and three seconds, sir," the wolf shifter who had tossed Serena over the side answered.

I was going to snap that fucker's neck with my bare hands.

Knox bent down and whispered in my ear. "If she made it to the bottom of the ocean, she would've fought at first. Her chest tightening with each passing second. The movement of trying to get out of her binding would make her heart pump faster, using up her oxygen. Then it would've become painful, the need to release the carbon dioxide overriding her brain. In a panic, she'd release what breath she had left. After three or four minutes, she would have lost consciousness, inhaling the water, letting it fill her lungs. Her heart is probably slowing to a stop by now. And whatever is left of her, the sirens will get."

As if in answer, an ominous song hummed through the night. The melody thrummed through my body, calling to me, beckoning me closer. The chimelike sound was soft, unthreatening, and ended with a light screech that was cut off when the siren dove under the water.

Serena was gone. I had tried to save her. I wanted to protect her from death, from me. One the end, because of me, she was dead.

"You will pay for this," I spat.

"No," Knox hissed. "You will."

This pussy cat may have brought his entire pack, leaving me outnumbered. He may even take pride in surprising me and making me bleed, which no one had done in decades. He forgot one thing: I was the Demon Lord.

My body relaxed—melting into the pain, the darkness. My mind blanked as I let my power consume me. I allowed my demon to give me the power to erase them from the face of the Earth.

They would pay if it was the last thing I did. I no longer felt, I no longer cared. All I wanted was their blood drenching my hands. With a guttural roar, my body shot up, pulsing with power.

The shifters got thrown off me.

My wings were mere ribbons, yet I no longer felt the crushing pain when I twisted them to pierce the clawed tip through the chest of a fox shifter to my right. They would not die a painless death like their brethren. I would make them hurt the way they hurt Serena.

Three shifters, two cougars, and a wolf barreled at me.

Fire shot from my hand, consuming two of them. They were a burnt crisp before they hit the ground with a crunch. I allowed the remaining cougar shifter a clear shot at me, but before he made contact, my hand lashed out. My clawed fingers wrapped around his neck.

His giant paws slammed across my chest, leaving deep claw marks. I felt nothing. No pain, just the roiling anger in my blood. Whether it was mine or my demon's, I didn't know. I didn't care. He wanted their blood coating the ground, and so did I. For once, we were on the same page, and I had no qualms about it. Let them burn, let them bleed... let them die.

My other hand grabbed the top of his skull, and I pulled. His head came clean off, spraying warm blood all over me. I dropped the lifeless body to the ground and rolled his head to Knox's feet.

Eyes hard, he stared at me with a mixture of anger and horror.

With a roar, they all attacked.

CHAPTER
Twenty-Four

I HAD SECONDS TO REACT.

A fireball burst in my palm, singing my other arm and part of the rope holding my wrists together. It wasn't long enough.

The cement block broke the surface of the water, making it easier for my body to follow in after it. I didn't even have a moment to gasp when the frigid temperature slapped me.

The fireball snuffed out.

My lungs constricted in response to the biting cold. I had little time to overcome it while I sank. Within a few feet, the pressure from the water pushed into my ears. With each passing foot, it increased, and what started out as discomfort soon felt like someone was taking an icepick to my inner ear.

With my hands behind my back, I was unable to pressurize my sinuses via blowing against a pinched nose. Instead, I frantically swallowed. Each swallow released the pressure a fraction, but I was sinking too fast to keep up.

The searing pain of the salt against my open wounds blended in, consuming me with torment.

I kept my eyes squeezed shut. It would be too dark to see anything anyways.

The block hit the sandy bottom with a thunk. My body drifted down a little more before naturally trying to float back to the surface. The rope around my ankles pulled taut, keeping me underwater.

I didn't thrash around in fear of using up my oxygen, and my chest already ached with a need for air. I focused on swallowing some more, until the piercing pain of my ears subsided into a dull throb.

Everything hurt. The water no longer felt cold, my skin having numbed to the sensation. It spread into my dislocated shoulder, making the sagging arm more tolerable.

A song swirled around me, like nothing I had ever heard before. The tinkling sound reminded me of angels and called to me like home.

My body warmed with each passing note. I relaxed into the swaying motion of the ocean swells. I didn't know where the sound came from. It was like it was from all directions, enveloping me in its euphonic blanket.

It broke off.

My mind cleared, and my lungs were screaming.

Shit. Shit. Shit.

My need for air outweighed my consciousness, and bubbles escaped from my mouth. I clamped my lips shut.

Think, Serena, think!

I pulled at the rope around my wrists, hoping I had burnt it enough to break it. My shoulder seared with pain from the movement. I opened my mouth to gasp, and it filled with salt water. I clamped it shut again, stopping myself from inhaling.

I tugged again, pulling with only my good arm, and the charms in my bracelet painfully pushed into my skin.

That's it! I had no way to grab it, and didn't know if it would work, but if I didn't try something soon, I was going to die. I envisioned the charm in my mind. It was the size of my pinky nail, the round silvery fish with indented eyes and four outlined scales.

Respirare, I thought.

Nothing happened. There was only one option left.

With the last of the air from my lungs, I enunciated every letter to the best of my ability. "Respirare." The word still came out deformed and gurgly.

There was a flash of light that traveled up and over my neck and face.

With a mixture of desperation and hope, I took in a breath. I was ready for my lungs to fill with water, to choke and pass out. To my relief, it didn't happen. Instead, the magic managed to extract the oxygen from the water and provide me with a much-needed breath of air.

"Thank you, Kyla," I bubbled through my mouth.

With my body getting what it needed, my panic subsided. I had one hour to get free before the magic wore off, and with the sirens in the water, I needed to get out a lot sooner than that. Hopefully, the fireball had deteriorated the rope enough.

I brought my knees to my chest, pulling me deeper into the water. Biting my lip, I worked my rear between my bound hands then wiggled my bound feet through. My dislocated shoulder screamed in retaliation. The added couple of inches from it hanging lower was what made it possible to bring my hands in front of me. The rope tying my feet together trapped my hands still, but keeping the rope tight and secure was exactly what I needed. I rubbed the binding of my hands along the strand back and forth. Soon, I added in extending my feet and pulling them back to my chest to get more friction between the ropes. I hissed from rope burn when it caught my skin instead of the wrapping.

The rope finally snapped, freeing my hands.

I tamped down my rising hope. Bending over, my fingers fumbled with the knot at my ankles. Within seconds, the rope loosened. A knot was easy after everything else. Instantly, my body rose, and I kicked my legs to get to the surface faster. Yes, I could breathe, but I wanted to be able to see.

I gasped when my head broke the surface. I could've cried. I didn't believe how close I was to dying, and I totally just saved myself.

Hell yes! I was a strong, independent woman, and no one could convince me otherwise!

Treading water, I peered up the cliffside and saw no one. Neither could I hear anything with the crashing waves against the rocks.

Another song came from behind me. This time it reminded me of a summer's day with the warm sun shining on my face. A soft smile broke across my face and I turned toward the sound, wanting to swim to this little piece of heaven.

A woman floated there with raven hair and turquoise skin. Her navy blue, bowed lips hung open, and the sound trickled out like fresh nectar.

I swam closer to her.

The corner of her mouth pulled up, revealing razor-sharp teeth. I wasn't scared. She was beautiful, she wanted to take me someplace safe. Her song got louder. When I was five feet away, her nostrils and gills on the side of her neck both flared, breathing me in.

Her onyx eyes widened as though fully taking me in for the first time. She sniffed again, and her song cut off.

I stopped swimming for her, reality slamming into me.

Her head tilted to the side, watching my every stroke of water. Gills flapping, she leaned forward and took another whiff of me. "*Pomacanthidae*," she hissed in a foreign tongue before disappearing under the surface.

I stared at the blank water. She was just... gone. There was no way I was planning to stick around to see if she came back. I turned and swam for shore like my life depended on it. Actually, it completely fucking did right now!

I hit the rocks and scrambled up their slippery side, getting out of the water as fast as possible. The waves slammed into me, making me lose my grip and cutting open my palms. I didn't stop until I was out of the ocean.

Pressing myself against the cliffside, I scanned the surface. There was nothing but water, and no songs inundated my mind. I searched the stony area and saw a small pathway, with a few rock scrambles, to reach back to land.

A roar stretching into a gut-wrenching cry sounded from above me.

Laz!

My heart tore at the mutilated sound. He was up there alone, taking on the shifters of *Tenebris*. What if he wasn't strong enough? Shifters were strong, especially when they worked together. He was capable of mass murder, but would he let himself go there again, risking the entire city? No, he wouldn't... he couldn't. This was our home. I hadn't seen Neferia or Azazel; he had no back up.

No, that wasn't true. I was his backup, and I needed to get to him. I needed to help him, save him by the sounds of it.

My hand held the arm of my dislocated shoulder in place as I ran.

My chest heaved as I scrambled up the last few steps. I was soaked, bloody, and a bit woozy from everything my body had been through. All I wanted to do was curl up in a ball and go to sleep, which between the head injury and freezing water probably wasn't a good thing.

My sluggish brain snapped back to attention as soon as I saw him.

Power seeped from Laz like primordial ooze trying to

eclipse the land. His wings were in tethers. Blood as black as the night sky leaked from them like a broken faucet, coating the ground. The tops of his wings were at a weird angle, the glint of white bone protruding from them.

Oh, Laz. Bile rose in my throat at the sight of them, and my vision blurred from threatening tears. His precious wings were butchered. I couldn't even call them wings anymore. No wonder he had screamed. He had told me they could bring the greatest pain or pleasure. How was he still standing? Still fighting?

His black clawed hand ripped into the chest of a wolf, pulling out the shifter's heart and lungs before tossing it to the side. The body crumpled, littering the ground with the dozen other bodies surrounding Laz.

He hit a fox with a fireball as big as itself. The shifter turned to ash.

Holy fates, I had never seen any Supe come close to that amount of power. I suddenly understood how he killed all those people. He was beyond anything this world knew, and somehow, he had kept it hidden. I knew he was strong, however, this was another level. A shiver lanced down my spine. I should have been terrified, running for my life, hopping in Kyla's car and never coming back. The thing was... I wasn't. For whatever reason, his all-consuming energy drew me towards him.

Laz threw his head back and roared into the night.

Despite the danger, shifter after shifter attacked him, a wave of fur and feathers. A hawk's talons cut his cheek, a wolf bit the back of his thigh, a cougar swiped at what remained of his wings. On and on it went.

Laz's power lashed out, a wave of energy crashing into everyone and flinging them backwards.

I cowered, arm coming up to protect myself, but it dissipated before reaching me. "Laz!" I screamed.

He didn't hear me.

"Laz!" I called again, racing towards him. At this rate, he'd kill everyone. I saw the ghosts in his eyes over The Great Genocide. He'd hate himself if I let him wipe out the shifters.

I joined the foray, and for whatever reason, the animals didn't attack me. There was one threat, and their pack mentality planned to kill him.

I grabbed his arm, and a jolt of electricity ran through my body. I whimpered at the contact. This wasn't the pleasant sensation I had come to know; it was raw power.

He swirled around, flinging me off him.

I skidded across the ground on my good side, the impact rattling my teeth. I sat up and swiped my hair out of my face to peer up at him.

Red eyes. Bright, murderous, and completely empty.

"Laz," I whispered.

There was no recognition, no sign of relief at seeing me. My heart sank. He had to be in there somewhere; the Laz I knew would never let something like The Great Genocide happen again. I had seen it in his eyes, I had seen his pain, his loneliness.

It matched my own. I needed to reach him, to let him know I was fine.

His clawed fingers stretched at his sides. He took an earth-shaking step towards me, bringing up his enormous hand. A snarl ripped from his mouth, spittle flying everywhere.

He was going to kill me! My chest seized with fear. This wasn't the Laz I knew and... cared for... I'd be damned if I wasn't going to go down without a fight, and hopefully save his ass in the process. A little fire wouldn't hurt.

A fireball formed in my hand, and I threw it, hitting him square in the chest.

It didn't even faze him.

I hopped onto my feet, another fireball at the ready and threw again.

It hit him in his groin this time. Still nothing.

Another fireball. Another hit. Another fireball. Another hit.

He kept walking toward me.

Two fireballs in each hand, and I aimed them both for his face.

He smacked one to the side but didn't see the second behind him. He bellowed in pain, closing his eyes from the embers exploding around him.

I used the chance to throw another. And another. And another. I hit his face over and over again. I didn't let up.

He stumbled backwards, and I moved forward. I hit him again. And again, tears streaking my face. "Wake up!" I screamed. "Wake up, Laz! It's me! Wake up!"

My arms ached from the power I wielded, the fire feeding from the pain and fear of seeing him like this. I didn't want to kill him, nor did I want to die. All I needed to do was reach the Laz that I'd come to know. The one who cooked me food and made me eat my vegetables, the one who could bring more pleasure than I ever thought imaginable, the one who loved his sister and had a best friend like a brother, the one who came here to protect me... not kill me.

All these emotions created one giant fireball between both my hands. Screaming, I hurled it at him.

It was so large that when he threw his arms up to block his face and chest, it still slammed into him, knocking him backwards onto the ground.

The shifter's used the opportunity to attack again. Yips, hisses, and caws echoed together as they charged forward.

No! With one hand, I threw a fireball at a wolf shifter. His fur caught on fire, and he ran away, howling into the night.

This didn't deter the others, though. They kept coming.

There were too many of them. They'd kill him, and then me the moment they had a chance.

I unleashed a blood-curdling scream as the fire magic took over my body. Using all the power I possibly possessed, fire ran down my arms. It shot to the ground, arcing into a circle around myself and Laz, blocking us from the blood thirsty pack.

He came for me when I needed him, and I would do the same for him. I wasn't going to give up on him, even if he gave up on us. There was no pact forcing him to come rescue me, and yet he arrived to do just that. He must care. Even if he knew the truth, a part of me felt he wouldn't kill me. He released me to protect me, I saw that now. Together, we were not alone. It broke my heart to do this, to attack and hurt him, but I was determined to shock him back to be with me. I cared about him too much to lose him.

The circle of flames were scorching, so hot that the hawks were unable to sweep down on us from above.

Exhaustion pulled at my limbs. I fell to my knees. My nerves were on fire from the overdose of magic, and my vision blurred.

The Demon Lord sat up.

CHAPTER
Twenty~Five

LAZARUS

FIRE. IT WAS EVERYWHERE, TOWERING INTO THE SKY. Burnt flesh and fur singed my nose.

No. My stomach plummeted. I did it again.

I pushed myself onto my elbows, struck by the towering flames licking the night sky like a lover. The heat was unbearable, even for me.

What happened? Was I dead? Was this hell? Or was my beast-self destroying the world and this was where I would be held in the corners of my mind as everything burned?

My demon had taken the lead again, not in full control but enough to where I barely remembered what happened. It wasn't a total blackout like before. This time I remembered the blood, the howls of pain as I murdered the shifters. I could recall relishing in his rage... my rage... as we killed. I let him take over. I was nothing more than a figment in the back of my brain. I really was my father's son. I was the monster he had wanted me to become no matter how much I fought it. I hated him for being right, but I hated myself more. Why was my demon gone now? How was I me again? Neferia and Az didn't come with me; they probably would have killed me if they had. I wouldn't have blamed them. It's what they should do if he took control, and here I was handing the reins over.

I scoured the area, looking for some kind of clue. Then I saw her.

On her knees, shoulders hunched—one lower than the other—and arms hanging at her side. Her body shook, red hair hanging limply in her face. Blood smeared across her pale skin, which had a bluish tint to it. Despite all the heat, she was cold. Her clothes were soaked, a mixture of saltwater and blood; I could smell it from here.

"Serena," I croaked.

Her head shot up, her eyes going wide.

We stared at one another, both of us in mild shock.

She had died, but she was here. This must have meant I was dead too. She'd ended up in the depths of Hell alongside me. I would do my best to protect her soul, but even I could only do so much.

Leaning forward onto her good hand and knees, she crawled closer to me in a daze. Based on her pinched face and shaking limbs, every movement was taxing for her.

I raised onto my knees, the movement wrenching my wings. I sucked in a breath, vision tunneling from the slicing pain. They were in ribbons. A swirl of emotion pressed on my chest. Rage, surprise, mourning, and sadness. What had happened to me? No wonder I died, except how could this follow me into the afterlife?

A slim hand pressed against my chest. It was cold as ice, so much so I could feel it through my shirt. I peered down at my little witch.

Tears brimmed in her eyes. "It's you," she whispered.

I cupped her cheek, wiping away the blood with my thumb. Every piece of her was frigid.

My shirt bunched in her grip. She held onto me like I was her only tether to the world.

Dipping my head down, I took her full lips in mine. I wouldn't have been surprised if she shoved me away and slapped me across the face. I deserved it; I put her in danger. She did none of those things. Instead, she kissed me back.

A buzz passed between the two of us. The tingling something I only felt with her, something we wouldn't feel unless...

We weren't dead.

Pulling at me, she pressed her lips harder against mine, devouring me like I was her last breath. She tasted of the ocean, which made her usual sweetness only shine more.

I swept my tongue across her bottom lip, wanting to taste more. She moaned against my mouth and opened up for me. I went hard. Her tongue entered my mouth, tracing the tips of my canine. I dug my fingers in her hair and pulled her flush against me. Her arm wrapped around the back of my neck, and I could feel every curve of her body.

I wanted her. I wanted all of her. I shouldn't have let her go. Losing her had done more damage than keeping her ever would have.

My magic snaked out, caressing her skin, trying to warm her body.

She melted into me. The feel of her was like nothing I had ever experienced. It was enough to where the pain from my wings was a distant sensation.

I could smell her wetness, not her clothes, but what was pooling between her legs because of me. I wanted to taste her, to relish in her, to make her feel more pleasure than she even realized was possible.

Every place we made contact zipped with energy. An electricity, a power, molding together and consuming us with ecstasy. My powers dipped between her legs, caressing her in a way I wanted to do myself.

She gasped, and a smile pulled at my lips.

I lifted her further into my arms to feel more of her.

A cry left her lips, one of displeasure. We broke apart.

My eyes scoured over her. "What?"

Her face dipped to the side. "My shoulder."

It was dislocated, and I had wedged it.

Carefully, I lowered her to the ground; she stayed pressed against me. The blue color of her skin was gone, and a healthy pink tinged her cheeks once more.

"You're alive," she breathed.

"Me?" I raised an eyebrow. "*You* are alive, my pet."

She released a breath and leaned into my chest. I wrapped my arms around her and kissed the top of her head. The flames continued to rage around us, and the sounds of animals yipped, growled, and cawed from the other side.

"What kind of predicament do we seem to have found ourselves in?" I inquired.

She pulled back, giving me a sheepish grin. "Yeah, the fire might be my fault."

Unable to contain my surprise, my eyebrows shot up. "You did this?"

She shrugged with her good shoulder. "What can I say? I have an affinity for fire."

A smile tugged at the corner of my lips. "So it seems, my pet."

"One problem." She chewed her bottom lip. "I don't really know how to make it stop."

I chuckled. "That is easily rectifiable." With a snap of my fingers, the flames snuffed out, leaving tendrils of smoke behind.

Surrounding us was a pack of animals, reflective eyes of ambers and greens just beyond where the circle of fire had been. They stared at us, gathering intel. We were still sitting on the ground, holding onto one another. Their hackles raised and noses rose as they scented our blood. We were weak, easy targets.

Or so they thought.

A cougar, Knox, pawed forward with his head held low. His shoulder blades bobbing with every soundless step. He stopped, dipping closer to the ground, never taking his eyes off us. He pounced. The rest of his pack followed, all of them moving as one to take us out.

Knox's hind feet hadn't even left the ground when I released my power. It ruffled Serena's now-dry hair before washing over everyone else.

The shifters froze, my power holding them in place.

Together, Serena and I rose from the ground. She still held onto me. Based on her bowing shoulders, it was from fatigue more than anything else.

I turned her toward me, ignoring the animals as they monitored us, unable to move.

Serena side-eyed them, not wanting to let her guard down, but I knew my powers would hold. My magic was like a river, constantly flowing and with extra to spare, and now that I was of sound mind again, nothing would touch me… or *her* unless I allowed them to.

"Serena." I drew her attention to me.

Large brown eyes stared up at me.

"I need to fix your shoulder," I said. I frowned at the arm still hanging at an odd angle. How long had it been that way? The blood flow to her arm could be disrupted, which would be a real problem. I tried to listen to the sound of her heartbeat, to see if I could pick up on the damage, except there were too many furious heartbeats around us to isolate hers specifically.

Her face hardened, and she gave a single nod. "Do it."

I could distract her in a number of ways, a couple of particular intrigue, but I didn't fancy an audience for what I had in mind.

I didn't hesitate, hoping to lessen the pain by taking her by surprise instead.

My powers lashed out, gripped her arm, and yanked.

She screamed, falling forward into me, and I steadied her with my hands. Serena took a few deep breaths before straightening back up. "I'm fine." Gasp. "I'm good." Another gasp.

I leaned down and whispered in her ear, even too low for shifter hearing, "Oh, my pet, if only you knew how good I could make you feel."

Her heart skipped a beat, but she didn't show her hand to the Supes surrounding us. No, not Serena. Instead, she laughed.

My body warmed from the sound, and a smile tugged at my lips. She may have been laughing now, little did she know I would be getting her to cry out my name soon enough.

Just you wait, I promised in my mind. For now, we had other matters to take care of first.

I sauntered over to Knox, whose eyes screamed murder, careful not to shift my wings too much. Each step took effort. I had lost too much blood. The damage to my wings would normally have me writhing; between blood loss and shock, I feigned strength. I was able to keep the shifters locked down, even as it took more energy with each passing second.

With my depleting power, I would need to feed soon.

These fuckers shouldn't have been able to do this much damage in the first place. That was my fault. I would never hear the end of it from Neferia and Azazel.

With a wave of my hand, my magic loosened on Knox. Not enough to where he could attack but to where he could transform back.

"We need to talk," I demanded. A growl rumbled in his

chest. My magic tightened around the hearts of every shifter in the vicinity. "Don't test me, cat," I spat.

As their Alpha, Knox must have felt the panic of his pack. He abided within moments and shifted back, clothed thanks to the witch's magic. "I will kill you," he snarled.

"You tried, you failed," I reminded him. "If anyone is dying tonight, it will be you," I promised. My hand shot out and wrapped around his neck. The tips of my fingers were already in claw form and pierced his flesh. "In fact, I think that is exactly what you deserve."

"It was within our rights to seek retaliation," he retorted, unflinching.

He was a strong Alpha, a good Alpha. The pack would be weakened when they lost him.

I barked a laugh. "Retaliation?"

"You killed dozens of my pack members without reason."

"Not without reason," my deadened voice rumbled. "You killed my warlock and then attacked a witch under my protection. It was within *my* right."

Knox's brows knotted. "I gave no order to kill your warlock, and your little bitch already fought and killed pack members for how she was treated, despite knowing the risk when she voluntarily chose to walk into my bar."

A smack echoed through the air. Knox's head snapped to the side, and a red handprint formed on his face.

I followed the hand back to a feral Serena. "Pet," I cooed.

She didn't take her eyes off Knox, even as he turned back to stare daggers at her. "Don't ever call me a bitch again," she warned.

Pride swelled in my chest.

Knox blinked and looked at me.

I shrugged. "You heard her." My fingers tightened around his throat. "You are lucky. I will make this quick, and none of your other pack members will die tonight due to obeying their Alpha. That is, unless they attack me again."

Fire licked down my arm; the orange reflected in Knox's green eyes. The sour scent of fear permeated the air around him even though he didn't flinch.

The flames were a few inches from his face when he broke. "Wait! I know who ordered the hit on the warlock!"

The fire crept forward.

Knox didn't hesitate. "Don't kill me, and I'll tell you."

"Or I kill you and work the information from one of your pack members," I countered. "I already know the wolves bought the serum, and it was a hawk who finalized the kill."

"You don't know all of it!" he cried out. "I know the truth, and if I die, this information dies with me. You will remain at risk. If you let me live, I will tell you and make a pack-promise to never attack you again."

I let silence fill the air as I thought. The shifters and demons weren't at war, but this world was dangerous. It didn't mean one couldn't break out at any time, and the more Supes, the more bodies I had ready to fight by my side, the better. This was how you stayed at the top of the food chain in today's world. I wanted to kill him more than anything for what he did to Serena, to me, but business came first.

"I let you live, you tell me what you know, and you make a pack-promise that you will stand by my side, and if I ever need you or your pack, you will be there without hesitation," I offered.

"Deal!" Knox hollered.

I reached my hand out and lessened my magic on him a little more.

He put his hand into mine and shook. The magic locked into place, not just binding him but his entire pack to my will. I felt every single life tether to me, to my powers. A pack-promise was very risky on an Alpha's part because not only did he put his life at risk but also every single shifter who did not obey the deal. If there came a time where I summoned them, any shifter who did not abide would drop dead. Maybe he wasn't as good of an Alpha as I thought.

His loss. My gain.

"Perfect." I smiled. "Now, tell me who murdered Darius."

"The vampires!" he blurted. "They gave an extra potent venom and told the shifter to slip it into the drink. He didn't realize what it was at the time when we gave it to the bartender to put in his drink. It wasn't until we heard of you investigating that we realized what happened."

The vampires? As in more than one? Alina had given me a single name; however, she was the owner of one of the more notorious clubs in town. Lips became loose when under the influence, whether it be alcohol, sex, or saliva. I would need to repay her a visit to ensure I got my money's worth. This excluded the fact that the bartender, one of *my* bartenders, distributed the venom into Darius's drink. This treachery went deeper than I thought.

I scratched my chin. "How do you know so much? Was it you who gave the orders?" I inquired.

Knox shook his head. "No, I didn't realize my pack was involved until the hawk shifter came to me with what had happened."

I raised an eyebrow at him.

"We interrogated him, and some problems arose," Knox added.

"I see," I said. "What kind of problems?"

"He died." Knox's throat bobbed.

Interesting. It was unlike the shifters to kill one of their own. And it seemed I had a certain bartender of my own to take care of too. I knew Baltic had supplied the venom, but he was too much of a low-life to give the order. Clearly, I needed to pay a visit to the Queen, but I would rather have all the information I could get first. "And the money?"

"Money?" Knox's brows drew together. "What money?"

Serena stepped forward, hand on her hip. "The wolves paid the vamps, and we assumed it was a transaction to get the venom."

Knox shook his head. "I don't know anything about any money." His eyes narrowed on me. "And you killed the person who would've."

"Ah-ah-ah." I wagged my finger. "I never killed your beta, and it's a good thing too because it seems we both have some questions that need answering. A beta doing dirty work behind his Alpha's back." I *tsked.*

Knox grimaced. "That son of a—"

"Do you know the vampire who ordered it?" I cut in. He could be pissed at his beta later. I was getting weaker with every passing second, getting harder to hold onto dozens of shifters. I needed answers fast.

He shook his head. "No, never got a name. The old pack member was given the vial by a skeezy bloodsucker and the name of a target, but that's all."

"Your pack member never told you why they agreed to it?" I asked.

"He was unable to answer the question," Knox said. "Died trying."

Damnit, so Knox didn't kill him. He should've said that earlier. Leave it to a shifter to still try to keep secrets despite a predicament not in their favor.

Baltic must have charmed him into silence, which led to his untimely death when he tried to speak. Demons had their deals, witches had their magic, sirens had their songs, shifters had their poison, and vamps had their charms. This was getting messy.

Serena listened to every word, taking it all in. "Why

Darius?" she mumbled to herself with the wheels turning in her head.

"Why indeed," I rumbled, staring down Knox. "You said I was still in danger. Why?"

"Your warlock had information, something on the vampires related to you. They wanted to make sure word didn't get out," Knox explained. "That's everything I know, I swear."

I could taste the honesty of his statement. This was worse than I thought. Had they managed to keep an angel blade hidden from me? Or was it something else?

My powers pulled at my chest, and my heart constricted, as it demanded more to keep holding the shifters. I needed to leave before I became too weak and unable to shimmer away.

I nodded. "I will have someone collect you later. We can question your beta together." The beta was more likely to talk if his alpha was there, either from a sense of false security or submission.

"Yes, sir," Knox said. His eyes widened at how he had addressed me.

I smiled again. People really should learn exactly what they are agreeing to. He may be Alpha of the shifters, but now I was the Alpha of him. The pack-promise made sure of that. I hoped he proved to be smarter in the future.

I faced Serena, who had stood by me the entire time, never flinching or reacting. She gave nothing away.

Good girl.

"Ready to go home?" I asked.

She stepped closer to me. "Let's go."

With her wrapped in my arms, I shimmered us away, dropping my magic holding the shifters in place a split second before we disappeared.

CHAPTER
Twenty~Six

SERENA

WE LANDED IN HIS BEDROOM. CRISP AND CLEAN, smelling of old books and with the fire already crackling, the room had the smoky flavor of him everywhere.

Adrenaline wearing off, my head was clear now—of the fear, the near death, and with my shoulder fixed even the pain was less. This left one big gaping hole, which anger filled.

I stepped away from Lazarus, needing a moment to myself to work through my roiling thoughts. He had cast me off, ended our pact like it was nothing, like I was nothing, like we were nothing.

Lazarus reached out, his large hand wrapping around my wrist, and pulled me back towards him.

I ground my feet into the floor and yanked my arm away. "Don't," I whispered. Yes, he had come for me. But I had saved myself, not him. I was always saving myself; I was always relying on myself and no one else. In fact, I was the one who saved him.

"Serena." His voice was soft, pleading, and traced along my nerves until I closed my eyes with a sigh.

"You can't expect things to just go back to the way they were." I stepped away, and to my relief, he didn't try to follow. With the space helping to settle my confusing mix of emotions, I met his penetrating silver eyes. "You saved my life, then pushed me away by trying to terrify me, then..." My voice cracked. "Then you abandon me."

None of this would have happened if it wasn't for him. I nearly died twice. Yes, he had helped save me from the shifter attack to then throw me to the curb like I was nothing. He shimmered me away and didn't look back until it was almost too late. Of course, I was happy that he was alive, but I felt far from free.

His hand, void of claws, extended towards me, while remorse knitted his brows.

I stopped him before he could get any closer. "You let me go!" I shoved against his chest. "You released me." Another shove. "You got rid of me!" Then he brought me back here, to his place, like it was nothing!

"I'm sorry," he muttered.

Should I have been surprised that the Demon Lord apologized to me? Yes. But I still wanted to punch him in the goddamn face. "Screw you," I seethed.

"I'm sorry," he repeated.

I peered up into his eyes, back to the silver swirls I'd come to know. "Don't pretend you want me."

His blood dripped onto the floor, the poison in the shifter claws making it hard to heal. "Serena." His voice was firm, and the way my name rolled off his tongue had me squeezing my legs together. Not pet, not witch—my name, and it dripped from his tongue like honey. "I was trying to protect you. I am so very, deeply sorry."

My anger lessened, which made me even more annoyed. I

just wanted to be angry, and here he was making it really fucking hard to continue to be. I was upset and just needed a moment to breathe.

Suddenly, Laz's eyes rolled into the back of his head. He collapsed to the ground, wings splaying out underneath him

My negative emotions evaporated like a candle had been blown out. I raced over to him and dropped to my knees to bend over him. I turned his face towards me. The usual spark between us was barely there.

He blinked his eyes open, and a shiver ran through him. "Get Azazel," he said.

"What's wrong?" I searched his body, trying to figure out how to help him. There was too much damage to know where to begin. I should've anticipated him collapsing; no one could sustain that much power. If anything, I should have been surprised it didn't happen sooner. Stupid.

"I..." he hesitated. "I need to feed."

My mouth made an 'oh'.

"Get Azazel," he coughed.

I pursed my lips. "Use me... feed from me." I bent down lower, holding my palm against his face to stare into the silver pools of his eyes, hoping I'd convince him. I didn't know what it entailed, but he wouldn't hurt me. I'd do what was needed to help him. Despite everything, I trusted him. Yes, he sent me away, but he showed up as soon as he learned my life was in danger.

He shook his head.

"Lazarus Morningstar. You are too goddamn weak to make it to your little brothel, or to wait for them to get here." And honestly, I wanted it to be me, although I would never admit that to him.

He chuckled, or what was a sorry excuse for one. "I don't think anyone has called me by full name in... well, ever."

"Let me help you," I pressed.

"You won't be enough," he said. "I could kill you by accident."

Like fucking hell he would. "Demon Lord." I smirked. "You have it under control. When I asked you to rein it in last time, you did. I trust you."

Before he could come up with any more excuses, I covered his lips with my own. He grunted in surprise, and I used the invitation to suck his bottom lip. I lightened up, giving him a chance to pull away if this truly was not what he wanted.

His hand came up, fingers wrapping into my hair at the back of my head to pull my face back towards his. His tongue swiped out, licking my lips, and I let him enter. His bonfire taste filled my mouth, and I moaned against his lips. This only made him hungrier for my mouth. He kissed me ravenously.

The thrum of energy between us ignited, spreading from my lips through my torso and down to my toes. My whole body tingled with panty-wetting power coming to life from his touch.

I threw my leg over to straddle him, like when we were in the sky. His hard length pressed against my core, and I burned with need. I pushed myself flush against him and ground my hips in a slow circle, moving with just the right amount of pressure and friction to where a rumble came from his chest.

My hands had a mind of their own, wrapping in his hair and moving across his chest. I pushed my mouth closer so I could taste more of him.

There was a sudden pull of my energy. It was invigorating, like every nerve in my body had been overloaded with endorphins and I was flying.

I gasped, breaking our kiss.

"Are you alright?" His gaze searched mine.

He had fed from me, taking some of my essence. It surprised me, yes, but it felt... good. There was no pain, there was no trigger from any blood, and I craved more. It somehow connected us, and it felt good to give myself over to him in a way I had never done with anyone else before, had never trusted to until now.

I pulled him into a sitting position and kissed him again. "Take more," I demanded.

There was a pause, and a second later, I felt another pull. The energy thrumming through me churned. It moved like a river from me into him.

His kisses became stronger, and soon instead of me holding him against me, it was he who pulled me against him. His cock throbbed with need.

"I want you," I said against his mouth.

"Careful what you ask for, my pet," he growled.

I pulled back, holding his face in my hands. "I want you."

His eyes flashed red, swirling dark with desire. "I need you."

With a snap of his fingers, our clothes melted away. Skin against skin, I let out a moan as my energy met his power, lighting up every cell in my body. This was different than when he bit me before. Now, it was like my energy wanted to mix with his, which was only proven by the pleasure radiating through my body. There was no pain.

He raked his canines over my neck, and when he breathed in, he pulled at my energy. "Fuck me," he whispered. "You taste even better than you smell."

A small smile pulled at my lips. I moved my hips, grinding against him, using my slick center to rub myself against his velvet cock.

He moaned. "Careful, pet, or I won't be able to hold back."

"Who said I wanted you to hold back?" I teased.

"Naughty little thing," he replied playfully. His lips trailed kisses along my neck, over my shoulder blade, and one of my peaked nipples slipped into his mouth. His other hand massaged my other breast, pinching my nipple.

I yipped at the sudden pain, and he licked it away, replacing it with pleasure. He went back and forth between my breasts, working them between pleasure and pain, while I grinded against his hard cock.

My need built up and up, and when I was about to shatter, he pulled away.

"No," I whimpered, looking down at his heated gaze with wide eyes. "Don't stop."

A devilish smile traced his lips. "I don't plan to, *amica mea*." His power wrapped around me, and when his mouth met my own, his magic flowed across my core and dipped inside of me while he took my nipples between his thumb and forefinger.

I exploded with his name on my lips.

His powers vibrated inside of me, absorbing the energy from my orgasm. The intense feel of it, a piece of him inside of me, simultaneously feeling his throbbing shaft pressed against me had a second orgasm crashing through me until I was left panting against his shoulder.

"Delicious," he crooned. He shifted underneath me, arms bracing me as he rose with me cradled against his chest.

Blinking my eyes open, the room came back into focus.

His wings fluttered behind him. They were whole once more, although the membrane was pinker with being so new.

Without thought, I reached out and ran my finger over them. I bit my lip with a smile at the same velvety softness. I did this; I was able to help heal him.

His wings shuddered under my touch, and he grunted.

I retracted my hand to my chest. "S-sorry!"

"Don't be. It felt good, really fucking good. They're just extra sensitive right now."

A swell of happiness lifted inside of me. I made him feel

good. And for once in my life, I could be touched without excruciating pain. I could relish and indulge in the pleasure someone else could bring. No, not someone... Laz.

He walked over and laid me down on his bed. His heated gaze traced over every inch of my body.

I blushed under his scrutiny. I wasn't experienced in this department, which was horrifying, but Laz looked at me like I was a goddess.

His eyes burned with desire when they met mine. "I want to watch you come for me. You have two options, my pet. You work yourself or I work you, which would you prefer?"

I was stunned into silence.

"You have three seconds or else I'll decide for you," he warned.

"Y-you!" I blurted.

His fangs glistened from his sinful grin. "You like when I work you, *amica mea*?"

I nodded.

"Good girl," he purred.

My center throbbed with need, and his eyes shot down to where I clenched my thighs.

He clicked his tongue, and it reminded me of what he could do with it between my legs. Wetness pooled between them. His powers shot out, pulling my knees to the side and exposing me to the room.

I gasped, and my hands raced down to cover me.

His powers leashed out, wrapped around my wrists, and held my arms above my head.

"I said I want to see you. How can I do that if you're covered?" He arced an eyebrow. "Do you remember our safe word?"

I nodded dumbly. How could I forget? I'd probably never look at a cantaloupe the same ever again.

"Good," he breathed.

This time when his eyes traced me, his magic followed. It trickled across my body, licking me like a flame, but instead of heat there was pleasure. When it dipped between my legs, it swirled around my clit, stroking it.

My legs shook with my building need, fighting against the invisible tethers of magic holding my limbs down.

Laz's powers expanded, and even though he continued to rub me with them, pieces drifted up my body until breaking apart to squeeze my nipples and wrap around my throat. His powers pressed in on me from everywhere.

His nostrils flared. "You're close."

"Yes," I panted.

"Ask me for it," he said.

"Laz, make me come."

His fangs elongated, pushing into his bottom lip, and fists curled at his sides. "Come for me, my pet."

His powers ramped up like it was voltage, but instead of electricity, it was pleasure.

Stars dotted my vision as I came, and when I opened up my mouth to call out his name, his lips were against mine as his body joined his powers, pushing into me from above. He pulled at my sexual energy, taking what he needed to continue to heal himself.

When my orgasm dwindled, his powers released me, and I liquified into the mattress.

His fingers twined through my hair as he watched me. "You are the most beautiful thing I've ever seen."

I had no words. I had spent my life in the shadows, pretending to be someone and something I wasn't. This was the most exposed I had ever been, and somehow, it was freeing.

I wrapped my arms around him and pulled him down for another kiss, which he happily obliged. I shifted underneath him, and without breaking contact, I reached down one hand and grasped his hard length.

It pulsed in my grip.

Laz's powers pressed into my core, using my wetness and natural flexibility of my opening to widen me for him. I relaxed into him, into his powers, and my body molded for him without any problem. His velvet tip lined up with my entrance and pressed inside. Inch by inch, he went further, filling me up. I inhaled sharply, and he paused.

"Yes," I moaned, urging him on. "More."

He pressed in further until he was to the hilt.

Tightening around him, every hard inch filled me. Opening up to him, I leaned up and covered his soft lips with my own.

He began to move. His pulsing hips rocked against my core, hitting every nerve in just the right spot. His hand ran down my side, pulling my right leg up and around his back so he could grasp my ass. With the new angle, he managed to dive deeper inside of me. He groaned against my mouth.

With each thrust, I got wetter until we could hear the slap of my desire for him.

"That's the best fucking sound in the world," he purred.

I moved with him. My head fell back with a moan, arcing my back and pressing my breasts against his bare chest.

"Fuck, Serena," he growled into my ear.

The deep tenor of his voice brought me higher. My nails dug into his back, and this only spurred him faster. Power and pleasure wrapped around us. He pulled at my energy, but what surprised me was how his energy moved into me as well. Whatever he took, he gave back.

Our energies mixed, becoming an inferno that had both of us sweating and moaning. A tangle of limbs and cries of pleasure, I didn't know where he ended and I began. We were alive and could burst into flames.

His hand reached out and grabbed the headboard. There was a crack, and splinters of wood fell across the pillows.

"Fuck me, Laz," I breathed.

With his name on my lips, he groaned. His cock thickened inside of me, bringing me closer to falling over the edge.

With one final thrust, I exploded around his throbbing cock as he came inside of me with a grunt. He continued to rock against my bare body. When he came to a stop, we panted in unison with the small shudders of his cock still inside me.

He raised onto his elbows to look at me. His wings flared behind him, his full strength having returned. "You truly are something else," he breathed.

CHAPTER
Twenty-Seven

Lazarus

Before the door shut, I peeked at Serena.

Her chest rose and fell with even breaths underneath the white sheet of my bed as she slept. Red hair covered the pillows, like flames devouring kindling.

Walking towards the kitchen, I rolled my shoulders. They were stiff from all the healing, but I still felt better than I had in years. Serena's energy was like nothing I had ever tasted. It was like a drug, and I wanted more. Every time I feared I was taking too much, somehow, she had more to give.

I had no idea how she did it—if it was that her witch magic matched mine, or her affinity for fire. Whatever it was, I was alive because of her. Now that I wasn't straining for energy or on the cusp of losing myself, there were quite a few things I needed to take care of. I made a mental list in my mind: have Azazel or Neferia find the bartender and bring him in for questioning, go visit Alina myself to see what more information she possessed and failed to provide, find out exactly what information Darius possessed that got him killed, which led me to visiting the vampire queen herself. I needed to do all of this as soon as possible before it got any more out of control.

Tired again just by thinking about it, I ran my hand through my mussed hair. I was pissed so much had happened under my nose without me realizing. Neferia and Azazel had been gone for a little over a month, and I had no one to assist me with my duties. I guess the Supes of *Tenebris* had gotten comfortable without them here too. I needed to be more diligent, pay more visits, and find more eyes and ears across the other districts. Everyone had a price, and I was willing to pay it to ensure the safety of myself and those I cared about. They were few, but the number had grown by one recently.

Rounding the corner in only boxer briefs, I stopped short.

Azazel leaned against the kitchen island with his arms folded. He wasn't bothered by my state of dress, but his attention drifted to my wings, which had fresh skin.

I was surprised they didn't scar; my compliments to Serena's energy again. I continued forward, saying, "Az, I need you and Neferia to go pick up the bartender from *Peonis*." Fates, I hated that name. Poor taste.

"What the fuck?" Azazel hissed, glaring at me.

"Don't look at me like that," I snapped. I grabbed a glass from the cupboard and filled it with cool water from the fridge. Serena would be dehydrated, and I planned on this being ready for her on the bedside table when she woke up.

"You could've died!" Azazel slammed his hands onto the marble.

"Hush!" I glanced to the hall that led to my bedroom. "She's still sleeping."

"You should've called me!" Azazel angry-whispered.

"There wasn't any time," I said, placing the glass on the counter.

"Bullshit. How about before you went and got ambushed by more than half the shifters in *Tenebris*? By the time I found out…" His hands clenched at his sides.

I noted a scent of something that wasn't quite fear, but… worry. My eyebrows rose. "You were scared for me?"

Azazel rolled his eyes. "Of course I was! You're my best friend, my brother. You may be hard to kill, but it's still possible. And if you survived, I didn't know which version of you I'd find."

"Ah." I ran my hand through my hair, and for the first time in days, there were no horns. A weight lifted off my shoulders, which seemed to have transferred to Azazel.

If I had continued to unravel, Azazel would've killed me.

"I'm sorry," I uttered. I've been saying those words more today than I had in the last five hundred years. "My intention is to never put you in that position."

"Then fucking don't!" Azazel pinched the bridge of his nose. "Next time, fucking call me so I can help."

He was pissed, fragmented; I don't remember the last time I saw Azazel this way. I nodded. "Of course." He was right. I even knew that the moment I arrived at the ambush, but I hated to admit aloud when I was wrong.

"They could've killed you," he repeated. He sounded exhausted, and his shoulders hunched as the anger fell away.

"They didn't," I reminded him, and it would've been difficult for them. "Plus, the only thing that could truly kill me is the blade of an angel. Thankfully, we are in short supply of those."

Azazel narrowed his eyes. "That doesn't mean it doesn't exist."

"You were by my side when we scoured Earth centuries ago," I noted.

"It doesn't mean someone didn't manage to hide one." He sighed, looking like he hadn't slept in weeks even though it had only been a few hours. "You're alright?" His attention raked over me again, noting all the places I was once wounded despite there now being new, smooth skin.

I nodded. "Thanks to the witch."

His eyes widened. "How? You killed over half a dozen succubi just from being aroused."

"I honestly don't know, but it's like nothing I've ever experienced," I admitted.

"Oh?" Interest flared in his face and in his scent. A small snarl escaped my lips. Azazel held up his hands in surrender. "Woah, there. I'm just interested."

"Take your interest somewhere else," I warned.

Azazel stifled his shock at my response, and I smothered my own. I had never responded, been territorial, over another being this way before.

"There might be an answer in here," Azazel said, pushing a manila envelope across the counter to me.

"What's this?" I asked.

"The witch's bloodwork you had me run when she was attacked by the shifters. I swung by to check on you and thought I'd bring this too. I figured you may want to know, and it seems it might be of even more interest now."

I picked up the envelope and slid my finger under the sealed edge. I pulled out the white paper. It had no name or information on who it came from, as whoever ran the test had no information aside from the blood sample. My eyes bugged from my head. "Who's read this?" I asked immediately.

Azazel shrugged. "Just the person who ran the DNA test."

"Has anyone else seen this?" My voice raised. "Did anyone else read this or were in the lab when this was run?"

Azazel's head popped up at my panic, becoming instantly alert. "Not to my knowledge. Why, what's going on?"

"Kill him," I said.

"What?" His jaw snapped open.

"Kill him and anyone else who may have seen it. Destroy the software," I said. With the paper crumpled in my hand, I headed for my room.

"Laz, what is it?" Azazel tried to cut me off.

I halted and turned towards him. "Do not speak to anyone. Do not read anything yourself. If you want to help, do this for me. Destroy anyone who knows and anything that contains this information."

Azazel stared, wide-eyed, but soon schooled his face into controlled determination, letting his assassin mindset take over. "Understood."

This was why I trusted him.

He shimmered out of my apartment without pressing for more. He was used to partial answers, knowing I would tell him if it was vitally important. This was a secret I wasn't ready to tell.

I marched to my room, and the bedroom door blew open from my power.

Serena bolted upright, clutching the sheet against her bare body as she frantically looked around. When she saw me, she stilled. "Wh-what is it?"

I threw the paper onto the bed.

With hesitant fingers she picked it up and scanned it, and when her eyes landed on the same place mine had, she froze.

"You truly are something else," I said, power radiating out of me. "You are not a Supe, you are something that hasn't existed in this world for a long time."

"I can explain," she whispered. Her body shook, and her sweet scent had me drooling.

I had tasted her and now I knew why it was so good.

"You're human," I said.

She looked up at me, trembling, but she didn't try to correct me.

My gaze dropped to the charm bracelet around her wrist,

the one she never took off. Concentrating, I sensed witch magic emanating from it, mixing with her own essence to make her seem like something she wasn't. It gave her the smell of Kyla and the powers of an elemental witch, hiding her in plain sight. I wouldn't make her remove it, though, because no one else could find out.

She was mine now.

My wings flared behind me.

"I'll never let you go again, *my pet*," I purred.

Secrets In The Streets

DEMON PACT BOOK 2

Trapped. Discovered. Totally screwed.

I need to find a way to escape. I had almost gotten away, until The Demon Lord read a report on my blood. Now, he won't let me out of his sights, to the point where he's made me move in with him. I need help; I'm still drawn to him. And the temptation is hard to ignore when I keep having dreams about him. Very, very delicious dreams.

No! Bad Serena! Focus.

First, unravel the mystery forming around me, which seems to be tied to my past.

Second, break my new pact with The Demon Lord.

Third, try not to sleep with him.

...Odds really aren't in my favor. Thankfully, I still have secrets he doesn't know about. I'm a survivor, and if I must, I'll kill him to save myself.

Order Book 2 Now!

Follow Me

The best way to stay updated on news, releases, and giveaways
is by following my facebook reader group!

Kacey Lee's Thirsty Readers (https://www.facebook.com/
groups/393866872107819/)
or
Follow me on Instagram (https://www.
instagram.com/authorkaceylee/)

The second best way is by joining my newsletter:

Join Newsletter Here (https://landing.mailerlite.com/
webforms/landing/a7f9z4)

Will a chain keep me captive or help set me free?

I was lucky to escape my last pack with nothing but a few scars--a cheap price to pay for my freedom.

It was supposed to be just another run to calm my wolf, but I wasn't going to ignore those cubs' screams for help--even if they were from a rival pack. What I didn't expect to find was a feral vampire, or the wolf who would change *everything*.

The Alpha who caught me is like all the others--all raging temper and muscles. And yet...his pack is different than mine.

But no matter how much my wolf cries '*mate*', I need to break free. It's time I accept the truth: I don't belong anywhere. My wolf will never settle for anything less than she is, and no other wolf will accept what I am:

Different, an anomaly...

A female Alpha.

Chapter 1 Bailey

"You're not from here, are you?" I winced as the words left my mouth, but what else was I supposed to say?

The diner was dingy and old, just like the forgotten highway outside. The parking lot was losing its battle to nature. Weeds broke through crevices of the parking lot, which was turning to gravel with each passing week. A root had shot up through one of the limited parking spaces, so only cars with high ground clearance could park there. More tangible evidence that this small town in rural Colorado was also slowly being reclaimed by Mother Nature.

I knew everyone who came into my diner. Everyone. Not only because the handful of regulars and their tips were my only income, but because I had to be vigilant. I had to watch for others like me.

But while this rumpled, stale-smelling man certainly wasn't what, or who, I was worried about, I hadn't been able to think of anything else to say.

His tired gaze lifted from his coffee as he shook his head and mumbled something about a road trip and California.

I sighed, missing the Golden State myself. The woods and the coasts specifically, and not the people I left behind. I wouldn't think about him. Not here.

At least that's what I told myself nearly a hundred times a day. Possibly more.

"Bailey, order up!" The cook, Louie, slammed a plate of greasy breakfast food onto the metal window separating the kitchen from the main dining area. If you can even call this hole-in-the-wall that.

Shooting the dull traveler an apologetic look, I hustled back to the kitchen, balancing the heavy tray of platters like I'd been doing it my whole life instead of months.

Louie wiped his hands on his apron. "I'll never understand how a tiny thing like you can heft all of that so easily."

I shot him a wry grin. I wasn't about to tell him my secret either. "I'll never understand how you can cook all day and be as skinny as a rail!"

Louie howled with laughter, even though I made the same joke at least once a week. The banter was safe though. It was familiar. Personally, I loved the laid back atmosphere and his willingness to pay me under the table.

Not having a bank account made hiding and moving a lot easier.

"Two eggs, extra bacon, and a Jimmy Dean omelet." I handed the ticket with the customer's order over before picking up the hot plate to distribute to table 2.

"Anything else?" I gave Mr. Foster—one of my regulars— my award-winning smile. His tips were shit, but he was the nicest old man.

"No, thank you." He picked up his fork to dive into the four sausage patties, buttered toast, five pieces of bacon, and extra cheesy eggs.

If he wasn't careful, his daily meal was going to take him to an early grave. But it wasn't my business, and I wouldn't be here much longer anyway. I had to keep moving or my past was bound to catch up to me.

The phone rang, and a pad of paper and pen were already in my hands by the time I picked up.

"Otto's Place, what can I do for ya?" I said. Otto was long gone, having left the restaurant to his son, Louie.

"Oh! Bailey! Is there any way you can cover my shift for me tonight?" Molly, one of the two other waitresses, begged me from the other line. Her nasally voice grated against my ear, and I pulled the receiver away slightly due to my sensitive hearing.

"Uh," I hesitated.

It was nearly the full moon and my body vibrated with the need for release. I knew I wasn't getting a certain form of release because of the lack of eligible men, so my desperation for a run was at an all-time high.

"Carter has a fever, and Chad isn't picking up, the piece of shit. I'll owe you one!" She pulled at all my sympathy cards: sick kid and shitty boyfriend.

"Yeah, sure," I said, sighing into the phone.

"You're the absolute best! Thank you so much!"

The line went dead before I got a chance to respond.

Circling around the counter, I stopped by different tables to see if the customers needed anything. The restaurant wasn't huge, so only two servers worked here in a single shift. There were six booths, four tables, and a long countertop with eight built-in chairs.

The place cleared as breakfast winded down before the lunch rush. In between, I refilled sugars and ketchups, wrapped cutlery, swept the floors and mopped underneath where an over enthusiastic toddler had had his breakfast. By the time dinner rolled around, my skin itched from the inside out.

I stared at the rising moon longingly, counting down the minutes until my wolf could run. The moonlight bled between the expanse of trees lining the highway. The restaurant was a pit stop on the outskirts of a tiny town and surrounded by state land, which is exactly why I chose it. Running in the woods was always at the tip of my fingers. No, it wasn't living free, which is what I truly dreamed of, but it was close enough.

"It's okay, girl. Soon," I whispered to myself. My focus shifted back to rolling silverware. It was a slow night, with only two customers total, which made this last-minute double shift that much more excruciating.

"What'd you say, darling?" Louie leaned his arms on the metal window with no plates in the way.

"Nothing." I gave him a small smile, placing a fork on top of a knife.

"Go ahead and get outta here," Louie grumbled. "It's a quiet night. I can handle any customers who come in."

I raised my eyebrows in surprise. This wasn't an usual offer from him. "Misery loves company" is what he always said while laughing his way back into the kitchen.

"Are you sure?" I asked, trying not to let my hopes rise like the moon outside.

"You look so wound up, so I'm pretty sure any customers we do get you'll scare away," he said.

I laughed at the comment, but the tension built in my shoulders. I hated when my need to run was apparent to humans, like my true nature would be blown at any minute.

Louie shook his head with a snort. "Get outta here already. I'll see ya tomorrow."

"Thanks!" I fiddled with my apron, and it landed with a clunk on the counter.

Louie raised an eyebrow at me.

I laughed sheepishly, pulling my tips from the pockets. *Oh yeah, I kind of needed those.*

With a wave, I was out the door. I didn't have a car, but luckily I found someone willing to rent a small room over their garage to me a mile away. The journey was quick, probably because I ran for most of it.

Once inside, I threw my tips into a shoebox I kept stashed under my bed. Not the best hiding place, but this tiny town wasn't known for theft. And it was a hell of a lot safer than where I had spent most of my life.

I peeled off my work clothes, leaving them rumpled in the corner. I didn't bother to shower, knowing by morning I'd be covered in dirt and leaves anyway, and threw on a summer dress with no underwear. It was simple, easy, and would cover me up long enough to get to the woods. That was all I needed.

A short quarter mile jog brought me to the edge of the forest. The woods sprawled across three peaks and hid a series of valleys. Reds and ambers tumbled around me as the earthy scent of the wild filled my nose. With each step my body relaxed. My bare feet sank into the leaf-littered ground, and my eyes closed with a sigh.

Home, my wolf whispered inside of me.

My pace quickened until I found my usual boulder pile to stash my clothing in. It didn't take long for my wolf to burst forward the moment the fabric slipped from my grasp.

I'm happy there were no breaking bones or immense pain like you see on TV shows. Being part wolf was nothing less than magical. The shift was a realignment of every atom of my being. It felt like briefly losing myself to combine with the world around me before solidifying into another form. It's hard to explain to anyone who hasn't taken a psychedelic before. Not that I have, but from what I've heard, the connection to the world seems similar. A shimmer, a vibration through my body, and then it's over and

I'm in a different form. Although, it's different if you fight it.

I shook out my fur, the color tawny brown like my hair, and just as unruly. My hazel eyes were definitely my best feature, and despite Louie making fun of my small stature, I could kill a man with my thick thighs.

My wolf whined until I let go of my thoughts, giving into my base nature to live in the moment.

A howl ripped through my muzzle and I took off, tongue lolling to the side in a dopey smile. A fallen tree blocked my path, but instead of skirting around it, I bunched my haunches and leapt ten feet into the air, clearing the top by several feet with an excited yip.

Up ahead in a clearing a small herd of deer grazed leisurely.

I didn't slow down for a second, bursting through the tree line until the glow of the moon radiated across my body. The deers' heads shot up in alarm, and they fled from my beast.

I am predator. Hear me roar!

Another long howl pierced the night sky as I chased after them. All in good fun, of course. There was no reason to kill a deer for a meal when I didn't have a pack to share it with.

A pang of loss jolted through my body. Wolves weren't meant to be alone, yet here I was. I knew it was for the best. But I missed being a part of something larger than myself, living and working together, raising pups.

Yet, here I was.

Padding through the undergrowth, I enjoyed the stretch in my limbs while I listened to the night music—chirping crickets, hooting owls, and other tangible sounds that reminded me that, here in nature, I wasn't completely alone.

Hours passed before my wolf was satisfied and my human worries took over once more. The sun would rise soon, and I had another shift at the diner today. I needed to get at least a few hours of sleep.

Taking my time getting back to my clothes, I nosed along the ground, catching the scent of a rabbit that had crossed this path about four hours ago.

My right ear twitched as it caught the flutter of a bird's wings fifty feet away.

Pack, my wolf breathed, when an earthy aroma crossed my senses.

I stilled.

With a tentative step, I lifted my head into the air and sniffed deeply.

Pack.

Two shifters had crossed here earlier, their scent oddly familiar.

My hackles raised, a small growl rumbling in my chest when it hit me. It wasn't just any two wolves, but ones from the rival pack. The Yellowstone pack.

Shit. Did their territory extend this far south?

If they caught the scent of me, they'd still recognize me as part of my old pack, the Yosemite Pack. And if that happened . . .

I shook out the shudder running through my body. What if they already knew I was here? What if they were hunting me? Or worse, told my old pack about me?

I was dead either way.

I raced back to the rocks where my clothes were hidden. I needed to leave now.

Stay. Fight, my wolf growled in my head.

I returned the rumble with a verbal one of my own. That need of hers, of mine, was exactly why I needed to flee.

If not for my sake, then for my mother's.

A howl emerged in the night.

I swore and ran for it.

Chapter 2 Derrick

The music was loud, and the beer flowed freely. I wasn't the biggest fan of parties, but tonight I had to suck it up. It was my party, after all.

The hanging white lights from the trees were a nice touch, filling the small clearing with a soft glow. Trucks parked around the edges, tailgates facing front to hold food and people. We had blankets and fold up chairs, plastic cups, and blue jeans. It was noisy—loud and exuberant, with children running around as adults laughed and danced. It was more of a tailgate than an engagement party, but I kept a smile on my face, trying to enjoy it.

I supposed I was simply still struggling with my new role as Alpha. I cared immensely for everyone in this pack, but socializing had never been my strength. Now that I was Alpha, their eyes followed me constantly. It would take some time to adjust.

Our pack lived loosely together deep in the forest, in small serviceable cabins we'd built with our own hands. We were deep enough in the wilderness that hikers couldn't make it out here, and we worked with the natural cover of the trees, which shielded us from aerial photography. It didn't seem like the best plan on paper, but hiding in plain sight had worked for hundreds of years for this pack. Or so I'd been told.

I was waiting for the inevitable moment when someone flew over with an infrared camera, looking for a lost hiker and instead finding what looked like some sort of commune. Then what?

This cookout was supposed to be a celebration of my betrothal to the previous Alpha's daughter, but it was mostly a drunken party in the woods. It was 1 a.m., and everyone was still raging. I was happy my pack seemed to be enjoying themselves, at any rate.

"You could at least pretend to be pleasant."

My mother shot me 'the look,' and I struggled not to

cower under her gaze, despite being twenty-seven and six foot five. I would hesitate to call her petite at 5'7", but most people seemed small compared to me. Her brown, curly hair was much lighter than mine, as well as her complexion. People usually said we looked nothing alike.

Until we got angry.

"Mother. Don't."

She sniffed, her eyes flashing yellow before she put her nose in the air. "If you can't be bothered to enjoy your own engagement party, then at least allow me my contentment. Should I remind you that you're the one who agreed to the match?"

I bit back the urge to growl, despite knowing she wasn't completely correct. Mating with Rebecca hadn't been my idea, but it had seemed like the best solution for everyone. Plus we were childhood friends. Rebecca was the only child of the old Alpha, and our betrothal had soothed over tensions after he had yielded the pack to me, however reluctantly.

Though yielded was a polite term for having one's throat laid out millimeters from my teeth.

I snorted, pushing down the euphoric rush that typically came with any reminder of my victory. Instead, I scanned the crowd for my intended, frowning when I didn't immediately see her.

Rebecca was beautiful, in a preppy, *Seventeen Magazine,* sort of way. Her blonde hair went nearly to her waist, and small freckles coated her light skin, which she was showing plenty of tonight with her short white dress. Her blue eyes had a way of pleading with you for the smallest things. Not that anyone would dream of refusing her. Seeing those red lips pout was the worst.

Rebecca was well-liked, beautiful, and we'd grown up alongside each other. Together, we would have strong pups with the bloodlines of both Alphas. The mateship had been her idea technically—a show of good faith in exchange for her father's life. Tradition usually dictated the losing Alpha died. A dead Alpha couldn't stage a coup after all.

I granted her request with the promise she would be my mate. I'd been proud of myself at the time. I was a new Alpha and had saved myself a tiresome search for a mate all in one fell swoop.

So why wasn't I happier?

"Derrick. Are you even listening?" My mother's curt voice pierced my thoughts.

My anger left me in a rush. I never could be truly cross with my mother. In the end, everything I'd done had been for her. She was one of the few people who got to see me as anything other than the Alpha.

I sighed, but brought my attention back to my mother. "Sorry, mama."

Her eyes sparkled with mischief, appeased for now.

"Where is Rebecca?" I asked.

My mother's hands flicked haphazardly toward the crowd, and I finally found her, holding court with the other female wolves. Her preening prickled me almost as much as my mother's, but I took a deep breath and let it go. Rebecca was entitled to how she acted. It would be her duty to keep up relations within the pack, just as it was my duty to protect it.

I grabbed another beer out of a cooler and downed it, crushing the can in my fist and tossing it to the ground. My mother huffed in irritation but said nothing. Not even the pack Matron could chastise the Alpha in public. Her eyes softened when my gaze caught hers, and she turned back to the other mothers.

I shook my head, happy at least that she had found purpose in being pack Matron. Her mate was dead, and I couldn't kill the wolf responsible. Speaking of the devil . . .

Rebecca's father skulked on the edges of the crowd which

was mostly concentrated around the large bonfire in the center of the clearing. Victor snarled when he caught me looking, but I only leveled my own glare at him.

Victor had the look of a once-proud Alpha gone to seed—his dark hair was flecked with bits of grey and white, his body long and lanky. His pale skin glowed from the fire. I struggled not to physically react to his scent. It smelled like something bitter, yet spoiled. Like a good plant left to rot. He lowered his head to the ground and slunk away.

Right. That was why I was Alpha; because Victor was a slimy piece of—

"There you are! Dance with me?"

Rebecca's small hand wound around my bicep. She flashed a vivid smile at me, and the red haze cleared a little from my vision.

My hand snaked around her waist, and I pulled her close. She smelled nice, if nothing else.

She gave a loud giggle in return, and I tried not to wince at the sound.

How could such a noise come from something other than a squealing rabbit?

The next sound she made was a soft whisper in my ear, and *that* was much more pleasing. Until the words registered. "I see you glaring at my dad. Stop it."

I growled, a deep rumble that shook my chest. I loosened my grip on her waist.

She blinked, a quick moment of fear radiating from her eyes.

I hated how they were all afraid of me, but it wouldn't stop me. Someone had to take control of the situation and protect my mother and the rest of the pack. "Tell your father to stop being such a useless bag of shit—"

"Stop it," she said, and my wolf flared at the mild challenge.

The urge to make her submit to me was strong, but I pushed it away. "You stop it, Bex. How can you defend him after what he did?"

Rebecca's pale skin flushed, and her gaze dropped to the ground in embarrassment. "You promised not to bring it up again," she hissed, claws bursting through her nail beds to grip the small of my back.

Arousal prickled into my awareness as her small claws bit into my skin, and almost as quickly she released me, her face flushing. Technically, she could be punished for drawing my blood. Which was unfortunate, because nothing turned me on more than a woman who wasn't afraid of me.

If such a woman even existed.

Rebecca whimpered, convinced she was in trouble.

Sighing and releasing my anger, I ran a hand gently through her blonde hair. "I'm angry at your father. Not you."

She nuzzled her face into my neck, and a surge of protectiveness rose in me. I might not have been stupidly in love with Rebecca like I'd seen with other mates, but I was content to protect her. It was what was right, and what duty called for. It was expected.

It was the only thing in my life that was apparently going as planned.

My plan certainly hadn't been to become Alpha, but after Victor lost his mate, he came after my mother. That didn't even come close to the fact that he'd killed my father a year ago to become Alpha in the first place. Stepfather. Fuck, what did it matter? He'd been the one who'd raised me, and Victor had easily beaten him in a challenge. Too easily. I'd always suspected foul play, because my father had always been the strongest Alpha in the pack. There was no way Victor could have fairly beaten him. I didn't believe it then, and I still don't believe it now.

It was bad enough Victor had stolen my birthright and my

father in one fell swoop. But to sniff after my mother, who had still been grieving at the time?

Alphas were supposed to lead and to protect the pack, not murder their way into the position because they wanted someone else's mate. It took me only minutes to pound him to a bloody pulp, at which point Rebecca had begged for his life, offering herself up as my mate in return.

And now here we were, eating cake and hotdogs and pretending life wasn't just one giant series of fuckups.

Rebecca huffed, exasperated. "You can't be angry at him forever, Derrick. It's over and you won."

My grip on Rebecca tightened as I tried to control the rage. "How about someone in the pack murders me to get at you? Then see how you feel about the situation."

She cringed at the nasty tone in my voice, but I wouldn't budge on this. Rebecca would learn not to bring it up, or she'd get the nasty Alpha wolf. I hated that side of me, but accepted it was now a necessary evil. Other packs respected nasty.

I just wished I didn't hate it so much.

My mother hadn't been too thrilled when I became the new Alpha, even though he'd murdered her mate. I wasn't sure what hurt more; that I'd lost the man who's raised me, or that my mother didn't believe in me.

"I should go. See you tonight?" Rebecca shimmied out of my arms, giving me a suggestive twitch of her hips. Our contract specified that we couldn't consummate the bond until the ceremony, but I also knew it was mostly for show. Rebecca would do whatever she needed in order to keep me from her father's throat. Screw the contract.

"Perhaps tomorrow," I muttered, ignoring the disappointment in her eyes. I wasn't in the mood for her company, even if it was likely to cheer me up. Despite everything, Rebecca always tried to please me. Yet it didn't feel right. It had never come close to the way my mother had described her own mate bond.

I supposed it was because Rebecca and I weren't actually mated yet. Regardless, I made a mental note to discuss it with my mother. She'd had two mates already, so if anyone was likely to have insight, it would be her.

Her stature was poised, confident as she spoke with the other females, putting a hand on another's shoulder to offer help or a bit of advice. Gods above, that woman's strength left me breathless. I couldn't imagine fleeing your pack with your child and leaving your mate behind, then being forced to take a new one for your own safety. I shook my head, not able to comprehend it. I barely remembered our flight from the islands and the ensuing whirlwind that ended up with us landing with the Yellowstone pack. We weren't exactly accepted as easily being foreigners. It wasn't our brown skin and hair, the pack was diverse enough, but English wasn't our first language. At least my mother had had protection as our new Alpha's mate. That protection hadn't extended to me when it came to the other cubs in the pack, so I quickly learned to become better than all of them—smarter, faster, stronger.

I sighed, trying to breathe out my stress. I missed my father, even if he had been my stepdad. Semantics be damned.

Looking around at everyone talking, laughing, and playing, I was flooded with a sense that everything would eventually come together. Rebecca would be my mate. I'd protect the pack and keep one eye on her murdering father. If my mother could make a mateship work that hadn't been her fated mate, then so could I.

After all, Victor clearly couldn't be trusted. The only reason I knew he wouldn't kill me was because he wouldn't jeopardize his daughter's position. She couldn't rise any higher in the pack hierarchy than being my mate, after all. He may be a murdering piece of shit, but all signs pointed to him truly loving his daughter.

I threw Victor one last snarl before I stormed off into the woods, seeking nothing other than my own company to be alone with my racing thoughts. Those closest to me followed me with their eyes but didn't say anything. They were mostly used to my moods, and knew I needed more time to run and settle my thoughts than the others did. Besides, Rebecca and my Beta would soothe everything over. They always did.

I let the darkness embrace me.

Chapter 3 Bailey

My eyelids were slow to pry open, like I was being woken from a coma.

What the hell happened?

My wolf was calm in my chest, but my heart was not as I remembered what had happened the night before.

"Shit, how long did I run for?" I whispered to myself, staring at my muddied bare feet, but my wolf gave no inkling as to what happened.

My fear of being caught drove her forward. I only had flashes of greens and browns as we raced through the night. I trusted my wolf. She wouldn't put us in danger.

Wind ripped through my hair, causing goosebumps along my bare skin as I pushed myself off the ground. I used the moment to take a whiff of the area, trying to gauge where my wolf had taken us, but I got nothing.

We weren't in an area I had been in before.

I tilted my head back to peer into the fir treetops, which was all I could see. We were high in elevation based on the trees and rock slabs, but too deep in the woods to see any discernible features like a mountain peak.

"Great," I mumbled.

My muscles ached from running all night, and hunger

pulled at my stomach, making both myself and my wolf more irritable than usual.

The wind shifted, bringing with it the scent of water.

My inner wolf's head perked up at the thought of taking a dip.

"We don't have time for that," I murmured. But we did need water. My tongue was like sandpaper. "No swimming, just resting."

Content enough, my wolf settled back down inside me, and I turned to march deeper into the woods.

When I first bolted, before my wolf pushed me deeper inside, I had been sure to give a wide berth to where I had smelled the wolves, while staying away from the roads and any cars that would see me. This could now pose a problem since it'd be harder to figure out where I was. Usually I could rely on my senses, never truly becoming lost, but I would most likely need to find a town to catch my bearings.

Damn wolf.

She let out a low snarl in return.

"You're right. You saved our ass, thanks." I chuckled, but my heart wasn't in it.

I had liked my little town, the diner I found a job at. It's the most settled I had been in a long while. I hated that I left Louie high and dry. I didn't have a cell phone, so there was no way to call him to let him know I quit. It was shitty, but in the end there wasn't much I could do about it.

A small lake glinted between the trees. I slowed my steps. Water sources were the best place to come across . . . well, anything. An animal that needed water, a shifter that needed water, or even a human out camping or fishing.

I snuck through the trees, careful to place my toes only where there was no leaf litter or twigs. Every once in a while I stopped to smell the air, but there was nothing but the smell of dirt and pine.

I found a smooth rock on the edge of the water beside a large boulder. It was a nice place to sit—difficult to leave my scent, and an easy place to take cover in case anyone showed up.

Settling down, a knot in my chest unwound with a deep breath. I always felt calmer near water, which was weird for a shifter. Don't get me wrong. I loved the mountains, but even in Yosemite, I found excuses to drive out west to the ocean when I could. Which hadn't been often.

I rolled my shoulders before putting my hands on my hips to admire the small grove. Tall trees circled the area, leaving little room between the forest and the water. A hawk sat on a branch to monitor its personal domain.

I nodded towards it, wanting to pay my respects to nature like my mother had taught me. Even if they couldn't shift and communicate the way we could, that didn't mean they didn't deserve appreciation.

A lump formed in my throat at the thought of her. *I hope she is okay.* I pushed it from my mind before guilt consumed me and made me do something stupid, like go racing back to her.

The water was clear enough that I saw shadows of fish under the surface. My stomach rumbled at the reminder of food. This was something I'd normally take advantage of, but I didn't want any splashing to alert the attention of unwanted companions. Slinking to the edge of the rock, I cupped some crisp water in my hand.

With a slurp, the melted snow water fortified my belief I was in the upper Rockies. My eyes narrowed as I focused on what my senses told me about my location.

It no longer smelled like Colorado, at least not a part I had ever been to. My wolf would've stayed mostly within National Forest territory, keeping me away from the Yellowstone pack.

So, I doubt we went west or south, and I was too high up to have gone east. But north . . .

I shook my head. North was stupid too. I must be south, even if the scent of the area didn't match, but it would've been the safest and smartest. The only way to truly know was to find a town, or even a city.

Normally I stayed away from larger cities, but maybe it'd be easier to get lost in the crowd or mask my smell in a larger place. Although the chances of coming across shifters there would be greater.

I chewed on my lip in contemplation. Gulping down another handful of water, I sighed with resignation. Either way, I needed supplies and clothes. Big or small, a town was my best bet. Afterward, I could catch a Greyhound bus and get as far away as possible. I should be able to scrounge up enough money for that—after all, it was a lot faster than walking.

I scooped another handful of water.

"I want to go home," a small voice cried out, distant but clear as a cold breeze.

I froze.

"I know. I'm trying," a slightly older, but still young, voice responded.

I ducked behind the boulder as two children stepped up to the water's edge across the small lake.

The older one couldn't have been more than twelve. He stopped at the water's edge with a frown. Beside him, a younger boy, perhaps eight, slumped onto the ground.

"My feet hurt." Tears pricked the little boy's eyes, and his bottom lip trembled.

The older boy crouched next to him, throwing his arm over the other's shoulders. "All we need to do is find a trail, and we'll be home soon."

Together, they both sniffed the air.

I grabbed the rock until my fingertips turned white, slowly scenting the air myself. I was downwind of them, which was good, and this allowed for their smell to travel to me.

My eyes widened. *Shifters.*

But they were so young. What were they doing out here by themselves? Unless they weren't.

I crept backwards, ensuring no sound reached their ears. I kept my eyes on them as I inched, carefully placing my feet on the ground. Once out of eyesight, I turned and hurried away between the trees, swift and quiet. The further away I got, the less constricted my chest was.

Then the small one screamed.

Protect. My wolf emerged on full alert, forcing a shift on me.

I gritted my teeth against the change. Pain sliced through me as I fought against it, reminding me of my first shift. Giving into it, accepting it, allowing it is what makes it not painful. But if any part of you tried to stop it, it felt like every bit of you was being torn apart by a grenade in slow motion, and you felt everything.

I dropped to my knees with a grunt, and a muffled cry wrenched from my throat with another push from my wolf.

Another scream in the distance.

My bones snapped as my body transformed, something I had rarely experienced because I never fought my wolf. My screams turned into a howl as my wolf finished the shift.

With a turn, I bounded back towards the lake, my instincts on override to save the children.

I ground to a halt at the water's edge, scanning the forest until—there! Movement. I dashed around the lake, the pounding of the little boys' feet and fearful gulps of breath driving me faster.

When I caught up to them, they crouched together against a fallen log. The younger one shook in the older's arms. Blood drenched the right arm of the older boy, and the tang of it hit my nose.

I growled, leaping through the air and over the log, landing in front of them with a turn.

That's when I saw the vampire.

His blood-red eyes roved over me. A tilt of his blue lips showed a red fang, a startling contrast against the milky white of his skin.

Red, white, and blue—God bless America.

He swiped at me and I growled back, every inch of me as threatening as I could get. What the hell was a vampire doing out here? And even though he was hidden within the shadows of the trees, it should be impossible for him to be out during the day. Confusion and rage warred within me.

Blood coated his mouth, matching the wound on the older boy. Their bites weren't fatal to us, but shifters were a favorite snack of theirs. Apparently we were a delicacy, so it wasn't unheard of for them to attack us. But their Queen usually kept them in check, decapitating any vampire who took an unwilling victim.

Not this one.

He pulled at the lapel of his suit. Yes, his fucking suit in the middle of the wilderness. Seriously, who was this guy?

His eyes lit up like I was a piece of candy. In a blur of movement, faster than I've ever seen any vampire move, he raced behind me.

A wail rang out, and I spun.

In his clutches, the youngest boy hung by his throat. His tiny hands scrabbled at the hold while his feet kicked uselessly in the air.

The older boy was frozen staring at them in abject horror, completely frozen in place, tear tracks on his dirty cheeks.

I gave a warning growl, bunching my haunches.

The vampire side-eyed me. "I'll deal with you in a second.

I like to savor my dessert." His voice, usually melodic to humans, were forks scraping against a plate for me. He opened his mouth, and I pounced.

I knew better than to go for his upper body. He could've easily turned and used the little boy as a shield before I could stop my bite. Instead, my jaws snapped around his thigh, and the satisfying crack of bone reverberated through my body.

The vampire hollered, dropping the boy to the ground.

The youngest was smart enough to backpedal away from us towards his brother, and both of them quickly hid behind the trunk.

The vampire lashed out and grabbed the nape of my neck, his claws lengthening until they pierced through my pelt. I tightened my teeth into his flesh, but when he ripped away at my neck, I gave an involuntary yip, which released my hold.

His muscles bulged in his arms as he flung me by the scrap of my neck.

I flew through the air, twisting in time to avoid smashing my head against a tree trunk, but my spine made brutal contact. I collapsed onto the ground with a huff, but I did not stay down for long. I sprung onto all fours, ignoring the painful twinge in my back.

He stood there, sole focus on me like the pups were no longer there, waiting for my move.

We both sprang at the same time. His speed was insurmountable, but my instincts drove me. The moment I realized his direction, I propelled myself a few feet in front of his blurred form.

We smashed together, which twisted my paw at an odd angle, but I took him to the ground. Successfully standing on his chest, I didn't hesitate. I couldn't with this freak of nature.

My jaws clamped around his throat, and I pulled.

His neck tore away, gushing blood all over my fur. He bared his fangs, and lunged for a bite of his own.

I dipped my head, so he missed his mark; but I did not. Pulling away, another chunk hung from my mouth and I spit it to the side.

The vampire's sharp fingers whipped out at lightning speed into my shoulder.

I yelped, burrowing my muzzle one last time into his neck. With a twist and a snap, I took his head clean off with a bellow of victory.

His hands dropped to his side, one red with my blood and the other dropping a golden flower. *Creep.* His body was ash before it even finished tumbling to the ground.

I shifted back in my human form and fell onto my hands and knees. Adrenaline raced through my veins as I took a moment to recover my breath. The metallic taste of the vampire's blood in my mouth twisted my stomach.

Soft whimpers from the boys were the only thing that gave me enough energy to move. With shaking arms, I pushed off the ground into a sitting position.

The little boys didn't even bat an eye at my nudity—something too common among shifters—and they ran right toward me.

My arms wrapped around them. "It's okay, it's all over now," I cooed. Now, I just needed to figure out where they were from, and how to get them home without being spotted myself.

"Step away from the boys," a deep voice growled from behind me, and I stopped breathing.

"Derrick!" the eldest cried out, and both of them wiggled out of my hold to race to the man.

To not expose myself completely, I only turned my head toward the newcomer. The man standing there was nothing short of a Polynesian god. Even fully clothed, his sculpted musculature was easy to see with the naked eye. His longer, wavy brown hair was pulled back, emphasizing a square jaw and sharp eyes.

His enormous hands landed on the little boys' shoulders. "You're safe now," he said to them, his voice softening.

I scoffed. *Yeah, thanks to me!*

His head whipped up, and when those deep brown, almost black eyes hit mine, I nearly choked from the power that wafted over me.

Alpha.

But I didn't look away. No. I straightened my back and narrowed my eyes at him.

Something like surprise flashed in his eyes, but it was gone before I could make anything of it.

"Who are you?" he demanded. When his eyes roved over my body with barely concealed curiosity, I flushed. It took everything in me not to shiver. The males in my pack had only been interested in one thing, and I would not give this one any similar chances.

My nostrils flared as I inhaled, and his scent rushed towards me. Pine, firewood, and . . . ocean? But the part that instantly raised my hackles and sent fear slithering into my heart was the indistinguishable smell of the Yellowstone pack, same as the cubs.

Shit.

Continue reading Chained (Rise of the Alpha Book 1) now!
https://www.amazon.com/Chained-Rise-Alpha-Book-1-ebook/dp/B09F6ZW31T/ref=sr_1_2

Message From The Author

Dear Readers,

Thank you, thank you, thank you! Your support, reviews, excitement, and taking a chance on the first book of a new series means the absolute world to me. I'm not able to do what I do without you, and your enthusiasm and love is really what helps drive me on those days where it's just a wee bit harder to write.

I truly hope you enjoyed Serena and Laz's story, and I think this world has so much to offer. I'm hoping all of you love this series enough to where I decide to do some spin-offs. Personally, I'm gunning for a Kyla story because I think she has so much to say and her strength will be very empowering to write and read.

Again, reviews and recommendations from you are the life force to an author, especially an indie author. I would greatly appreciate it if you left one on Amazon on Goodreads (careful of spoilers for other readers!). Thank you in advance if you decide to do this.

You rock, and most importantly, happy reading!

Kacey

First and foremost, I want to thank Becky Tama! You have been by my side since day 1 of starting my author career. Who knew you'd be a gold mine as a beta reader, facebook reader group partner, friend, and coauthor. Your support has gotten me through all the lows and highs, and I owe keeping extra pieces of my sanity to you. Go check out her bookstagram account (@becky.tama) for more PNR recs.

Also, a huge thank you so much to Kendra, another amazing bookstagrammer (@a.literary.affair), for beta reading! Your repertoire of romance books, especially PNR, gave you such a wonderful insight and really helped drive this story further. Also, I'm so excited for the ideas we hashed out for Book 2! Not only is she an amazing reader and mother, but opened her own brewery in Fall 2021 in Tomball, Texas! If you are ever near there, go check out Paradigm Brewery, which is family-friendly.

Thank you to my editor, Ashley Olivier. Line and copy editing are not my forté, so without you my book would be far from where it is now. Thank you for all your encouragement and kind words, as well as being very timely with everything. It makes the release much easier.

Finally, thank you to my amazing husband. You are my rock, and give me undying support no matter what I decide to tackle. From moving across the world (multiple times), to pursuing Master's degrees, to deciding to become a published author while being a full time teacher, you do nothing but encourage me. Thank you for being you.